I0730220

TO RIDE A STORM SURGE

READY TO GO?
BOOK THREE

LISA HATFIELD

To Ride a Storm Surge

Copyright © 2025 by Lisa Hatfield

Published by High Plains Wordsmith LLC

Paperback ISBN 978-1-7368941-8-7

Hardback ISBN 979-8-9925405-1-2

Ebook ISBN 978-1-7368941-9-4

Audiobook ISBN 979-8-9925405-0-5

All rights reserved.

No part of this book may be reproduced or used in any manner without the written permission of the copyright owner except for the use of quotations in a book review. For more information, contact Lisa at Lisa@LisaHatfield-Writer.com.

This is a work of fiction. Names, characters, places, and incidents either are the product of the author's imagination or are used fictitiously. Any resemblance to actual persons, living or dead, events, business establishments, or locales is entirely coincidental.

In addition to telling a story, the book aims to provide information and to stimulate action. The author and publisher make no claim to provide any type of professional advice. The author and publisher hope the contents of this volume will be helpful to readers. But readers must take responsibility for their own choices, actions, and results.

Published by High Plains Wordsmith LLC
First edition July 2025
Cover and interior design by Gordon Saunders
LisaHatfieldWriter.com

This book is dedicated to:
The resilient people of the Mississippi Gulf Coast,
especially in Hancock County and Harrison County

CONTENTS

What readers are saying:

"Valuable wildfire information intertwined with a personal growth and love story. I enjoyed reading *To Starve an Ember* (Ready to Go? Book 1) and came away with a better sense of how to prepare my property against fires. A must read for all who care about our land and protecting it." *Arlene M. Fisher-Olson*

"Lisa has a talent for weaving together a multi-dimensional story that includes not only exciting action, but deeper, heart-level stories within stories within stories." *Angie Curry, M.A. English Composition, Language & Rhetoric*

"Hatfield's latest novel, *To Ride a Storm Surge*, reads like it was written by a local. Likely the closest anyone will get to experiencing Hurricane Katrina from the front row like we did, as it turned every single aspect of our life upside-down and inside-out." *Meridith Bang - Longtime Pass Christian Parent, Community Member, Teacher, School Principal, and District Administrator*

"*To Ride a Storm Surge* is an exciting, suspenseful novel that weaves together so many different things a teenager faces. The author infuses many practical tips and reminders that will cause the reader to be more aware and prepared for unexpected situations." *Jenny Horsey, elementary school teacher and Gifted Education Specialist*

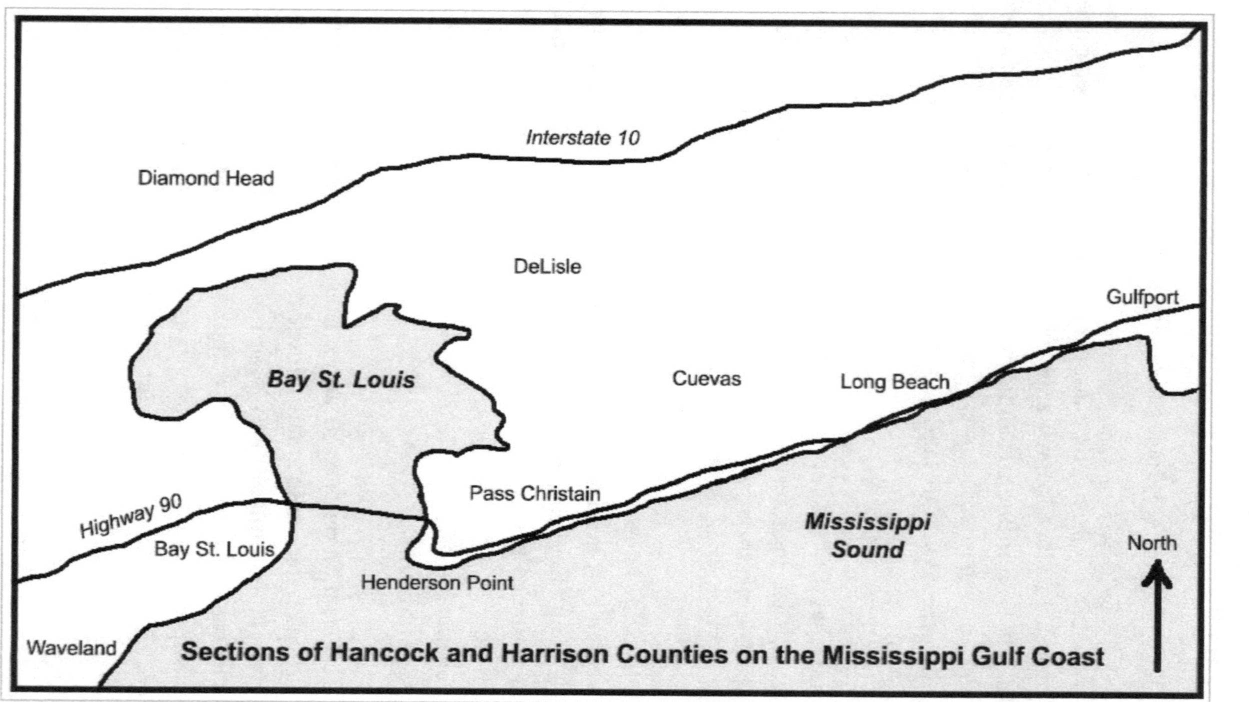

Interstate 10
Diamond Head
DeLisle
Gulfport
Bay St. Louis
Cuevas
Long Beach
Pass Christain
Highway 90
Bay St. Louis
Mississippi Sound
North
Waveland
Henderson Point
Sections of Hancock and Harrison Counties on the Mississippi Gulf Coast

Tuesday, August 23, 2005 - evening

Grandma yells at her chickens in Cantonese because she loves them, so that must be why she yells at me in English. I climbed the steps to the apartment and as I opened the door she got in my face. "Jessie, why you late home from school?"

Instead of answering, I held a heavy plastic bag out to her. "Look what I got!"

She squinted at me, not the bag. "What you got?"

"Red snapper, fresh caught." Fish water dripped out of a rip in the side and landed on the brown apartment carpet.

She accepted the bag but didn't look at it. "How you get this? You go near ocean?" she accused.

"Grandma, it's not the ocean. It's the Gulf of Mexico."

Her narrow black eyes pierced me, while her lips made a grim line. "Still big, dangerous water. Name not matter."

I swallowed. "Yes, it does. That is not the ocean out there. It's the Gulf, or the Mississippi Sound." But Grandma's universe was the only universe. No one else's opinion mattered, and she glared at me. I took a step back. "And anyway, I didn't even go near it." I'm taller than she is, but just barely. I hoped I would keep growing enough to be way taller than she was, and soon. She would hate that.

"How you get it? You steal it?" She still hadn't looked at the fish.

My eyes burned. "No, Grandma." Darn it, I had let down my guard. I had broken the first rule of living with my crazy Tiger Grandma, which was: Be Prepared for Unfair Questions. I should have had a joke ready about how I stole that fish right out of the water or something. Not that she would laugh, but at least if I could laugh, that would help.

But it was too much pressure. I couldn't think of a thing at that moment, so I caved and told the truth. "I earned it."

She tipped her head to peer down at the thick fish whose red and silver scales showed through the light plastic bag. "What you mean, 'I earn it'? You no have job, lazy girl." She wrenched the fish out of the bag by the tail and threw it in the sink. "You lie to me!" She was daring me to come up with an explanation that suited her.

"Miss Doreen gave it to me when I helped at her seafood store…"

Grandma took this and ran with it. "She think we poor? She think we need food so she give away old fish to us?"

I don't know why I bother talking sometimes.

Grandma pointed to the wall, and I fetched what she wanted down from its hook—the board with the clamp to hold the fish by the tail. Meanwhile, she started chopping vegetables like they too had insulted her, then cleaned and filleted the snapper in no time, just like Miss Doreen would have done, except instead of her laid-back style, Grandma worked with angry, sharp movements, then handed me the plastic bag full of fish guts. The bag felt heavy with blood and bones and scales. It felt heavier than it had when it was a whole fresh fish.

"Go feed chickens."

I hadn't even taken my backpack off yet. Welcome home, Jessie.

I attempted a joke. "What if the chickens aren't ready for dinner?"

She turned her back on me by going to the refrigerator.

I went out the glass sliding door to the apartment balcony on the back corner by the kitchen where chicken wire reached from floor to ceiling to stop them from flying into the bayou below us. Chicken poop and old grass clippings and newspapers covered the wooden deck boards like a layer of cement. Pretty soon I would have to scrape that stuff up to be used as fertilizer in her vegetable garden that I could almost see from the balcony though it was hidden behind the apartment buildings.

One slimy bit of entrails at a time, I picked the guts out of the bag and dropped them on the floor. Every time I dropped a glob of guts, the chickens pounced on it. Their sharp beaks scared me, a little, so years ago I'd made up a song to sing to myself when I was out there working. The tune sort of followed "The Farmer in the Dell," but the words were, "Poop rhymes with coop. Scales rhymes with gales. Feather rhymes with weather, and the coop is full of poop." I preferred singing to the chickens to make myself laugh, instead of yelling like Grandma did.

I also liked daydreaming. My brain took me all sorts of places away from her.

My friend Mary was the kind of friend who would tell me when I had dirt on my nose or accidentally had put my shirt on inside out. Her dad and mom came from Vietnam. He was a shrimper, so he was gone for stretches of time, but at least he was home more often than my dad, who was gone at least a week at a time as a truck driver. Mary didn't go on her dad's boat because she hated the smell. The salty sea creature smell blew all through the Pass constantly; it was part of the air, but the smell was even stronger on her dad's boat. She was my friend, and I didn't tell her she also smelled like shrimp all the time, whether she avoided the boat or not, because there wasn't anything she could do to fix it, not like an inside-out shirt. They were a nice family. Even her annoying little brothers were not so bad. Maybe they would help their dad someday.

Even though I'm only a middle-schooler, I wondered if maybe Mary's dad would hire me to help with the shrimping. Going out on the boat would have been a great adventure for me and I would have loved to have somewhere to be away from Grandma. It would have been awesome to have fresh-caught shrimp to bring home. But Grandma would have been mad if I went on the open water to get it. As it was, sometimes I borrowed one of those small round nets to cast from the shore or the pier, but I never held the edge of that nasty net in my mouth like some shrimpers did.

Mom said Grandma, her "Mama," was like that in San Francisco too. They lived within sight of the Bay, but Grandma never took her to see the water.

Why did Grandma Jiexen (JEE-shin) ever move to Mississippi?

I wished I had a brother or a sister. There went my imagination again.

I kept the plastic bag looped over my left wrist as I moved to the nesting area on part of the balcony close to the kitchen to look for eggs. Grandma had gotten Dad to stack plastic tubs sideways, so the openings were on the sides, and at night, the birds hopped up into them to roost. She put the lids on the sideways tubs as if they were doors, and took them off every morning.

I picked up two eggs, both covered with blobs of chicken poop, and put them in the empty fish guts bag. Then I went inside, washed the eggs, and set them gently in the dish in the refrigerator.

Grandma didn't look my way, but in those few minutes, she'd already cooked up a frying pan full of homegrown vegetables and pan-fried egg noodles with the red snapper, and she had made me a plate.

"Thanks." I slid my backpack onto the table next to the sofa and sat at the counter.

She prayed silently over her food and began eating. I did the same.

"Can I have some more?"

She gestured for me to help myself, then put her plate next to the sink and sat on the chair by the living room window, looking out in silence, watching me with the eyes in the back of her head.

I washed everything up and put away the leftovers for my mom when she got home at around midnight from the convenience store a few blocks from here. It was west of here, to be precise. Dad was the one who made me learn the compass directions by saying "Never Eat Soggy Waffles" to help me remember the order of the North, East, South, and West points and what it meant in real life. He said things like, "Just because you're twelve doesn't mean you shouldn't know which way is up, right?" I loved learning anything and everything, especially from Dad, and so whenever I went anywhere, I thought about which direction I headed. For practice.

He was in town for a few days, so he was spending time with Mom at the store again tonight. He was probably telling jokes and giving her a shoulder rub while she stood at the cash register.

Grandma didn't look at me when I picked up my backpack.

"Bye, Grandma. See you later." I let the front door slam on the way out, pulled my bike out from where it was parked next to Grandma's, and rode to the public library to see Miss James, who had learned my name the first time she met me six years ago. This afternoon, in no time, she helped me find that *Magyk* book that just came out so I could be the first one in seventh grade to read it. Then I rode to Mary's so we could do our homework together.

Wednesday, August 24 - 7 a.m.

"I'LL ONLY BE GONE a week, kiddo," Dad said, as we ate breakfast. Mom was fast asleep in their room, and Grandma was probably out in her vegetable garden already so she wouldn't have to say "Good morning, David," to him. He got the coffee maker ready to go, and I pushed the button for him. He scrambled fresh eggs in the skillet, and I made the toast with lots of butter, all the way to the edges.

Around a bite of toast, I said, "I know, Dad. It just feels longer when you're gone." It was hard to think about. Hours felt like days, at home. "Where are you going this week?"

He sat next to me at the counter. "Maine! It's only twenty-seven hours away. I could make it in just over a day." He chuckled, seeing I had believed that one. I should have known better; he's been teaching me about the U.S. interstate highway map. "Nah, it'll take three days just to get up there, because I do want to sleep at night, not drive straight through."

Oh right, I forgot about that.

I nodded. I'm practicing asking follow-up questions. That's what my teacher Mrs. Drummond calls them, when you're enjoying talking to someone and you don't want it to end. "Do you have a load to bring back?" I asked. I didn't like it when he did, because he had to stay away longer to drop it off on the way back to Pass Christian (kris-CHAN).

But he did get paid for it.

"Not yet, but I'll check the boards," he said. "Even if I do, I'll be back by Monday, most likely."

I picked up a forkful of eggs, then set it down on my plate. "I'll be fine. I mean, we'll be fine until Monday." I've observed that I tend to live my life in small increments like that.

I like to notice things.

For example, Mom drove her little olive-green car to get to work and do errands. Dad called it her "clunker" because it was rickety. A long time ago, I noticed that when we made a turn, the blinker always turned off, but it didn't always turn on when we were about to make a turn. Why? Was that because it was a clunker? Nope, I watched for days as I rode with Mom and finally figured it out! The blinker was working fine, but she didn't always flick it on before she made a turn.

That made me feel powerful, noticing that. Last week, Mrs. Drummond taught us a proverb, "In the land of the blind, the man with one eye is king." Maybe I'm not blind. Maybe I have one eye!

Dad nudged my shoulder. "Jessie? Hello? I said, how's your mom doing when I'm gone?" he asked.

Back to reality, oops. I shrugged. "She does okay." He and I both knew she wasn't okay, but we didn't know what to do. She had no oomph, and she slept so much when she was home with Grandma.

It's not like we could kick Grandma out.... Could we?

His big arm scrunched around my skinny shoulders. "You're looking older, Jess."

I shrugged again and finished my eggs.

He fumbled around for something supportive to say, like he always does. "I'm glad you're in the scrap metal business."

It was an exaggeration to call the metal collecting a business, but it sounded good when he said it that way. A good exaggeration, not a bad one. "Me too. It's fun to do with Mom when she's free." I would collect stuff during the week on my bike, and then every so often, we'd load up her car and take it to Waveland or Bay St. Louis. And get ice cream. And go to the beach.

He added, "It's good to have something else to do besides school."

"But I like school too, Dad," I said. Why did I like it? Well, it was organized there. It was easy to follow directions, and the teachers were happy with me. They didn't change the directions at the end and judge me for not doing it that way from the beginning.

Unlike Tiger Grandma. I never knew when—or why—she would pounce. Mom, Dad, and I used "Tiger Grandma" as our secret nickname for Grandma Jiexen.

Dad grinned at me. "I know you like school. I'm glad you inherited that from Anna. My mother used to say..." And now he tried to imitate Grandma DeGroot's voice and Dutch accent... " 'Da-*feed*, you bedder start like vorking vid dees milch cooows, eev you not going vork harrd in skoool'." He smiled and looked around, remembering his mother. I had really liked her, too, when we lived with her and Grandpa DeGroot. He said, "I never told her how much I hated those cows," he laughed again. "You're a strong kid, Jessie. You can do school with your eyes closed. You can do anything you set your mind to." He hugged me. "It's just good not to put your eggs all in one basket."

I didn't know what to say. What did he mean by that? I had so many questions that were too big to ask in between scrambled eggs and him driving away in his truck. So, I just said, "Thanks, Dad."

He smiled. "Do you know what a great gift you are to me and Anna, Jessie?" He squeezed my shoulder again, not waiting for me to answer, which was fine, because I had no answer to that. None whatsoever, because I knew it was the opposite of true. I was their whole problem. The reason for the way their life was now. Great gift. Yeah, sure.

We took turns in the bathroom to brush our teeth, then met by the front door. His deep blue eyes twinkled at me and he gave me a hug and kissed the top of my head. Dad will always tower above me, even when I grow up to my tallest height. I inherited my petite stature from my mom and my grandma and centuries of Chinese women. Yes, I said Chinese. One thing Mom and Grandma agreed on was that they didn't like being called Asian women. They were both 100% Chinese DNA, even if they didn't want to live in China.

Grandma appeared outside the front door while Dad was giving me one more hug. "Jessie, you take out garbage now."

Why was she always surprising me out of nowhere? "Yes, ma'am," I said. It's not like I never do what she says. I didn't understand why she thought I would forget this chore when I did it every single morning. I was on the honor roll. I'm a good kid.

I would do each task just like she said, but then she would change what she told me and act like it was my fault, just like a tiger pounces on a fawn in the forest, with its teeth stuck in the back of the fawn's little neck. One day she would tell me, "You not sleep enough. Grow strong. Need sleep more." But the next day she would yip at me, "You go to bed too early. Why not get more homework done?" She would never be happy with what I did.

Why didn't Grandma take a chill pill?

As I had been daydreaming, Dad had picked up his duffel

bag and was halfway out the door, but when he saw I was paying attention again, he looked me in my eyes, gave me another smile, and only then went down to the "Pete," his Peterbilt truck—just the engine and the sleeper cab—in the parking lot. I got my backpack and the trash bag, followed him down the five half-flights of stairs, hopped on my bike, and pedaled over to the dumpster across the parking lot to throw the trash away. I could follow the Pete west on North Street and watch him turn into the Pre-Stress parking lot where they made concrete parts for bridges and stuff. They'd attach a certain kind of trailer there and load it with cement pilings or girders for him to deliver. Dad told me depending on the customer's location, sometimes they sent the girders on a barge instead of on a semi-trailer, but I just didn't understand how a boat that weighed that much didn't sink. I guess I was glad Dad drove a truck with a trailer instead of a barge. I followed the Pete out of the parking lot.

I had gotten away before Grandma put my hair in those too-tight braids this morning, so the wind blew my hair all over the place. It was only a fifteen-minute ride, and I loved riding my bike. I could ride forever. But now my hair was getting all snarled up. I wondered if Mary would have an extra rubber band I could borrow when I got to school. She had long brown hair just like mine, and her mom put it in two braids for her every morning, like Grandma did, only more gently.

When Dad got back home next Monday, I planned to give him a hug so big it would knock him sideways. Then he and Mom and I would go out for dinner at a restaurant, maybe at the open-air fish place perched on stilts, twenty feet above the Pass Christian harbor. That would be great, because Grandma wouldn't join us since it was close to the water. We would watch the shrimp boats, and the people fishing from the pier, and Dad would get me a drink with a little umbrella in it. And he and Mom would hold hands and watch the sunset. We might even spot a few dolphins if we were lucky!

Wednesday, August 24 - 8 a.m.

The Mississippi Sound was within sight of my middle school. I really liked the sound of the gentle waves and the salty, fishy smell, so after I followed Dad's truck, I rode south and went a few blocks out of my way to put my toes in the sand before school. I watched the shrimpers heading out from the harbor nearby, wondering if Mary's dad was going out now. Knowing him, he probably headed out before the sun even came up in the sky. Mary's dad always said, in his combined Vietnam/Mississippi accent, "Shrimp don't gonna catch themself."

Grandma would freak out if she knew I was here. What was her problem with being close to water, anyway? How could she be so smart and so fearful at the same time? I knew she could swim, because that's how she escaped from China, but the rest of that story was a secret.

Grandma's mean reactions to my best efforts were hard on me. I tried so hard to do things right, but she always found a new fault in me, the "incurable" child as she said. Last December, after a bad fight with her, something about her hidden vegetable garden, I really considered running away. I could just have gotten on my bike and ridden north, all the way up to the farm in Nebraska where Dad grew up, where we lived when I was a preschooler. But I remembered it was the middle of winter up there then, with snow and icy wind, not like here on the Gulf Coast. And it was really, really far from Mississippi to Nebraska, even in a car.

Today I replayed her stupid reaction to the red snapper I'd brought home. Maybe I should skip school and just keep heading west out of the Pass and across the bridge over Bay

St. Louis. One time, when Mom and I were over there on the weekend to turn in the scrap metal, we found a quiet, clean park in Waveland. We ate ice cream, and Mom talked about starting a community project to paint murals on the edges of the skate park and the big garbage bins. Maybe I could just go there and watch the Gulf.

Nah, school was not the problem, and anyway, there was a test today in Mississippi Studies. It was about hurricanes, and I studied a lot for it since it's relevant. I liked that word. Mrs. Drummond encouraged us to expand our vocabulary. I've lived on the Gulf Coast since I was six, and we've had more than one hurricane every year, along with lots of tropical storms. Usually, the surge-prone areas would flood, and we got a day or two off from school. Sometimes the bayou filled up and spilled water into the parking lot at our apartment complex. What could be more relevant than that?

I got to homeroom in time to watch Hook TV. Mary gave me a sideways smile, didn't even say anything, and handed me an elastic band. I looped my snarled hair into a messy ponytail. On the screen, Tamika stood up for the pledge of allegiance and we followed along in our classroom, and then co-anchors Katrina and Tyrell did the Pirate Daily News.

Katrina read her script. "Another tropical storm has formed in the Bahamas." She giggled, adding, "It was called Tropical Depression Twelve yesterday, but now it's named Tropical Storm Katrina." Her pale cheeks blushed bright pink, knowing there was a tropical storm with the same name as hers.

Tyrell, who had the most beautiful brown eyes and brown skin, read the teleprompter. "The National Weather Service in Jackson says we will get a lot of rain out of this storm, as usual." They moved on to reading the school lunch menu for today—meat lover's pizza or tuna salad sandwich, corn, applesauce, and fruit cocktail.

The bell rang, and Mr. Hartman asked if we had any last questions about the hurricane unit or the study guide, and then we put our heads to work on that test. The last question was a short essay: "What part do oceans play in the formation of weather systems such as hurricanes?"

I wrote, "It all starts with warm ocean waters, thunderstorms, and winds." Just because you have a tropical storm, it doesn't mean you'll get a hurricane out of it, and even when you do, hurricanes come in different categories. Our big hope was that the tropical storms never made it into the Gulf at all. The last Category 5 hurricane to hit here was in 1969, which was Hurricane Camille, and it smashed all the towns right along the Gulf. In War Memorial Park, there used to be a monument to all the people killed in World War II, but Hurricane Camille even destroyed that. They rebuilt the monument later, and now there was also a monument to all the people killed by Camille.

The five miles of water between here and the barrier islands was super shallow, so it was warm all the time. Mr. Hartman said the shallow water in the Sound was one reason the storm surge from Hurricane Camille got so deep and reached all the way to the railroad tracks in the middle of town. Plus, all the rain, too. It flattened everything along the Mississippi Coast and killed more than 259 people. Hurricanes like Camille were called hundred-year storms, because people said they only came around about once every hundred years. So, we had a while before we had to worry about anything that serious again.

I didn't write all that on my test sheet, but I'd read about it, and I remembered it.

Oh geez, did the bell ring? Now I'm late for pre-algebra. Story of my life.

2

Thursday, August 25 - 11 a.m.

Mrs. Drummond's journal prompt for today told us to "Describe yourself and your life situation in one paragraph." I had already thought about this a lot, so, I wrote my answer quickly. "I'm Jessie, age twelve going on thirty according to my teachers. So why does Grandma blame me for everything? I couldn't help being born and ruining her daughter's life. Maybe I should give up like Mom has—I could just disappear on my bike. Then I wouldn't have to hear Grandma's yelling or her noisy chickens. Dad gets to disappear for days at a time in his 18-wheeler. So, who's in charge around this crazy apartment, anyway? Not me. I'm not in control of anything. I'm just bobbing up and down on the rising waves, and holding on for dear life." Yep, that about summed it up.

At lunch, rain spattered the windows, and we heard that Katrina, now designated as a Cat 1 hurricane, had hit Fort Lauderdale directly over the office of the National Hurricane Center. That's about six hundred miles away from here, not a big deal for us this time, but it was a problem for those people in Florida. Nine people died, and over a million people lost electricity there today.

As we ate, Mary and Pam did more imitations of my grandma which were funnier to me than when I did them. "Why you not help me cook food, you lazy girl?" joked Mary.

Pam chimed in with the contradiction that always came next. "No. You don't cook food right way. Stop cook now. Go do homework."

This was my life. She would say, "Go make egg drop soup," so I did; it's not complicated, but then she would say, "You do wrong," and re-do everything I just did in a whole different way: which broth to use, how to stir the eggs, how to cut up vegetables. "No, too small," and then the next day, all the same except now it was the opposite, "No, too big."

We all giggled. Pam snorted and her chocolate milk came out her nose all over her pizza.

I put down my drink and pushed some paper napkins over to Pam, who now had snot plus milk dripping out her nostrils. Disgusting.

My stomach hurt from laughing so hard.

I tried to think about what the pastor said at church about praying and forgiveness and breathing, but I could only breathe so much before I wanted to strangle Grandma just like the way she strangled a chicken when its days were over. That was not a very Christian thing to think, but I couldn't help it.

Right after lunch, we had a tornado drill. We do those all the time. Our principal Mrs. Favre and all the teachers led us into the hallways on the lowest floor. Technically, we're also supposed to be away from the windows in case they get broken, but that's hard to do, since there are so many windows and so many of us.

While we sat on the floor, talking, waiting to go back to

class, the speakers crackled and our principal said, "Attention, Pirates. Thank you for your attention. Listen up." That was not usually what she said when a drill was over. Usually, she said what a great job we'd done or something. "This was originally just a tornado drill, but that hurricane that hit Florida is spawning rain and tornadoes, and we are now officially under a tornado warning. We need to stay put." We sat there for ages. Some kids even fell asleep.

By the time we left for home, and our principal had said, "Thank you, students for your cooperation. You did a wonderful job today. Once a Pirate, always a Pirate.'" It was way past our usual dismissal time. We hadn't heard anything disastrous happen outside, but as I rode my bike out of the school parking lot, I saw tree branches had been ripped off and thrown into buildings. I went past Miss Doreen's seafood shop, and her place looked okay, but Mr. Bourdin's plumbing store had some broken windows, and so did the Chinese restaurant across the street. Branches and leaves lay scattered, as if nature had thrown confetti instead of beads in a Mardi Gras parade.

I picked up speed on my bike and went out of my way to see my mom at the Quik Mart. The wild sunflower patch, tucked along the fence behind the building, was okay. I'm sure Mom had planted those "wild" flowers again this year. Cars waited on both sides of the pump to get gas. Inside, five or six people waited in line to get chips and bottled water and Slim Jims. And cigarettes, of course. Mom saw me and smiled with her eyes, but her mouth was more serious. I went behind the counter and gave her a side hug while she rang up people's purchases.

"Mom, are you okay?"

She smiled and sighed, hugging me back. "Sure, Jessie. I'm just kind of tired. The new kid didn't show up for his shift today."

I hugged her harder. She turned away from the customer to pay attention to me, and it made my tummy feel warm. "Mom, I meant the tornado." She looked surprised, so I said, "We had to hunker down at school for a long time for a tornado warning. They just let us out."

She looked out the window, as if she could see something now. "What? A tornado?" Her eyes didn't focus on anything. "What time is it?" She turned back to the cash register. "I didn't know about it." More people came in, and a man stood inside the doorway, saying in a loud voice something was wrong with gas pump number two. "I'll be with you in a minute, Jake. These people are ahead of you." She gave me a true Anna smile and a long hug, filling me with happy energy. "See you tonight, Jessie my girl. I love you!"

"I love you too, Mom." I lit out for home. She might see me tonight, but I wouldn't see her, because I was always asleep long before she got home.

Grandma was napping in our room when I got to the apartment. The answering machine by the living room window blinked at me. It's the old kind with a tiny cassette tape in it to record the messages. It used to belong to Grandma and Grandpa DeGroot, but when we moved out of their house to go to Mississippi, they gave it to Dad. They used to leave messages all the time, telling him about stuff on the farm with the cows and the neighbors, so he could listen at home in between trips. Sometimes he would find a pay phone at a truck stop and call us. With Mom and Dad's goofy schedules, and since Grandma and Grandpa DeGroot were always out in the barn with the dairy cows, that worked for everyone to share short stories with each other.

The other thing they gave Mom and Dad when we moved was this frilly pink and white glass dish. Grandma DeGroot always put candy in it on the coffee table in her living room. I think I was the only one who ate that candy, but maybe she did it just for me, her little granddaughter. Mom cried when Grandma DeGroot gave it to her, which I didn't understand. In Mississippi, Mom put it in a glass cabinet in the apartment and didn't fill it with candy anymore.

When we lived in Nebraska, tornadoes came through all the time, and we always went to the basement and waited until it was over. Afterwards, Grandpa and Dad would fix missing shingles from the roof, cut up fallen branches, or repair the fences.

But last year, it was different. That time, the tornado hit their house and barn directly, and they both died, along with a bunch of the dairy cows. Now Dad's older brother Joe ran the farm. He didn't ever leave messages on our machine.

I had just listened to Dad's message from today at lunchtime, checking in from somewhere in Pennsylvania. Then the phone rang. I picked up right away, and Dad's voice said, "Hi Kiddo!"

I know I squealed like a little girl, because I was his little girl, even though I was almost thirteen. "Dad!" I said. "Daddy!!!"

He laughed his big, happy laugh. "Well Jessie, I just saw you yesterday. Do you miss me that much?"

"Yes! Dad, I always miss you, but guess what?" I didn't even let him answer. "We just had a tornado!"

His voice got serious. "Well, actually, that's why I was calling again. I heard about that new hurricane and the spin-off tornadoes along the coast." He cleared his throat. "So, you had one there? How are you all doing?"

"We're okay. Grandma's asleep, so she might have missed the whole thing." We laughed. "I stopped in to see Mom." We both grumbled about the new hire not showing up. I had applied for a job there this spring, but they said I had to be sixteen, even though I'm definitely more reliable than that stupid kid.

I could hear Dad changing the subject. "Want anything from Maine? Or even Pennsylvania? That's where I am now."

I shook my head. "Just come home, Dad."

Friday, August 26 - 8 a.m.

On Hook TV this morning, they told us that the Pirate Pride contest started on Monday, and everyone was supposed to wear red, blue, and white all week, and the homeroom that collected the most food for the food pantry would win a shrimp po' boy party from Kendal's Seafood—Miss Doreen was famous for her generosity, and she always told me, "I love this town." They said for lunch today, we could choose among nachos grande, a Mexican burrito, or a chicken fajita, and we could add cucumber slices with ranch dip, rice, or pinto beans.

I loosened my hair out of the two too-tight braids Grandma had done and put it into one ponytail instead. Relief.

Mr. Hartman gave back our hurricane tests. "You all did well. We're in the middle of hurricane season, and I'm glad you're taking this seriously." He looked around the room. "Part of these Mississippi Studies classes is what we called emergency preparedness." We must have looked back at him kind of blankly. "Preparedness is like 'pre-deciding' what you're going to do when a disaster happens. I remember learning that from my teacher Mrs. Lipp when I was your age." It was hard to imagine him ever being a middle school boy. He smiled at me, saying, "Jessie, I'd like to congratulate you for getting the top score in the class. You just missed two."

Pam nudged me and whispered in Grandma's accent, "Why you not get 100%, you lazy girl?" and cracked up. Her mom never asked her about her grades at all, and her dad was not around much, and sometimes Pam could eat like a pig at lunch time. She even looked a little like a pig with her bright pink skin and pudgy fingers, but she was my friend, and there was nothing she could do about either how she looked or whether or not I was her friend. None of us ever talked about our looks, because we had so much in common on the inside, and besides, we all had eyes, a nose, a mouth... Shapes and colors didn't matter. Though we did tease if someone tried to wear makeup or started to get acne. That was funny. "Middle school is a really awkward time of life, so just get used to it," Mom told me.

In language arts, Mrs. Drummond taught us a new idiomatic expression, "To weather the storm," which meant to deal with a tough problem without being harmed or damaged too much. That's idiomatic, not idiotic. We had to write out all the new expressions and vocabulary words in meaningful sentences. I wrote, "To live with my grandma is to weather a storm, because there's no way to know what she's going to be angry about next, no matter how hard I try, but I keep trying. Is that dumb?" I predicted that Mrs. Drummond would draw a happy smiley face next to that one in purple ink when she read it.

At lunch, we all told stories and laughed at how ridiculous each family was. I treated lunch time like a talent show. I would never go on stage to tell stories, but I could do it at the table with my goofy, awkward friends. I did an imitation of Grandma Jiexen yelling at her chickens in Cantonese, and then Pam imitated her dad when he showed up four hours late and acted like nothing was wrong. We laughed at that too. What else could we do?

After school, Mary and I stopped at War Memorial Park. Sometimes people didn't pay attention and would mix me up with Mary. She was short like me and had brown eyes and brown hair like me, but her nose was small and cute, just like her mom and dad's Vietnamese noses. They came from Vietnam, but she was born here, in Mississippi, kind of like when Grandma and Baa came to the U.S. from Hong Kong, and then my mom was born in San Francisco. My eyes still look kind of Chinese, but Dad said I had a big Dutch nose like his, and I was born in Nebraska on the DeGroot's dairy farm, just like Dad was.

I'm digressing again. The park. It overlooked the beach from the other side of Highway 90 and Scenic Drive, which both parallelled the beach. Mr. Hartman got us to notice that we were about eight feet above sea level at our school, and the park was about the same, but lots of other parts of the Pass were only between one and six feet above sea level. Like our apartment complex.

The other cool thing about War Memorial Park, and all around the Pass, was the mammoth live oak trees. Mr. Necaise taught us they were called "live" because they didn't go dormant in the winter. In the park, a dozen of them had their own individual names: George Washington, Betsy Ross, Abraham Lincoln, and other famous Americans. Mr. Ellis pointed out there was a registry of these trees throughout the city, telling the address, the name of the tree, and how old they might be. The oldest ones were six hundred years old! I didn't understand how they survived Hurricane Camille when they were so close to the beach.

I loved to sit at the picnic table under the trees and look out over the Mississippi Sound, with Cat Island, one of the barrier islands, in the distance. The sun shone on the peaceful waters of the Sound, and it smelled like fish and sand and salt water. Mary said, "I could sit here forever." Yep, same here. I just nodded.

At home that night, I turned on the television after Grandma made dinner and I cleaned up. Long ago, I had figured out that if I did the dishes immediately and then turned on "Dancing with the Stars" on Friday nights, Grandma would sit on the sofa to watch it with me, and it didn't turn into a lecture about anything. Bliss.

But the local news announcer interrupted the show as soon as it had started.

"The National Hurricane Center has shifted the possible track of this hurricane from the Florida Panhandle to the Mississippi/Louisiana coast, as the storm continues to strengthen in the warm waters of the Gulf of Mexico," she said.

Grandma sat up straight and shooshed me. I hadn't even said anything. Why did she always have to assume the worst of me? Despite how annoyed I was with her, I listened too.

"Voluntary evacuations are issued for low-lying areas. The Mississippi Gulf Coast is now directly within the cone of uncertainty for this hurricane," the meteorologist said, pointing to a map with Waveland, Bay St. Louis, Pass Christian, Long Beach, and Gulfport front and center.

I pondered the irony that for a tornado, you're supposed to hunker down in the lowest level of the building, but for flooding, that's the exact worst place to be. Hm.

The reporter said, "We experience hurricanes frequently in our area, but we recommend you leave town for this storm. If you do not evacuate, at least move your vehicles to higher ground and your valuables and important papers to a higher level in your home, in case of higher-than-normal storm surge. Go ahead and get the plywood back out to protect your windows," she said. "Make plans to pick up sandbags as soon as possible. Double check your emergency supplies, because grocery stores report they are running out of supplies like batteries, bottled water, bread, and other non-perishable goods." The banner on the screen said, "Hurricane Katrina headed toward this viewing area. Immediate evacuation recommended."

Grandma's eyes didn't leave the screen. "When Anna get home from work?"

"She won't get home until after midnight tonight, Grandma." She never did. Why did she ask questions I didn't need to answer? If I didn't answer, though, she'd say something like "incurable child make me weep bitter tears."

So unfair.

"We need get out of here," she said. "Get me phone number for her work," she said. "I need call her." She switched off the television.

I knew the number by heart, so I dialed it and handed the phone receiver to Grandma.

She stood up with importance for the phone call, and I heard Mom's far-away voice answer, "Quik Mart, Anna speaking."

"Anna, come home. Now!" She switched to Cantonese, telling her about the updates on the hurricane.

I could hear Mom on the other end of the line blowing out some air before answering. She answered in Cantonese too, but I could tell pretty much what she said when Tiger Grandma responded by slamming the phone back on the base. She switched the TV back on to "Dancing with the Stars," but her eyes looked out the living room window instead of at the screen.

I heard her and Mom arguing late at night after Mom got home from work.

Saturday, August 27 - morning

For the first time in months, my mom woke up before I did. She sat on the edge of my bed, speaking with a cheery tone I hadn't heard in a long time. She'd even washed her hair this morning before braiding it. How early did she get up? "Jessie, sweet girl, would you please get up and help your grandma with breakfast?" She said this in a voice that meant she was trying to be awake and pleasant even though she was exhausted. Her eyes gave her away.

But, hey, she was taking charge around here, even a little? I could totally live with this!

I rubbed my eyes, changed into my weekend shorts and tank top, and went to the kitchen.

The television was on in the living room, which was open to the kitchen, so the news was in my face before I was ready to listen. For weather information, they liked to watch the news station in Biloxi. I know I'm just a seventh grader, but this new weather announcer looked like he was not much older than me. He said, "The National Hurricane Center is forecasting Hurricane Katrina will drive directly toward the Mississippi Gulf Coast."

That's what they said last night, but sometimes they change their minds. We do pay attention to hurricane forecasts, but we can't be concerned about every one that comes along. That would be like the Boy Who Cried Wolf. But now this one was heading straight toward us. I started toward the sofa to sit down, but Grandma pushed past me and sat next to Mom first.

I could have sat in Dad's chair, but instead, I went to the kitchen, turned on the faucet, and ran water into the teakettle. Grandma turned to glare at me. What was her problem? Everyone could still hear what he was saying, and I had a feeling that everyone was going to need hot water for tea.

He kept talking. "Hurricane Katrina has reached Category 3 intensity. The storm tracks now predict a Louisiana and Mississippi landfall." His voice cracked again, just like a high school boy.

"Ha!" I laughed at his squeaky voice, but I shut up again when Grandma shooshed me.

The announcer said, "There is not a mandatory evacuation yet, but authorities highly recommend that you board up your homes, move vehicles to higher ground, collect your vital documents, and evacuate farther inland, away from the storm surge flooding." He showed photos of lines of flooded roads and cars parked along the interstate and at schools. "Leave as soon as you can!"

Grandma said, "Anna, we need..." but Mom waved her hand and shooshed her and kept her eyes on the screen. Why did my mom, who was usually so depressed, have enough energy to disagree with Grandma today?

Then they showed a video of people filling sandbags. "County workers are filling sandbags to redirect some flooding around specific vital infrastructure. Residents can fill their own sandbags at public facilities along the coast. However, as you know from past storms, this is no guarantee, and officials encourage you to leave town instead of trying to ride this one out."

A random piece of knowledge from the hurricane test percolated to the top of my brain. When all the floodwaters receded, those sandbags could not be emptied back onto the ground. Nope, they had to be treated like toxic waste because of all the gross stuff that collected in them from the floodwaters — bacteria and toxic slime. Epically disgusting.

I had to agree with Grandma, at least in my head. Time for us to get out of here.

Mom stood up and shut off the television while Grandma stared at the screen. I poured the boiling water in with the loose tea in the pot. Outside the open window, the air was completely still. The gigantic branches on the palms and live oaks didn't move.

Maybe I had a premonition. We'd just learned that word, meaning a feeling of evil to come. I felt this image of us on an overloaded highway, trapped in Mom's green car, which was packed full of pecking chickens. I couldn't believe Grandma hadn't started in on Mom yet about how we need to leave, but for once, Mom got her speech in before Grandma started hers.

"Mama and Jessie, I know we have all agreed as a family that when they tell us to evacuate for a hurricane, we will do that."

I nodded. Grandma looked ready to talk, but Mom pointed a finger at her, stopping her. Whoa! What was Mom about to say?

"David and I know full well that when they tell us to get out, we need to listen. And I'm about to try to get him a message and tell him what I'm saying to you now," she paused. "While I'm gone today, you two can pack up what we need and get ready to load the car as soon as my shift is over." She looked at both our faces. "We'll leave early this afternoon." She was smiling.

That was not what I expected.

I started to ask my question, but Grandma shooshed me again. "Anna, you not smart girl. We need leave right now! Why you want go to work?"

Mom laughed, catching us both off guard. "Mama," she said. "There's no one else working at the store. That new kid never showed up, and the manager left early this morning with his family to go to Jackson. He told me last night."

"That not our problem, Anna," said Grandma. It would be too painful to actually agree with her out loud, but she was right.

Mom had this wistful look in her eyes. "I can help those people who are staying," she said. "If I help keep the gas station and the store open one more shift, a lot of people who have nowhere to go, or the ones who don't want to leave, can get what they need to ride it out." She listed things. "Batteries, food, water. We even have a stack of plywood in the parking lot for them to board up windows." She looked excited. "Goodness knows, even the ones who are evacuating need to gas up their vehicles before heading into those traffic jams."

Grandma and I both opened our mouths at the same time, but she kept going. "Stop. Stop it, you two." Another move totally unlike Mom. "I filled my car gas tank last night, so you know. The storm is not supposed to hit until Monday morning. We have two days before it gets here," she said. "Our pastor is always reminding us to give a little more than we think we can, to help those around us who really need it, right?"

I nodded. Grandma didn't.

"This is giving a lot, but it will be fine." Mom kept going. "This is a time when I can really help," She was talking to herself as much as to us. "I'll come home early this afternoon, and you two will have everything ready, and we'll head north, okay?" She addressed Grandma. "Mama, you know what we need to pack. You've done this before."

Grandma pressed her lips tight into a line, but she nodded. What did that mean, she'd done this before? We'd all done this before, closing windows, packing, heading for high ground. Was something different?

"Now, I've got to call David."

She couldn't call him directly when he was on the road, but she called Pre-Stress and left a message for him on their answering service, saying, "David, we're going to evacuate this afternoon. I've heard the hotel situation is bad. There's nothing between here and Jackson." When did she figure that out? Did she hear it at the convenience store last night? Was she up making phone calls this morning while I was still asleep? Did she even get to sleep? "We'll just drive straight through and meet you at the farm in Nebraska with Joe. If this turns out to be a false alarm, meet us back at home here after the storm. Love you, honey."

She hung up and smiled at me and Grandma. "I'll be home by one o'clock at the latest." She took her purse and left me with Grandma.

State of emergency, big deal. Grandma and I were in a state of emergency all the time. Why couldn't it just be a normal Saturday where Mom and I could go to Waveland and hang out, or Dad and I could play some miniature golf?

No, instead we had to pack up and leave, except we couldn't leave right away, because today of all days, she had the guts to say a "big fat no" to Grandma and love everyone just like Jesus did. Forgive me if it made it hard for me to understand about Christianity when it made people act crazy and illogical. Or hypocritical. I liked it when the pastor talked about sharing love with others, but then I looked around at the people in church and remembered how they acted the rest of the week, more like Grandma. Then I was just confused.

She was so distracted today, she didn't even try to braid my hair. Relief. I combed through it and put it in a ponytail holder. So there.

Saturday, August 27 – later morning

I went in the bedroom and looked out at the sky. It was a beautiful Gulf Coast day. Not ominous at all, looking at it from a third-floor apartment less than a mile from the beach. We had time to get ready.

Grandma's voice broke through. "Jessie, you hear what I ask you?"

Apparently, I hadn't. "No, Grandma."

"You get all school books?"

"Yes, Grandma." I pointed at my backpack by the bedroom door. When did I pack those? But, she would never give me points for being ahead of the curve.

She kept frowning. "You pack up all good food from refrigerator?"

"Huh?"

She said, "We bring the food. It go bad if we gone long time."

Okay. Not a bad point, not that I would ever say that to her. She cooked all the time, really good food, too, and sometimes we brought homemade food to share with people at church or gave it to neighbors. Mom said Grandma's need to cook so much food had something to do with when Mao got everyone to kill all the sparrows in China and it caused a famine. People had no food, and some ate grass. Jiexen's school had a tank on the roof to grow algae, so they would have food to eat. Algae? Mom said, ever since she swam away from China to Hong Kong, she cooked food all the time, first at the noodle shop, and now here. So much food. I remembered *The Sorcerer's Apprentice* movie, where the enchanted brooms wouldn't stop fetching buckets full of water, even when the house was flooding. Hm.

"Jessie! You need work!"

I went to the front hall closet, got the blue ice chest and dragged it over to the kitchen, flinging all the little containers of leftovers in there. Onion pancakes. Almond jello. The red snapper from the other night.

She stood and watched me work, shaking her head.

"Grandma, you don't have to stand there and watch me do this."

She crossed her arms over her chest and her sharp, black eyes told me to keep on packing.

"Fine! All done!" I got the last two containers to fit but then remembered the freezer. When I opened it, I saw at least four more plastic containers of frozen leftovers.

This could not be happening with her standing there

watching me. My chest hurt. I reached for the stuff from the freezer, but she pushed me aside. My eyes burned.

"No, you do it wrong." She reached in the cooler, took out all the refrigerator containers that were partially full of left-overs: spaghetti, egg salad with pickles in it, spicy tofu with peanuts, and chicken vegetable stir-fry. She combined them into fewer boxes and fit them all in the cooler. "See, more room now. Get all them now," gesturing to the freezer.

I squeezed my eyes to keep the tears inside.

This was gross, having all the different flavors of food touching. What a stupid way to handle this. I did it anyway. No point arguing with a crazy grandma. Or an army of enchanted brooms like the ones in *The Sorcerer's Apprentice*. My chest felt heavy and hot inside. I kept squeezing my eyes closed, but tears leaked down my face.

Apparently, she was talking to me again, wagging her finger at me. "And clothes to wear while we gone to Nebraska?"

I shook myself back to reality. "Yes, Grandma."

She sniffed. "It very cold there. You bring warm clothes?"

I laughed through my tears, which felt great. "No, Grand-ma." I laughed right in her face.

"What you mean?" She looked at me, hard. "Why not? Go get warm clothes. Winter coat."

The joke was on her for a change. "It's summer in Nebraska, just like here. I haven't had a winter coat since kindergarten."

She cleared her throat, pursed her lips, preparing to peck at me some more.

A little voice told me this would be a good time to pray for help instead of saying one more word. Our youth leader said it was better to pray than to say something you would regret, but it was hard to remember that with Grandma in my face, pecking at me.

I went in the bathroom to blow my nose, and I laughed again, imagining Grandma was shaped like a chicken, wearing a winter stocking hat with a big pom-pom on it, hopping up and down the apartment stairwell, clucking and looking for bugs. Please God, help me not laugh any more. We just had to make it until Mom got home, and then she would get us out of here.

Grandma got money and papers from Mom and Dad's room and her own desk, and a box of papers in Chinese calligraphy that I've seen her sit and look at sometimes, and she stuck it all in an old blue plastic flight bag decorated with a white globe-shaped symbol, but the lines were curved wrong. Mom had told me it was a logo from Pan Am, a company that didn't exist anymore. Grandma had it with her when she surprised all three of us by showing up in Mississippi that day when I was six. She had never told me a story about China that was positive, so what memories did those Chinese papers have? No clue.

Back in the front hall, I had an idea about something Grandma hadn't hollered at me to do yet. I grabbed the laundry basket and put in her rice cooker, the coffeemaker, and the special black tea Grandma ordered from San Francisco. I didn't want to be on the road with her for days if she was whining about her tea.

Correction, I didn't want to be on the road with her for days at all.

Why couldn't Mom just stop being such a perfect angel and we could have left already? I had a premonition Grandma would find a way to make this my fault.

We made a stack of suitcases, bags, boxes, and the laundry basket full of small appliances by the door ready to take down to the car. Now we waited for Mom. I looked out the living room window. The sky was still blue. The air was steamier than usual, and it was completely still. Nothing to worry about yet.

Grandma went out to the balcony and talked to the chickens. Odessa, the white and black one, was her favorite, the one she took for walks with a leash and a little harness she'd made. But she didn't try to get her or Penelope or the others into the tubs. They would not willingly do that in the daylight and it was too soon before we were leaving, anyway.

I plopped down on the sofa with my backpack and took out the *Magyk* book that I'd scored from the library before Mary could get it.

Grandma appeared next to me. "Jessie."

"Huh?" I guess she was done hanging out with her chickens. How long had she been standing there?

She spluttered at me, "Why you no get all the vegetables from garden?"

"What?" I was not expecting this.

"If storm come, all vegetables broken by wind."

I shook my head at her with confused eyes.

She nodded her head back at me, hands on her skinny hips. "We need take them in car. Give to the brother in Nebraska."

I had not seen Uncle Joe since we moved away, back when Grandma and Grandpa DeGroot ran the farm. From what I could remember of Uncle Joe, he did not eat a vegetable if there was another option, like meat or potatoes or dessert.

"Grandma, I…" was all I got out of my mouth.

"You don't argue with me, Jessie. I say, you go do. Now."

My eyes burned again. I squeezed my eyes, but I did not stand up. It wasn't even a decision. Instead, I found myself not obeying her commands. Instead, I turned back to my book, trying to hide from her in plain sight. All the muscles in my throat felt tight.

She snorted, got the garden snips and small wicker gathering basket from the closet, and held them out to me. My eyes tried to read the words, but they were getting blurry. My arms stayed where they were, holding the book.

"You take!" She dropped the snips and basket right on top of the book, but I tipped the book so they fell off my lap and onto the floor.

Next, I felt like I was watching myself do things from a viewpoint up by the ceiling. Through a fog, I saw myself jump up from the sofa, leaving my book and backpack there, and bolt right out the front door to the landing and down the flights of open stairs.

I'm sure Grandma's screechy voice yelled behind me, but it was just background noise.

I joined up with my own body again and felt my flip-flops landing on each step, felt my legs running down toward the parking lot. From far away, Grandma's voice yelled at me to get back inside, but it was just words I could not obey this time.

I jumped on the bike seat and flew away from the building, wondering where my bike was taking me.

3

Saturday, August 27 - afternoon

I didn't notice the rain at first because of the tears running down my face. I couldn't even see where I was going. I just went. Away, away, away from that crazy lady who saw me as a big, incurable mistake. I pedaled like mad, not paying any attention to where I was riding. I just went.

The longer I rode, the madder I got at Grandma, and at Mom too, and I couldn't even see straight.

The railroad tracks ran in a completely level line for a hundred miles between New Orleans and Gulfport. They ran on their elevated path, right through the bayous and swamps and towns. The streets crossing the tracks all had to slant upward to get over the tracks and back down the other side. And today, I didn't remember to hold tighter to the handlebars as I plowed up that steep slope.

I lost my balance and crashed on my right side.

Slam!

The rain soaked my shorts and tank top, and even though it was a hot day, I felt cold and shivery. And shaky. I got myself disentangled from my bike and dragged it to the side of the road, limping. A huge sob spilled out of me. I hunkered down there for a long time, until my throat was sore and no more tears came out.

Blood leaked from some scrapes on my right elbow and knee, and the rain ran red rivulets down my arm and leg. I picked up my bike to keep riding and winced. I must have hit my shoulder, but I didn't remember for sure. I closed my eyes, took some deep breaths, and tried not to cry again.

Where was I going, anyway?

Mary's house. Whenever it was crazy at my house, I could go there, and her mom would feed me, and her little brothers would act like idiots and distract us, and then I would feel better. That's how it always worked.

Whenever Mary came over to our apartment, the only difference was I didn't have any little brothers, and we would usually walk the few hundred feet across the parking lot and the grass to the wooden dock that stretched out into the bayou behind the apartment building. We'd drop leaves and sticks in the water and talk about stuff.

I focused on that, figured out where I was, and rode a few blocks to her family's little cement block house, just two steps up to the door, not up high on stilts like a lot of the newer houses were. I wiped the leftover tears off my face, and when Mary's mom answered the door, said, "Hi Mrs. Ngo. I'm sorry to bother you…" I loved saying her mom's family name. To say "Ngo" felt like swallowing the end of the word "bongo." Nothing like an English sound. Delicious.

But, whoa, I'd never seen her cry before. She was what Mr. Necaise called a tough cookie. "I'm …" I forgot what I was worrying about, seeing her so upset like this. "Are you okay, Mrs. Ngo?"

"What you still doing here, Jessie?" Her Vietnamese-style sentences sounded a lot like Grandma's. "You need get gone!

Katrina bad storm!" She didn't even notice that my hair was wet, and I was bleeding, but she ushered me inside.

The television blared a news channel. Mrs. Ngo pointed to a bag and a suitcase just inside the front door. "Jessie, be good girl, help take this to car for me. Then you go home." I stood there with my mouth open. She gave me a quick hug and then nudged me away. "You need leave. Now!" She patted my shoulder, then sniffled and went in the bathroom, where a loud nose-blowing sound came out of her tiny, flat nose. Impressive volume. When she was done, I went in for a tissue too.

The TV announcer said, "The national weather service in Jackson has just issued a detailed Special Weather Statement to raise awareness and recommend preparedness activities. A large swath of sustained wind speeds around 60 miles per hour and higher, including the potential for sustained hurricane-force winds over 75 miles per hour, will be possible over areas east of Interstate 55 and south of Interstate 20 Monday evening and Monday night."

That meant the entire eastern half of the state was going to be blown away. It was Saturday afternoon, so this was not for two days, which was good, but the goosebumps on my wet skin made me hug my arms around myself.

The man said, "For now, if you're still in a flood-prone area, decide which part of your house is safest and create a family disaster plan. Check your stock of canned foods, first aid supplies, drinking water, and prescription drugs." Pictures of the items flashed on the screen. "If you have not already evacuated, make plans for possible prolonged power outages and loss of water or other utilities."

I breathed a little better. Okay, that didn't matter, because we were going to leave today as soon as my mom got home. I didn't move, just kept my eyes on their TV and tightened my arms around my chest, still sniffling a little.

Then the announcer said, "This just in." They showed the casino in Biloxi that looked like a riverboat which floated on a barge. Huge crashing waves surrounded it. The casino boat moved up and down next to the wharf, in real danger of smashing into it, with those crazy waves stirred up in the shallow water of the Sound.

"For those of you on the road or about to head out, be aware that Interstate 10 along the Gulf Coast is closed through the entire state of Mississippi due to high waves endangering bridges along that route. Repeat, as of three o'clock this afternoon, you may not travel on Interstate 10 along the Gulf."

We would still be okay. Mom said we were going to drive north, not east or west, when we left today.

Saturday, August 27 - a little later in afternoon

I took the stuff outside and put it with the other things next to the car. I didn't see how they would all fit. Maybe they would ride with boxes on their laps. Finally, Mary came outside with a little brother hanging from each hand. They were squirrelly little guys, and I was glad I didn't have to ride in the back seat with them like she had to now.

Mary came over to our apartment a lot. Her two little brothers didn't listen to her mom at all, just her dad, but he was always out shrimping in the Sound. Mary and I took turns escaping to each other's houses, or else we rode our bikes around the Pass together and looked for scrap metal to sell. Of all the people in the Pass, she and Pam were some of the few who had met my grandma, besides the people at church, but church people aren't allowed to judge each other's embarrassing family members, at least not until they get home. All my other friends must have thought she was a wicked stepmother character I stole from the Hansel and Gretel story or something. I think I would have died of embarrassment if they met her in person, because she was just too unbelievably unpredictable. And she smelled like too much garlic. I'm digressing again, aren't I?

But Mary understood, and she was pretty good at imitating Grandma's accent, making a sour face and laughing at the same time. "Why you not perfect, Jessie? Why you not make million dollar and buy big house for me to live?"

Back to reality. "Hey, Jessie," she said. "Want to go to the beach today and hang out?" She tried to be her usual funny self. It didn't work.

"Where are you going, Mary? Where's your dad?"

"He's heading toward Lake Pontchartrain to float the shrimp boat up the Pearl River."

I sucked in a breath. "What?" I thought people were supposed to avoid going on the water during a hurricane.

She read my mind. "It's farther upriver, so it might survive the hurricane there." She didn't sound like my mischievous friend at all anymore. She sounded so serious.

Her dad's shrimp boat was called the *Free in America*. He had painted the name on the prow of the little boat by hanging upside down from the deck to fill in the letters, one at a time, with shiny blue paint. He told me, "Before this, I have red letter on boat, but sun make them look pink. Now I change to blue." He smiled a wide smile that showed all his teeth and all the gaps where there weren't any teeth. The words looked like they were painted with an ink pen in calligraphy, the kind that reminded me of Chinese characters I couldn't read. The *Free in America* was his pride and joy. It took a long time to get the money to buy his own boat, and that was why they waited until they were older to have any kids.

My throat was frozen. "Oh, geez," I said. I just stood there, thinking about her dad, out on that little boat with the long-reaching outriggers folded in, and what it would be like when the hurricane-strength winds hit, the ones Miss Bernie described so well.

I realized Mary was looking me right in the eyes. Sometimes, I felt like we could communicate telepathically. I just shook my head a little, keeping my eyes on hers. I didn't want to hear what she was going to say.

In a very grown-up voice, she said, "Mama said her friend Tu Phan has a cousin in Hattiesburg who has space in her basement for some of the shrimper families."

I must have made a face.

Mary nodded and grimaced. "We're going to be jammed in like sardines in a can…" she chuckled a little. "But at least we're going to have some great food to eat." Her mom was even a better cook than my grandma or Miss Doreen. She glanced at her little brothers and got all businesslike again. "I better make sure they brought some games and stuff. I gotta go."

They loaded in the car, and her tiny-but-mighty mom could barely see over the steering wheel. From the back window, Mary's eyes found mine, and she'd never looked that serious in her whole life. Then one of her brothers must have pulled her hair or something because I saw her arm come up and thwack him. I stood there waving as if I had all the time in the world, as if I'd see her at school on Monday or Tuesday when it re-opened, or whenever we got back from Nebraska.

The rain hit me in the head and face, waking me up finally. The pictures from the news all finally reached my brain. Highways full of cars. People filling sandbags. Lines at the gas station. Food shelves empty. Boats being pulled out of the harbor and hauled away on trailers, or lifted on frames to hold them above the water or flooded up river.

Oh geez, did that announcer say it was already three o'clock?

Saturday, August 27 - 3:30 p.m.

I had forgotten about my bike crash and my sore knee, so those first few pumps of my feet on the pedals hurt a lot, but I just yelled into the wind.

The wind? It's windy now too?

The rain made it hard to see, and the back wheel flung water up from the street onto my back. It didn't matter. How did it get so late? I peddled faster, amazed at how many carloads drove north past me.

Why didn't I just stay and deal with Grandma, so we could have left on time?

At the apartment parking lot, I didn't see Mom's little olive-green car in her usual place. Maybe she'd gotten delayed. Some of our suitcases sat next to Grandma's bike. I parked my bike by the stairs and ran up, dreading every step. Grandma confronted me at the top landing. "Where you go Jessie!?" she yelled. "Why you be gone so long?"

I tried to get things back on track. "Where's Mom?"

"She drove! She look for you!" Grandma yelled. "You carry box down so we leave when she come back."

I started hauling stuff, and when it was all downstairs by the asphalt, I stayed there next to my bike, far away from Grandma. It took forever, but then I heard Mom's little car pull in the parking lot. When she saw me, she parked right by the steps and hopped out into the rain.

"Jessie! You're here!" She hugged me. "Oh, I'm so glad you're here." I couldn't believe how nice she was being, even for her. I knew I was late. She noticed the scrapes on my arm and leg and raised an eyebrow.

"Bike crash." I started to explain the rest. "Grandma and I had a big…"

"Nope!" she stopped me, holding out her hand flat in my face. "Mama said the police came by to tell us to evacuate right after you ran away," she filled in. "Mandatory evacuations. Mama told them we were leaving soon, and that's still the plan, whatever happened to you, so let's do that." She popped the trunk. "Mama!" she hollered instructions up to Grandma in Cantonese. She turned to me again. "As soon as we get this, we can go."

I kept loading stuff, and she bounded up all five half-flights of steps to get Grandma and lock the door. I thought they'd come back in a minute, but they didn't, and instead I heard some yelling up there, so I went upstairs too.

Oh my gosh, chickens ran everywhere. The sliding door to the balcony was open, and gusts of wind blew the rain inside. The fluffy chickens, Grandma's best friends, were not dumb cluckers like some people thought. They were not going to jump in Grandma's arms if she wanted to stuff them in a tub in broad daylight. Penelope landed on the lamp next to the sofa in a flurry of black feathers and chicken dust. Mom and I looked at each other and tried not to laugh. That was the best moment of the whole day so far, but there weren't many to choose from today, either.

Mom got one of the other tubs from the balcony, and she and I ambushed one chicken at a time, working as a team. Once we got hold of one, I hooked my fingers around both its feet, held it upside down, stuffed it in the tub, and held down the lid with a few books. Six chickens in two tubs. Crowded.

Mom said something in Cantonese. I picked up one tub, and Grandma got the other one, went out to the landing, and started down the steps. Mom locked the door, and we hurried to the car. The warm rain came down harder now, and we had to struggle against the wind to get the doors open and closed again. We were all soaked.

I rode in the back seat with the tubs of hens, and I wondered if we'd brought some chicken feed to keep them quiet. If not, this was going to be worse than Mary having to sit next to her brothers, for sure.

Mom read my mind. "Once we get out of the traffic farther north, we could stop at a grocery store and get some vegetables for them, okay Mama?"

Grandma kicked into high gear. "I tell that girl, get vegetables to feed chickens in car, but she not listen. She run away."

Not true! "No, Mom! She said the vegetables were for Uncle Joe. She didn't say anything about…"

Grandma interrupted, "Anna, sometimes you smart girl."

Well, that was a rare statement. If Grandma actually said Mom was "a smart girl" for once, maybe there was hope for me, and she'd stop saying I was lazy. Not today, but maybe one day.

Mom didn't try to sort it out with Grandma. Not worth it. I gave up, too. If we could just get going, maybe we would be okay. I pictured the highways all clogged up with cars like I'd seen on the news and wondered how far Mary's family had gotten. It would be many hours before we would stop for vegetables for the dumb cluckers. Maybe they would decide it was night time and fall asleep in the tubs.

Mom started the car and pulled forward so we could turn back south and get to the road. I closed my eyes. I always practiced our driving route in my head, because Dad quizzed me on that sometimes. He would say, "Before you learn to drive, you have to know the names of the streets, Jessie my girl."

Once we got to North Street, we would go east to Menge Avenue to get around the east side of the bayou and go north out of town to Interstate 10. Maybe we would go north on 49.

But hey, the car wasn't even moving. I opened my eyes. We were still in the parking lot, not even on North Street yet. Just stopped.

Mom made tight noises in her throat and pushed her foot on the accelerator, over and over. The engine was running, but we weren't going anywhere.

Grandma said, "We go now, Anna."

Mom sounded choked. "I'm trying, Mama."

We still didn't move. I looked up at the apartment and saw we'd left the light on in the kitchen. Oh well.

Mom turned off the car and got out. She kneeled to look under the engine. I got out to see what she was doing.

"Oh no," she said. "Oh no, this can't be happening."

"What is it?" I asked, as Grandma got out too. We both looked where Mom was looking.

A puddle of thick, dark liquid spread out under the front of the car and mixed with the rainwater on the ground. Mom ran back toward the stairs.

She was halfway up when she turned around and hollered down at me, "Bring the car keys up to me, Jessie. I can't get in here." Her voice sounded strangled and weak.

I took the keys from the ignition and got up to her as fast as I could.

She flipped through the phone book. "The car won't move," she told the man at some random service station. "It was red, or reddish-brown." A few more sentences and she hung up.

She looked at me and Grandma. "I'm so sorry," was all she could get out. Tears spilled out of her eyes. She could barely say, "We'll try to get a ride or something." Mom pointed to me and gestured for me to go down to North Street to try to flag down a car. Her voice would not come out of her throat anymore.

Oh my gosh. Our car wasn't working? But that was the plan. To drive north in the car. My eyes felt red and burning, just like mom's looked. Finally, I said, "I'll go see if I can find a ride, Mom." The first person I thought of calling was Mary, but they were long gone and had zero extra room for three people, a bunch of suitcases and boxes, and two tubs of angry chickens. Besides, they left hours ago.

Yeah, hours ago. If I hadn't let Grandma get to me, we wouldn't be stuck like this. Hours ago, we could have found a ride. Now it would be like "trying to pull a cow up a tree," as Grandma said.

After about twenty minutes, Mom joined me on North Street. "Grandma and I took the chickens back up to the balcony, but everything else is still in the car, in case we find a way out tonight," she said in a quiet voice. "I looked to see if anyone had lights on in any of the other apartments, and I knocked on some doors, but I couldn't find anyone still home."

The rain beat on us. We waved at any car that went by, but they were few and far between. It got dark, and the cars did not stop, until one pulled over and rolled down the window. It was my friend Pam with her whole family, the car packed to the gills. Her dad was actually with them, and he said, "Sorry kid, we have to get going. I'm so sorry." Pam gave me a thumbs-up through the back window.

We were stranded, and it was my fault.

4

Sunday, August 28 - morning

I am so smart in school but so dumb in real life. I heard Mrs. Drummond's voice in my head, "A day late, and a dollar short." Even sweet Mrs. Drummond would agree it was not my smartest move to run away when we were about to evacuate, even if Grandma was horrible to me. And I'm sure you can just imagine what Grandma has been saying to me ever since yesterday.

I stayed hidden under the covers Saturday night, even though it was hot under there. From under the sheet, I thought I heard the chickens walking around inside the apartment, but that couldn't have been right, because they would make a mess of everything. If Dad were here, he'd be saying, "We'll never get our security deposit back!" I thought about where Dad might be and if he knew yet about the trouble I caused.

Another expression Mrs. Drummond had taught us that applied to me now was, "It never rains but it pours," and if that were true, we were far from being "out of the woods," since now we had to ride out this hurricane, which sounded bigger, and closer to being right on top of us, every time they talked about it on the news. By 7 a.m., the announcer said the National Weather Service declared Katrina a "potentially catastrophic" Category 5 storm and predicted "devastating damage."

My stomach ached with the unfairness of it all. It wasn't my fault that Mom went to work for one more shift or that the car broke. It was just bad timing, but I knew the timing was my fault. I pulled the pillow over my head and tried to pray, but I was too mad. And scared, too. I knew what a Category 5 hurricane meant, in my head, but I didn't want to observe it in real life.

I tried to focus on something I could control, and I wondered if Mrs. Drummond would give me extra credit for all the idiomatic expressions I'd been using in meaningful context. I wondered where she was now. She had said her kids lived in Memphis, Tennessee, which she pronounced "TEN-ah-see." Was it true that "Every cloud had a silver lining"? Hm, probably not this cloud.

I dozed off and then woke, remembering what Grandma said to me very late last night as we hauled our supplies back upstairs from the car. "Confucius say you 'horse that harms the herd.'" Was that really true? If so, I sure didn't harm my family on purpose.

I thought about taking a shower and getting the snarls out of my hair, but I couldn't find the energy, even though I was so sweaty and my brain felt bleary.

The television finally got me out of bed when they announced that our school district was officially closed tomorrow. Well, how about that? What took them so long?

Then the news got worse. Worse than a Cateogry 5 hurricane heading straight toward us? Yes. They said that by 10 a.m., besides the inland hurricane warning, they "emphasized the horrific impacts Katrina would likely create for southeast Louisiana and coastal Mississippi. Devastating damage is expected. This is a most powerful hurricane with unprecedented strength, rivaling Hurricane Camille in 1969."

So much for hundred-year storms.

Mom and Grandma sat next to each other on the sofa, holding hands. The announcer said, "Most of the area will be uninhabitable for weeks, perhaps longer. At least half of all well-constructed homes will have roof and wall failure. All gabled roofs will fail, leaving those homes severely damaged or destroyed."

What did they mean, uninhabitable? How could it be uninhabitable when people were in the middle of living there? The muscles in my stomach twisted up some more.

Grandma whispered, "What gabled roof?" but Mom ignored her. Penelope and Odessa pecked for crumbs between the sofa cushions. Rosita, Big Fluffy, Jing, and Lily wandered around in the apartment, pooping and finding crumbs or bugs. Yuck.

"The majority of industrial buildings will become non-functional. Partial to complete wall and roof failure is expected. Concrete block low-rise apartments will sustain major damage, including some wall and roof failure."

Was that our kind of apartment? I had a feeling school would be closed longer than just tomorrow. As in, would we ever be able to go back to school again? Ever?

"High rise office and apartment buildings will sway dangerously, a few to the point of total collapse. All windows will be blown out. Airborne debris will be widespread and may include heavy items such as household appliances and even light vehicles. Sport utility vehicles and light trucks will be moved."

I stood with my mouth open, behind Mom and Grandma. Then I went to sit on the floor in front of Mom, who took the comb from the end table and slowly worked on easing the knots out of my long hair while more bad news announcements came, one after another. She was so gentle with my hair, and maybe it was relaxing to her too, because before I knew it, she had it in one long braid down my back.

"The blown debris will create additional destruction. Persons, pets, and livestock exposed to the winds will face certain death if struck. Power outages will last for weeks, as most power poles will be down and transformers destroyed."

It dawned on me that we did still have power, to watch this on TV.

"Water shortages will make human suffering incredible by modern standards."

Grandma jumped up and pointed at me still in my sleeping t-shirt and undies. "You, get dress, now!" Then she headed to the bathroom, running water in the bathtub. She was going to take a bath? She was definitely illogical. Maybe something was even wrong with her brain, like what happens to old people sometimes, but she wasn't that old. I shouldn't have had to wonder about questions like that. It was not my job.

Grandma left the door open, so I couldn't hear all they said about all the trees being snapped off or uprooted or totally defoliated, but it was bad. He meant the live oaks in War Memorial Park, and the ones by the school and our church.

I put on clean clothes, my shorts and a Pass Christian Pirates t-shirt. Mom came out of her room wearing similar clothes. We went back to the TV and tried to hear over the noise Grandma made filling the bathtub.

"Few crops will remain. Livestock left exposed to the winds will be killed."

Maybe that was why Grandma kept the chickens inside this time. She had the tubs stacked up inside the sliding door in the kitchen, instead of in their usual place out on the balcony.

Oh. I am such a dumb-head.

Sunday, August 28 - still morning

"The inland hurricane wind warning means winds will reach near hurricane force, sustain for more than one minute at a time, or frequent gusts at or even above hurricane force, are certain within the next 12 to 24 hours. Once tropical storm and hurricane force winds onset, do not venture outside."

I was glad we had already moved all our boxes and tubs back up to the apartment, and none of us was going outside again until this was over. The winds were crazy enough already. I looked out the living room window at the tree branches swinging wildly in the rain. Over on the other side of the dumpster, Mom's green car sat where it had failed us, blocking the way if any other cars wanted to drive out that way. There were a few other cars still parked, but nobody was around to drive them. Where were they?

I had seen it before, how the water from the bayou rose high enough that it crossed the grass, floated the little wooden dock kind of sideways, and then invaded the parking lot in a gentle flow. It only took a few minutes for the first inch to cover everything in a smooth, wet wave a few inches high. That was usually where it stopped. The apartment manager always had to repair the dock after a tropical storm or hurricane.

Usually, Mom's car was parked in its spot near the apart- ment, not on the other side of the lot. It looked abandoned over there by itself, water all around and under it, rain whip- ping the air and the windows. It was stuck in the water, like steers and heifers who had been grazing in the fields and got surrounded by tall snowdrifts in Nebraska, and the farmers couldn't reach them with more hay. They would just have to wait it out until the drifts melted enough they could walk to the barn and get some hay to eat, like the dairy cows got. If it took too long for the snow to melt, they could starve to death, Grandpa DeGroot told me once.

I sat down on the floor next to the sofa. One chicken, I think it was Rosita, pecked my foot, hard, but I hardly even noticed. She let me pet her reddish-brown feathers for a while. How long would we be in waiting mode this time? Every storm was different, but this one sounded like none we had ever dealt with and there was nothing I could control. I just had to wait.

Grandma came out of the bathroom where she'd finished filling the bathtub.

"You, fill up all bucket with water. Pitcher. Cooler. Bowl. All fill with water."

So, I had to wait and also obey orders from Tiger Grandma. "Yes, ma'am." I was not going to argue with her, but we could never drink this much water even if we were stuck here for a week, so what was her reason for it? Whatever, it would get me away from this stupid chicken that just pooped on the carpet.

It wasn't fair. Even though I got an A on the hurricane test, maybe I didn't know what we should be doing now that we were really trapped and had such a big hurricane about to hit us. Who was I to question Grandma? Maybe she was right about me being just "a child with head in clouds." I had no idea what to do except follow Mom's and Grandma's commands now. From where I stood by the kitchen sink with the water running, I could still hear the man's voice.

"… will result in human suffering and devastation," he was saying.

That's a new one. Every year we have at least a tropical

storm or two come through, and most years there's at least one hurricane that erodes parts of the beach, makes super high tides, and washes out parts of roads. Last month, Hurricane Cindy came, and the eye hit Waveland, west of us. They got a bad deluge of rain, seven inches I heard. We got less, but the storm surge still covered the parking lot with water like it was doing today. Well, maybe not as much as today. It was foggy in my head now.

The very next week after Hurricane Cindy, Hurricane Dennis plowed through surrounding states and in some places made a huge storm surge, almost six feet of water, and dropped a foot of rain. We didn't have to evacuate for that one, but it did so much damage around us Mr. Hartman told us they were retiring the name "Dennis" so it couldn't be used for hurricanes anymore.

The announcer's voice sounded stressed. "If you have the means to evacuate, get out now. There is still time," he said. "Traffic congestion is prevalent on all major northbound highways and roads. All bridges along the Gulf Coast are closed to east-west traffic due to high waves threatening the structures."

A photo from a space satellite showed what looked like a white spiral of clouds taking over, and it was so wide it touched both Cuba and Louisiana at the same time. The center of it, the eye, which looked a hole in the middle of the white monster, was heading right toward where we sat in our living room with Grandma's chickens and a bathtub full of water, was a gigantic white spiral, spinning counterclockwise, almost filling the Gulf of Mexico.

Sunday, August 28 - noon

It was hard to sit and wait around when we saw we were at the center of a gigantic target on the map. This felt so different. We were not just waiting for it to be over this time. So, what else were we waiting for? Maybe we were waiting to see if we could make it through this one. Oh gosh.

The phone rang, and Mom and I dove over there to answer it. Mom won.

"Hello? David?" she said right away.

His voice was loud enough I could hear him even though I didn't have the phone to my ear. "Anna, oh geez, I hoped you wouldn't answer, babe. But you're still there? In the apartment?"

Mom said, "Oh honey, we're stuck," a big sob made her stop talking. "The car broke down, and it was too late to find a ride by then." She sat down on the floor next to the little bookshelf where the phone was. She had her eyes closed and kept crying. "I was up all night, trying to call people for help, but everyone's gone already." She sobbed and sobbed, sitting on the ugly brown carpet.

He asked her some more questions, but she could barely take a breath, so she handed the phone to me.

"Dad? It's Jessie. Where are you?"

He said, "Oh, that doesn't matter right now. The big thing is where you are. I hoped when I called, you three would not be there to answer the phone."

I gulped. Well, here we were. "I'm sorry, Dad."

"This really is turning into a bad one, Jess."

"I wish you were here," I said, then changed it to, "No I don't. I don't wish you were here. I wish we weren't here, but I wish we were together."

He chuckled. "Me too, Jess. From the looks of the news, it would be better if we were all in Nebraska, even if Joe's there." We both laughed, a little.

I said, "Dad, it's all my fault we're still here. I'm so sorry."

"What? No way, Jessie."

"Yeah, it is." I told him what happened yesterday, all the

fights and the bike accident and the chickens and then the car breaking. In the background, Mom shook her head, but Grandma nodded her head and frowned at me, the horse that harmed its own herd.

Dad said, "No, Jess, you can't blame this on yourself. There was a lot going on, and you all did what you had to do yesterday." He took a breath. "You know, you three need to stick together right now." He didn't usually give me speeches like that unless it was serious, like when his mother and father got killed in the tornado. I was afraid what he would even say next. "You've got to be a team, more than ever. You, Anna, and Jiexen." It scared me when he used their real names instead of saying "you, Mom, and Grandma." I swallowed, hard.

His words made my eyes fill up with tears with the impossibility of it. There was no way Grandma and I were on the same team. If she were the coach, she would have me sent down to the minors by now. Or Siberia. "Dad, you don't understand how it is. She..." but he didn't let me go down that path, and then Mom was feeling better and signaled for me to give her the phone back. I sniffed. "Okay, I love you, Dad. Bye."

I don't know what else Mom and Dad talked about, because I ran into the room I shared with Grandma and closed the door so I could be alone. I'd accidentally left my *Magyk* book out on the sofa, but I was not going to go back out there and get it, because that would give Grandma another chance to peck at me.

The rain clattered hard outside the window. On this side of the apartment, from mine and Grandma's room, I saw the raindrops getting bigger, and bigger, and louder. While I watched, it seemed like the water got even thicker, like it was being poured from buckets instead of just droplets.

I've seen rain before, but I wondered where all this rain would go when it hit the ground.

Mr. Hartman told us the problem with storm surge and rain is that when "a volume of water that large" comes to one place all at once, you run out of places to put all that water. It tries to flow and level out, but the storm surge from the Gulf was exactly like a pile of water on top of the land, sometimes in a wave, or it could just... well... rise quickly all around you. It gave me the shivers. That's too much water. Instead of being in the Gulf, it literally piles up on the shore, on top of the land, for blocks and blocks and blocks inland, not just the beach, crushing things and pushing them out of its way as it tries to get back to the sea. Maybe even a few miles inland, he had said. And on top of that, you have gobs of rainwater coming from the sky, adding to the pile of water on the ground with nowhere for it to go.

When you look at a map of Pass Christian, it's on a peninsula, surrounded almost on three sides by the Sound or the bayou. It's six miles long and only a mile wide. How much water would it take piling up to cover our whole peninsula? I didn't want to find out.

In our apartment, we were just a few feet above sea level. Looking out our bedroom window, I should have been able to see Johnson Portage stretching west toward Bay St. Louis, but there was too much rain blowing sideways to see even that far.

If I went to the front door on the landing, I should have been able to see the wooden dock stretching out into the brown water. That's the bayou where the water always comes from when the parking lot floods. It's probably already got water across it like it has so many times before. But there's no way I'm going to open the front door and go out there and check it out. A scrawny girl like me would be blown away, and besides, Tiger Grandma was out there in the living room. No way.

All I wanted to do was hide.

Mom knocked on the door. The rain still pummeled us, but now it was almost dark outside, not just from the rain, but because it was Sunday night. I must have fallen asleep. "Jessie, honey, let's have some dinner, okay?"

I fumbled my way out to the kitchen, and Mom gave me a hug.

We ate, and then I stood behind Mom's dining room chair so I could comb her long black hair out for her, too. I hardly got to do this for her, with her crazy work schedule. I made a long plait down her back, and then I wound it up and stuck a pencil through it to make a bun on the back of her head. Grandma always did her own hair bun with a few quick flicks of her wrists. She didn't even use a pencil or chopstick to secure the bun.

The wind came from the east and whipped the rain into the windows of the living room. It was loud enough now that when we talked, we had to speak up to be heard, and Mom turned up the TV volume when the guy on the news said, "the feeder bands have reached the coast," meaning more and more inches of rain were coming. The worst of the rain was yet to come, is what he meant. And those fingers of the swirl of the gigantic hurricane were touching us, getting ready to slam into us.

This was different than a puny little tornado. This was like one million tornadoes all working together to rip up everything in their path.

Monday, August 29 – darkness before the dawn

Overnight on August 28, WFO New Orleans/Baton Rouge began issuing hourly short-term forecasts to provide information on the location of Katrina along with wind and rainfall information. It was back to Category 3 when it hit Mississippi. All night, the stupid TV was on, and the wind and rain never stopped banging on the windows and the roof. Wind and rain. Wind and rain. Rattle, rattle, rattle. I wrapped a blanket around my head to block the noise, but it got too hot and I ripped it off again, and I just lay there staring in the dark, staring at my clock radio on the desk by my feet.

Early in the morning, I smelled food cooking. Grandma and Mom cooked food out of the freezer like crazy. I didn't know who they thought was going to eat all that today. Maybe they expected Dad to show up and save us and be hungry? I didn't know. When they were talking in Cantonese, I couldn't keep up, especially if I was in the other room trying to ignore them.

At 5:27 a.m., August 29, WFO New Orleans/Baton Rouge issued its first Extreme Tropical Cyclone Destructive Wind Warning for Katrina. The news said the eye wall of Katrina would hit St. Tammany parish in Louisiana, and Hancock and Harrison Counties in Mississippi in the next few hours. There would be extremely violent wind gusts up to 135 miles per hour. That was us. Harrison County, Mississippi.

Grandma bossed Mom around some more out in the kitchen. Why didn't they just go back to sleep? We had so much waiting to do for this storm to be over, like we had done before.

"Persons along the Gulf Coast in these areas need to take shelter in an interior room as soon as possible." Well, duh, I guess. A huge gust shook the windows.

My clock radio clicked to 5:40 a.m.

Then the numbers disappeared.

And the living room went silent.

No more electricity.

The best thing about that was we couldn't watch the news reports on television anymore. But the bad thing was the reason the electricity was out was the hurricane was landing right on top of our heads. We didn't need a news report. We just needed to look out the windows. Or hide in bed under the pillows until it all went away.

I had a feeling that was why my mom stayed in her room sleeping so much. To hide from her mama, the most unpredictable, relentless storm in the world, that mom had been bracing herself against since she was a little girl. She'd been dealing with her for almost twenty years longer than I had. No wonder she was exhausted

The rain made it sound like the whole apartment was being pushed through an automatic car wash. A gigantic one, big enough for two bedrooms, a living room, and a kitchen to be pushed through. Almost, but not quite big enough, so the windows shook, and the roof rattled, and we had absolutely no wish to open a door or window. Or even get out of bed, but I was tired of staring at nothing, especially now that the lights were off.

I went to the dark kitchen.

Grandma sat on the stool at the counter, eating sour-fermented-spicy *pao tsai* right out of the container. This batch she'd stored in a plastic container with a screw-on lid. That was one thing Dad insisted on with Grandma, that the most pungent/horrible/foreign smells needed to be contained with a screw top so they wouldn't contaminate the smells of the other foods. Or invade his big Dutch nose. But I liked *pao tsai*. It was like the Vietnamese *kimchi* that Mary's mom made. You could spread it on top of any food to liven it up: eggs, rice, chicken, whatever. But Mary and I had both figured out—the hard way—we had better not eat *pao tsai* or *kimchi* in the morning before going to school, because the spicy-garlic-fermented smell lingered with you all day, in your breath and on your clothes, and it made it hard for the other kids to bear sitting near us.

But we loved it. So we saved it to eat after school or on weekends.

Grandma handed me a mixture of leftovers that should never have been put in the same container and was definitely not a good idea for breakfast. "Eat food now. It still hot." It was all good food, but the combination was disgusting.

My head hurt. My heart hurt. I was not hungry. And I may have been a dufus when it came to hurricanes. But I ate that spaghetti-tofu-peanut-stir-fry all up, sitting in the dark at the counter next to her, because Grandma told me to, and if I were going to be trapped in here with her until the hurricane was over, I might as well just give in.

She told me to get dressed, as if I couldn't figure that out myself. For lying around the house waiting for the hurricane to be over, I chose shorts and a tank top like I had yesterday, even though what I wore yesterday, when we thought we were evacuating, turned out to be a mistake. I wouldn't tell Grandma that. I winced at the thought of hitting the pavement. And I didn't re-do my hair. I left the nice soft braid in it that Mom had made yesterday. Today we were not going to set foot out of the apartment.

5

Monday, August 29 - 8 a.m. or so

As the wind got stronger and stronger, I sat in the living room watching the rain hit the window. Grandma said, "Not go close to window. Wind break it!" We didn't have any windowless rooms in the apartment except three closets and the bathroom, so I backed up against the refrigerator and watched from there.

Hurricanes spin counterclockwise in the Northern Hemisphere, did you know? So right now, the wind came from the east because we were on the north side of it. After it went by us, or over us, the wind would switch and come from the west. I was conflicted. I didn't want to be alone in my room anymore, or hiding in a closet. But I didn't want to be out here with Grandma and Mom. I was trying to read my magic fantasy book using the light coming in from outside, but it was so gray, and so loud, I just couldn't think. I couldn't hear the wizards and mysterious travelers in the book talking, even though their voices should have been plenty loud inside my head.

The wind felt like it was a solid object, hitting the building over and over with such force.

And the wind was full of solid objects that it picked up and whipped around like they didn't weigh anything. Big tree branches, plywood ripped off people's windows or scooped up from the pile in the parking lot at the Quik Mart, parts of roofs, things that were just too big to be flying at all. It was unreal. Impossible. I remembered the scene from the *Wizard of Oz* where Dorothy sees all the people and cows fly by her before she's knocked unconscious by the tornado.

Slam.

Slam.

Slam.

The harsh sound of wind blowing into everything hurt my ears.

On a field trip last year, Miss Bernie told us on our tour, "Wind blowing seventy-five miles an hour is no joke. To be classified as a Category 1 hurricane, a tropical cyclone must have one-minute sustained winds of at least seventy-four miles per hour. That would blow leaves and branches off trees."

Our eyes got big. That was already faster than cars on the interstate!

Josephine Zibilich spoke. I just loved saying her name, Josephine Zibilich. Her family came from Dalmatia, Croatia (also fun to say), a long time ago, and they were oyster farmers, which was cool. Anyway, she asked, "But you said the hurricane wind simulator was 72 miles per hour, Miss Bernie, but that felt like the wind would rip all the hair out of my scalp." I remember, we all laughed. Yes, it was uncomfortable for that one minute of wind blasting, and when Zeke went in, his glasses blew off his nose and broke against the inside of the machine.

She said, "For Category 2, the winds must reach between 96 and 110 miles per hour."

No way. That sounded terrible. She asked us what effects that kind of wind would have.

Josephine's cousin on her mom's side, George Catanovich, spoke up. I knew they were cousins because they stuck together in school and out, and they liked to remind us how their families had lived around here for a hundred and fifty years. Mr. Cohen had taught us about that in social studies, but we all knew who was related, too. Lots of cousins in our school. "That would rip shingles off the roof," he said. "That's gettin' scary."

Miss Bernie nodded. "Yes. Now for Category 3, a major hurricane, sustained winds reach 111 to 129 miles per hour." She looked around. "Have any of you experienced that?" Most of us had been through hurricanes, maybe a few each year, but they hadn't been that strong, and we always stayed inside and so we didn't feel the wind like we had in the simulator. "By then, the palm trees are bending sideways and some are breaking off. The roof is pretty well destroyed. This would cause extensive damage."

She looked around to make sure we were listening.

We were.

The scale kept going up: Category 4 is 130 to 156 miles per hour. That would basically flatten all the houses, blowing them off the face of the earth. "That's the difference between 'extensive' damage and 'extreme' damage," she said.

And Category 5 is 157 miles per hour or stronger, causing "catastrophic damage," she said. "Whole roofs would be ripped off, and some buildings would be blown over, and massive evacuation of residents would happen because of the potential flooding." I remembered thinking, on the field trip, that I didn't know why anyone would want to still be there if the storm was predicted to be that big or strong. I heard there were people who chose to stay when there was an evacuation order, but Mom and Dad had always planned to evacuate when predictions were that bad.

So much for that plan.

Earth to Jessie. Come back to the real world, Jessie.

I vaguely noticed Grandma had put on a sweatshirt, even though it wasn't cold out.

I saw a flag whip past the window so fast I could barely see, but it was the Pass Christian city flag, like the one Mr. Bourdin hung on the balcony at his store a few blocks from the coast, and once a year he came to the schools to tell us about our town's history. It had a white Lone Star in a blue square in one corner, and a big white magnolia blossom in the other corner.

Was our history going to be blown away by these winds, starting with Mr. Bourdin's balcony?

Monday, August 29 - 8:15 a.m. I guess

My next question was, why were we still up here on the third floor? I kept wondering. What if the roof got ripped off the building? What if something huge hit us right in the windows and came in here? Then the wind and rain could get in too.

But it wasn't like we could go to the lowest part of the building like we do in a tornado, to the first-floor neighbor, Miss Roslyn. Nope. I hoped she had escaped days ago.

In the parking lot, the water kept flowing in. It was now above the hubcaps of Mom's car, but the top of the tires still showed. It looked more like a river now, as wide as the whole parking lot, as if the water in the bayou were higher than the parking lot and had to flow downstream into the low parking lot.

What? The parking lot was lower than the bayou?

I couldn't see the wooden dock at all anymore. When did it disappear, and where did it go? Oh, there, I saw it floating behind the two-story building east of us, crashing into the lower-level walls and windows.

Was it my imagination? Every time a wave surged, the dock lurched and crashed, and every time, it hit a spot a bit higher on the building. The water from the bayou was rising fast enough. I could notice it getting higher, an inch at a time, if I stood there and focused.

Pretty soon, the water would hide the tires on Mom's car. Then it would get into the inside, and the engine. I didn't think salt water would be good for a car engine.

"Mom, and Grandma, you need to look at this." I showed them.

As they came over, I noticed that Mom's t-shirt today was one Dad had brought her from San Francisco. It was gray and had a giant red crab on it, with "Fisherman's Wharf of San Francisco" in a circle around it. She always wore that shirt when she missed Dad. Sometime I hoped she would tell me why they liked San Francisco so much. Not today.

Mom found a view out the window in her and Dad's bedroom, where we could see the water lapping up against the open stairwell. Grandma said again, "Away from window, Anna!" but Mom ignored her.

"Look," she pointed. "It's at the bottom step now. We need to keep an eye on the stairs to see how fast it's coming up."

I'd hoped I was wrong when I observed that. This would be a great time to be wrong. Maybe the water wasn't rising as much as I thought. "Mom, I don't want to just sit here and watch the water go up. I wish there was something we could do!"

Mom tried to laugh. "Like what exactly, Jessie? Leave in a helicopter or something?"

I tried to laugh, too. "Yes! Let's contact our private, on-call helicopter and ask them to come pick us up." My stomach hurt, but I was so glad Mom tried to help me relax. I didn't want her to fade out on me and go hide in her room, leaving me with Tiger Grandma. "I'll put in an order for them to have double cheeseburgers and cokes for us all when we get on board."

Mom laughed. "Okay, sounds good. With life jackets on the side, right?" She and I both laughed, but then it wasn't funny.

"Mom, what should we do?" I looked at the stairs, and the water was halfway up to the next step already. This was all happening way too fast.

Grandma had been watching the water intently the whole time, and she kicked into gear again. "Water get high, more high. We need be more ready." She paced up and down. Big Fluffy and Lily scurried away from her with a puff of white feathers.

I hated to listen to her, because even though I got an A on the stupid hurricane test, I had no other ideas at all. I was furious about getting us trapped like this.

She took charge. "Firs', you two, need wear shoes. No sandals." She waggled her foot in the air to show us what real shoes looked like, as if we had no idea: sneakers with the laces tied.

"Grandma, we aren't going anywhere, are we?" I said, but Mom motioned with her eyes that we should follow her mama's orders. She got her socks and shoes on, and I got mine.

Tiger Grandma didn't let up. "Take water jugs from here," pointing to the kitchen counter where I'd left all the filled bowls and pitchers and containers, "and put up on the top," she pointed to the top of the cupboards near the ceiling. She nodded and pointed, waiting for me and Mom to act. We took too long. "Do! Now!" We did it.

I climbed up and stood on the counter, and no one even yelled at me for getting my shoes on the counter. Unbelievable. The rules change when there's a natural disaster, I guess. Mom handed the containers up to me, and I wedged them up on top of the cupboard.

Meanwhile, Grandma took boxes of crackers and cans of food out of the lower cupboards and handed the boxes and cans up to us to store safely on top of the cupboards where the water couldn't reach.

I didn't believe this was necessary. The water would never come up here. But I needed something to do, and meanwhile she wasn't yelling at me, so that was good.

Huge things kept flying through the air, some missing the building, others hitting the walls or windows. Parts of houses that were already broken, a real estate sign, a kid's scooter, and part of what looked like a mast from a sailboat. None of this should be in the air at all. It should be on the ground. I heard windows breaking in old Miss Akana's apartment next door; she was our closest neighbor, but I hadn't seen her in a while. She must have left.

No idea why our windows hadn't broken yet.

I hoped Mary's dad was somewhere far enough up the Pearl River that he wasn't slamming into trees or a bridge or anything. Would he tie up to something, or would he just float around in the shrimp boat like a raft on the rapids of a river?

Mom and Grandma had to yell now to be heard, it was so loud.

"What?" I yelled, climbing down to the floor again.

"Take, and put up on top," Grandma yelled, handing more canned food to me. Was she just being irrational as usual, or did she know what she was doing? I climbed back up and stashed it above the cupboards.

Mom yelled from her bedroom, "Look at the steps, Jessie!"

I climbed down, moved to the window, and looked. In the few minutes it took to get that stuff stashed up on top, the water—the Gulf rising onto the land—had covered, no, had engulfed two more steps.

Monday, August 29 - 9 a.m., give or take

While my eyes grew heavy watching the storm as it got scarier and stronger and louder. I decided to go back, in my mind, to a "sea level" school field trip we took last year. I had a gruff teacher named Mrs. Porter who was as large as a walrus. She said that herself, so don't yell at me. She never smiled, but she did sometimes raise her left eyebrow at one of us when she was impressed that we answered a tough question correctly. She was a fascinating teacher.

The beach was less than a mile south of our apartment, but we could never see the actual water from here because of all the trees. However, when we did our sea level field trip, just a few blocks from school, we didn't even take a bus, we just walked from the middle school to the beach, on the Mississippi Sound, on the Gulf of Mexico. It was a super hot day, as usual for August.

Mrs. Porter had us set up our outdoor classroom, with our towels and lunches in a circle around her demonstration area. Then she got us all to wade right into the Sound together, holding hands. It's hard to hold hands when we're covered with sunscreen and then get wet, but as new sixth graders, we all did what she said. We walked straight out toward Cat Island. You might think the farther you went out, the deeper it would get. But the sandy brown water stayed shallow. I'd done this bunches of times with Mom and Dad, but the new kids were surprised at how warm the water was, and how it just came up to above our knees, even though we were a hundred yards from the beach.

After we played in the water, we gathered around her demonstration on an upturned box, where she set up a shallow pan with a handful of small rocks in it. She had asked one of the kids to carry a gallon jug of fresh water from school, and then she poured water into the pan, slowly. She asked us to notice how the water crept up the edges of the dry rocks, using surface tension to grip the sides, so the surface wasn't even flat. Later in the morning, honeybees flew to the pan, perched on the edges and sat on the rocks, delicately sipping the clear water from the pan. Some of the water had already evaporated, and she said we should notice how the water moved when she poured more into the pan.

She poured slowly so she wouldn't drown any of the bees, and some of them almost got washed away but climbed higher on the rocks just in time. The water didn't slosh into the pan in one big wave. It filled in evenly around all the rocks, and in the blink of an eye, there was not very much dry rock space for any of the bees to sit on. If she kept pouring slowly, they flew off, but some were slow and almost got swamped. She blew on them, and they all flew away, safe and sound.

It was a demonstration of the way storm surge rises, sometimes. "Let me ask you, young scientists," she said, "if you were stuck on that rock in the middle, and the water surged up around you, what would you do?"

For a bunch of noisy sixth graders, we were all pretty quiet. One kid said, "Mrs. Porter, I don't think I'd want to be on that rock. I would want to be at my uncle's house in Wiggins. High and dry."

Her left eyebrow arched up. "Exactly! When the water is surging, the best place to be is elsewhere!" Mrs. Porter always commanded us, with a smile, "When in doubt, think harder."

Okay then, Mrs. Porter. I have a lot of doubts right now. Like how many feet of storm surge this was turning into, and how high the water would come up toward us, perched on this little rock.

I looked over to try to find Mom's car out there, but all I could see now was the top edge of the windows and the olive-green roof, about to disappear under the water. Was it floating? It seemed like it might be moving up and down? Or maybe it was the waves? It was hard to see.

When I looked again a minute later, I couldn't even see a hint of it. In the last forty-five minutes, the water completely covered the cars out there and was about to touch the first-floor landing.

It was coming faster and faster. How could the surge be speeding up?

Oh my gosh, when would the water stop rising?

For the test, we learned about "Camille the Destroyer," which was classified as a Category 5 hurricane when it hit Waveland in 1969, and not only that, the mammoth storm surge came in two destructive rushes, solid walls of water with "rolling breakers swirling on top," and they hit during the dark of night. People died as they slept in their beds, or when they got outside, the night was filled with lightning, and the winds were over 200 miles per hour.

Mom and I watched from her bedroom. At least it was daytime and we could see what was happening, and we knew what was coming next. The water reached the first landing at the first half-flight of steps, covering it, heading for the next landing as fast as it could. It sloshed against the building and then against the first-floor windows as I held my breath. Higher. Higher.

The wind blew, and the water went up and down and sideways. It flowed like a river but in every direction at the same time, as it came from the bayou and the sky and all four directions around us.

The wooden dock got dragged clear across the parking lot, over the spot where the trash dumpsters should have been, and crashed against our building, over and over again. Now I could hear it breaking windows and walls in the first-floor apartments. Right below us, the biggest section of the wooden dock, floating on the waves, slammed hard, and the sharp corner of the dock got pushed right into the window of Miss Roslyn's apartment on the first floor. We watched from above as the water surged in through the broken window and must have filled her bedroom and living room with brown, muddy, boiling bayou water.

I wondered where Mrs. Porter was today. Did she leave town and get to a safe place, as she warned us we should have done? Or was she creeping backwards on a rock in the middle of the Gulf, hoping she didn't run out of dry ground to stand on before the water decided to stop rising? Like we were? If it got this high, we couldn't fly away like those bees could. It just had to stop rising!

Something huge, big, and flat, slammed hard against the living room window closest to the TV. What was it, a road sign? Or a sheet of plywood? It smashed flat against the building and broke the glass out, then fell away into the churning water.

Wind and rain blew into our living room and swirled all the loose papers and light things and yes, the chickens, around, just like a jet engine cyclone.

And then, in the whirlwind, three chickens got sucked out the window into the hurricane before we could take a step to save them. Lily, Jing, and Big Fluffy disappeared, torn away from us by the wind.

Monday, August 29 - 9:30 a.m.

"No!" Grandma cried out, "Big Fluffy! Jing! Lily!" But it was too late. She screamed so plaintively.

I realized then she must have had a heart, because I just heard it break.

Those chickens were her best friends. Now three were gone.

I couldn't move.

Outside, the whole Gulf of Mexico, the entire Mississippi Sound, and the bayous and estuaries were full of water, and all the heavy, raging water was squeezing onto the shore, right on top of Pass Christian, into our apartment building. Water flowing uphill. Waves ready to engulf us altogether. It was going to stop being "outside" and change to "inside," right here in our third-floor apartment. It was happening right before our eyes as the water kept rising toward the second floor.

Grandma must have changed her sadness about the chickens, or her past hatred of the water, into pure anger, which got her moving first. She started giving orders. Fast.

"Anna, Jessie, get backpacks."

Most of the boxes we'd packed for the car were still near the door. Grandma didn't have a backpack, but she had that blue plastic flight bag, the one she'd put money and papers in, and she hung it so the strap went across her chest and the bag hung at her back. But why did she put it on? Where did she think she was going to go now? We could not leave. She was totally crazy.

Mom looked with wide eyes out the broken window at the surging, rising water below us but getting closer. Then she finally moved, taking her backpack off the pile and rooting around inside it first for something, then opening the other suitcases right there on the floor by the front door and adding two more plastic zip bags full of papers she got from there into her backpack. I glimpsed a water bottle and a kitchen knife in there, a shirt, and who knows what else.

She picked up her car keys, but then Grandma wrenched them from her hand and threw them back on the table by the front door. "Stop, stupid girl."

Mom froze and looked shocked. Grandma was mean, but did she have to be that mean, when we were so scared already?

Grandma pointed out the window at the flooded parking lot full of drowned cars. Oh. We had no car to drive. Car keys useless. This could not be happening. This was not real. This was not possible!

We all watched as the building east of us lost a big chunk of its roof as a wind gust ripped it off, just tore a big section of the corner away from the rafters and carried it off, very nearly hitting our building.

Mom closed her eyes and nodded slowly. She looked down and opened the small pocket on the front of her backpack to make sure her wallet was there. Then she slung the straps over her shoulders.

But why put it on at all? My family was definitely going crazy. We were not going out in the hurricane. We would die. Wearing backpacks inside the apartment?

I hadn't gotten mine yet. There was nowhere to go, and I was not going to wear my backpack for no reason.

A picture of Dad came into my head. He must have been going nuts, hearing about all this on the radio, knowing we hadn't been able to evacuate. We hadn't been able to tell him anything since then, but what was there to tell even if we talked to him right now? Yep, we're surrounded by storm surge and trapped in the apartment wearing backpacks? Maybe that was to weigh us down so we would drown faster. I had no idea.

I went to the unbroken window to look at the water coming up the steps, while the wind swirled inside the living room, and I thought something was wrong with my eyes. The water was already approaching the third landing, sloshing up and down like a raging river full of debris rushing all around the apartment building, a whirlpool of muddy, brackish water preparing to wash us away. The second-floor windows were submerged. Across the parking lot, waves engulfed all the second story apartments.

I tried to do some mental math to calm myself down. The logic of it always calmed me down.

If we had five half-flights of steps, and each one had about five steps in it…

Ack! I couldn't do it. All this wind made it hard to think. My head wasn't working.

Try again, Jessie. Think!

Okay. If the first half-flight of steps was about as tall as I was, that was about five feet tall. And if there were five of those half-flights to get to the third floor where we lived, that would be twenty-five feet. Then you had to add the few feet that it took the water to get up from the bayou to the parking lot. And add a few more feet if the level of the water came up past the counters in our kitchen, which, I began to realize, was what Grandma imagined coming next.

That could not be right. If I'd figured that out right, we already had more that twenty-five feet of storm surge. That was not possible. That didn't happen here. We usually got a few feet, maybe six feet when things were really bad.

In 1969, Hurricane Camille, we had just learned, created a twenty-four-foot storm surge. It was a Category 5 hurricane when it hit this exact coastline, flattening absolutely everything. It was the second most intense hurricane to strike the United States since 1935, we had memorized. But even though I knew those numbers, until now I hadn't really understood what they meant. Or how they felt.

And now it was 2005, and Hurricane Katrina was pushing Gulf water on top of us. Was it worse than the nightmare of Hurricane Camille? We were on the third floor, wondering how we could survive. But what about the people who didn't have a third floor or even a second floor to climb up to? An image of the whole Gulf Coast came into my mind, zoomed out like in a photo taken by a Hurricane Hunter flying into the eye of the storm to gather data and show an aerial viewpoint of the destruction. The shore was now inundated with all this extra water pushing everything and everyone wherever it wanted to with so much vicious force. What was happening in the rest of the Pass? What about around us in Bay St. Louis, Waveland, Long Beach, and the big cities of New Orleans, Gulfport, and Biloxi?

How many others were fighting for their lives right now?

6

Monday, August 29 - 9:35 a.m.

"Jessie, get backpack!" yelled Grandma, grabbing my shirt sleeve, dragging me away from the bedroom window and into the front hall where all our stuff was.

I picked up my pack and almost dropped it, trying to remember what heavy items I had packed in there yesterday that seemed so important when we were going to evacuate. I opened it to see what was in there, because right now, with my foggy brain, I had no idea. I dumped it all onto the floor.

Oh. Three thick school text books, so I could do my homework while we were up at the farm. An opened package of black licorice, which now spilled across the floor. My calculator, a pencil box, and my spiral notebook showing Kim Possible, the global crime fighting cheerleader doing a karate move and saying, "Deep breath and take the plunge," which until today seemed clever. Right now, that notebook just made me feel stupid. If we got out of here but could never come back, was my Kim Possible notebook the thing I wished most I would have saved? But I had just thought we were packing for a long weekend in Nebraska, so I had brought things to do while we waited.

I had learned so much since yesterday.

"You lazy girl, why you make such problem?" yelled Grandma, using her sneaker to poke at everything on the floor. "You need put in things to help you not die!"

Not dying. That was a good idea. I didn't want to die in a hurricane. My life was just getting going. I was finally getting a clue. Pastor told us when God started a great work in me, He would be faithful to complete it on the day Jesus came back. But what about right now? If I wanted to "not die" today, what should I pack in my backpack? It was too late to pack a set of wings so I could fly away.

I must have frozen.

Mom wasn't frozen, though. She wasn't hiding in her room, either. She moved to help me. She took my backpack and took charge. I was so proud of her just then, and so grateful, I really wanted to cry.

She got some more water bottles from the kitchen and stuck them in Grandma's bag and then her own and mine. Cans of soup — I noticed that she checked that each had pop top lids and didn't need a can opener. A little framed photo of me when I was a baby, cuddled on her lap, with Dad, and Dad's parents squeezed close by. From the shelf in the front hall closet, she took a plastic gallon zip bag labeled "Jessie's Hurricane Kit," in my messy grade school lettering, that Mr. Cohen had made us create in fifth grade. I'd forgotten about making that kit and couldn't remember what was in it. My brain was not working right. Why were all my thoughts so fuzzy and slow?

I watched her pick up a tiny plastic flashlight, which she clicked on and off to make sure it worked. She ran to her bedroom and got a folding knife from Dad's dresser.

"Mom, I don't know what to do with a knife!" I protested, as she threw it in my pack. My brain felt so numb, I could not imagine how a knife would help if I were swallowed up in the storm surge. Then that scary image of myself drowning really washed all the coherent thoughts out of me.

I realized Mom was saying, "You never know, Jessie. You can carry it, and maybe we'll need it later. You take it. I don't have room left in my bag."

I kept watching her pack for me, like I was a toddler going off to nursery school. Yep. My brain was not working at all.

Grandma said, "Get school ID, Jessie." I got it from my desk and zipped it in the front pocket. My tummy hurt.

My overwhelmed brain now helpfully reminded me of other times I'd been helpless, as it brought forth a few images from when I was a toddler. Mom or Grandma DeGroot would get me all dressed, playing games to get me to point my toes so they could get my socks on my feet. "Hide and seek, where's Jessie?" they said, when they pulled my little fuzzy shirt over my head. Getting me to close my eyes when they pulled the car seat strap over my head and buckled me in. Handing me a tiny container full of oat circles cereal to keep me occupied on the long ride into town to the kids center where Mom worked and I played and life was bliss.

Mom handed me my newly packed backpack. I put it on and clipped the front buckle to keep the other two straps on.

The water reached the next landing and showed no signs of stopping.

At the rate this was going, with the storm surge continuing to slosh up, it would be up to the ceiling of our very own apartment if it didn't stop right now.

Approaching thirty feet of water was all sitting on top of the dry land and couldn't find a place to flow down. It couldn't find a way out or a place to go. It could only keep going up, until the rain stopped and the hurricane stopped pushing so much water into the life of our town.

No bees. No helicopter. It was "just us chickens," as Grandma DeGroot used to say, and chickens don't float, either.

Monday, August 29 - 9:40 a.m.

"If water come here, no touch it!" Grandma ordered. "Bad water to touch it."

That made me remember what I heard about the sand in the sandbags getting contaminated with toxic waste, getting full of gas, oil, cleaners from every house's kitchen cabinet that got flooded. Every box of junk in someone's yard full of stuff they meant to get rid of. The cars and trucks floating in the water with their gas tanks gashed open. The Quik Mart and Walmart full of chemicals, pollution, and goo. Even the cemetery, I just realized — the one I rode by every day on the way to school — must be under more than twenty-five feet of water now. What if everything there, in the graves and in the concrete vaults with doors, you know what I mean, the skeletons, was getting swept out the doors and into the inland sea flooding the entire Pass? Did this happen during Camille? Not only was the water crushingly heavy, it was polluted with even more than I'd thought about already.

Rising. Rising. Rising. It was past the fourth landing now, almost to ours.

And not just like a gentle swimming pool, or a bathtub. Not like Mrs. Porter pouring the clean water gently from the gallon jug. No. The water climbing up the steps toward us churned, seethed, sloshed, like water pouring into a tub from all directions at the same time, and we were right in the middle where it all crashed together. It even sprayed through the cracks around the windows.

Grandma stood in the hall, and Mom and I just stood by the unbroken window, watching it come. The waves. The wind blowing things up against the buildings.

The next building over, where the part of the roof got ripped off a minute ago, was only two stories tall, not three like ours, so all we could see was the rooftop in the water, and the waves surging in and out of the attic over there

"Oh no!" I gasped. Now I could see two people crouched in the attic over there, where the hole in that roof was. They held tight to each other against the buffeting winds. I had met them a few times. They were Grandma's age or older, and they'd lived in the Pass a long time but had to keep moving to a cheaper apartment, like ours. The lady was so friendly. I think her name was Miss Boisclaire. She told me she'd been around for Hurricane Camille and it could never get worse than that.

"Mom, look!" She and Grandma looked over there with me. I felt even more helpless. The couple must have crawled up into the empty attic space above their apartment to get out of the water, and then the roof blew off, leaving them out in the ferocious winds gusting higher than I could even guess, like they were up on the roof of that big semi-trailer zooming down the highway at twice the normal speed. Strong enough to pull buildings apart.

I hated even having this thought, but they had to solve this for themselves right now. We had to work out our own problems. But what else could we do? If there was anything else we could do, Grandma had to be the one to think of it, because I was not having any ideas at all. Well at least I didn't trust my own ideas anymore, and neither did Mom.

However, Grandma sure did. She hollered, "You get chair and climb up there!" She pointed to the kitchen ceiling.

"Huh?" I didn't understand. My brain felt like it was full of molasses, and my eyes wouldn't focus right.

Mom understood, though. She pulled the chair over, lifted it on top of the counter and put another chair on the floor next to the counter. She motioned for me to step on the chair.

"Jessie," Mom said. "Climb up there and see if you can reach the ceiling." She ran to their bedroom and rustled around in the closet, coming back out with Dad's basic tool kit she got him last year for Christmas. I remembered it, because he said something about how he hoped he'd get to do home repairs when we finally got our own house instead of living in an apartment. The two of them had looked at each other for so long with this mushy, lovey-dovey expression on their faces, I had to turn away. It was so gross. But I could tell they loved each other, which was good.

From up on the counter, I could see out the window and I looked for the people in the next building, but they weren't there anymore. Where did they go? Were they hiding under what's left of the roof?

No. Now there wasn't anything left of the roof. They were gone.

Monday, August 29 - 9:50 a.m.

The horrible wind picked at our roof, pulling, pulling, pulling on loose bits of something, banging it over, and over, and over again, loosening more bits and bigger sections, ripping chunks of the roof away and sending them far into the sky, heading west toward Bay St. Louis, because the wind hadn't shifted directions yet. That meant we were not even halfway through this hurricane yet, but the building was coming apart.

And the water was almost into our apartment.

No. Now the water was here.

It sprayed in, pushed by the pressure of the waves hitting

the door. Pushing, sloshing, pulsing. The heaviness of that much water. The weight of it.

Did you know, even a single-serving water bottle gets heavy if you try to hold it out at arm's length for ten seconds? Or twenty seconds. Mr. Cohen made us do this for sixty whole seconds once, while he talked to us about how chronic stress could be just as debilitating to a person. Don't believe me? Try this yourself, and see how much your arm hurts after just one minute. That was just one little bottle of water, and its weight hurt enough to put a cramp in my arm. But now we had a thousand football fields of land suffering under the weight of almost thirty feet of churning brown water. My tummy really hurt.

The water squeezed under the door and through the gap along the side too. The brown carpet was already submerged inches deep.

"Jessie! Climb up!"

Mom climbed up on the counter with me and took my hand, then helped me stand up on the chair so I could reach the ceiling with Dad's hammer. "Smash the ceiling, Jessie! Smash a hole in it!"

Down on the floor, Grandma started screaming at the ankle-deep water. She didn't have anywhere to go to get out of it. I heard her running through it with some purpose, but I didn't look down. I didn't want to get dizzy and fall off my step, way up above the counter. I smashed and smashed, finally making a hole in the white ceiling and getting dust all over my face. I coughed and sneezed.

Mom hollered into the noise, "Keep going Jess, you're doing great!"

I pounded some more, pulled down the ceiling and pink insulation and what I thought might be mouse droppings. I choked and coughed some more. When I looked up again, I could see it was light inside the attic. A piece of the roof was missing, right over us in the kitchen. I felt the rain and wind coming down at me through the hole, besides what was coming in sideways through the broken window.

Grandma yelled in a frantic voice. "We go up! Climb up!" She had been trying to get the last three chickens gathered up into a tub, but they got away. Finally, she got hold of one of them, Penelope, and stuffed her inside her zipped-up sweatshirt, but Rosita and Odessa fluttered away, landing on top of the television. I knew they couldn't float very well, because I'd tried an experiment with that once with one of the chickens, maybe it was Big Fluffy. The chicken survived and Grandma never learned about what I'd tried with her precious chicken.

Maybe Grandma was not crazy, but I had never seen her this scared. Actually, I had never seen her scared at all. Angry, impatient, tired even. But not scared.

The water coming in under the door now filled the apartment to the middle of her shins, and Grandma actually jumped from the floor onto the first chair, and then up onto the counter, standing up next to me and Mom. I understood now why Dad once told me, "Jiexen is a wiry old lady." Hm. She was definitely younger than Grandma DeGroot, who would have had to climb up, slowly, using a chair for help. But not Grandma Jiexen. She just hopped right up there. She called to Odessa and Rosita, but they were nowhere to be seen already, and the wind blasting in from the living room window didn't help.

A big swell as wide as the whole building surged toward the east side. It blew waves up against the windows now, against the glass that was still there, like we were in an aquarium, but on the third floor. And with a huge crashing sound, it came through the broken window, water pouring in, washing the phone and answering machine off the table, sloshing toward the sofa.

Another crashing surge, and it broke the entire wall wide open, pushing the front door out of its way.

Swirling water rushed through the space where the whole door had been. It was a wave two feet high, swallowing up the brown carpet and spreading throughout the living room and kitchen, heading for the bathroom and our bedrooms in the blink of an eye. I heard the two missing chickens squawking back there through the wind.

I stuck my head and shoulders up through the hole, pushing off with my feet on the cabinet shelves and then the top of the cabinet, getting my knee up, and hoisted myself up to sit on the horizontal wood beam in the attic. The beam was only two inches wide and really uncomfortable. Mom took the hammer and made the hole bigger so she could get through, in between that beam and the one that ran next to it. First came Grandma with Penelope stuck inside her sweatshirt, then Mom. They climbed on the chair and used the cupboard shelves as a ladder, then pulled up on the wood beams in the attic, and I reached to help them balance when they got up there.

We perched up here like chickens in a coop, except we didn't have claws to help us grip the wooden beam where we tried to sit. I saw through the hole below us, through the ceiling into the kitchen. The furniture pitched up and down as the waves wrenched everything from their places and spun them, shook them, drenched them, ruined them.

The disgusting brown seawater took over our home. Faster than ever.

The water kept climbing. It rose higher than the countertop, and, sadly, a dead cat washed across it and kept going into the living room. It took my breath away, and I closed my eyes.

When I opened them again, the water reached the bottom of the cabinets above the counter, and the microwave above the stove. The entire refrigerator moved up and down like it might fall right over, but I couldn't see from here because the ceiling was in the way.

Huge waves crashed inside our third-floor apartment, like the spin cycle in a washing machine. Waves from the Gulf sloshed at us outside and came closer and closer to the ceiling.

I remembered our friend Mr. McDermott warning us, "You can get out of the wind, but not the water. That's what will get you in the end."

Grandma never dared to go near the water, but now the Gulf itself had come to Grandma.

Monday, August 29 - 9:53 a.m.

I was balanced on my hinder (you know, my butt!) on this wood beam in the attic, hopefully far enough above the rising water to stay safe until it stopped. But my brain was taking me away, away, away again. Sometimes I just needed to be somewhere else in my head, away from my body. It helped when I decided to choose a certain event and relive every little detail as a way of pretending I wasn't hiding under the roof with Mom and Grandma and hoping the water wouldn't get any higher.

This time, I thought about a day after school about a week ago. Maybe it was even the first day of seventh grade? I had just come home and gotten myself a glass of iced tea—with just enough sugar and a fresh mint leaf from the garden —and sat down at the kitchen counter, daring Grandma to say a word. Or even hoping she would ask me about my day. As if.

She chopped up one more carrot, then put down the knife and got the plastic laundry basket from the front hall closet with her trowel and gloves inside. She took her dorky floppy hat from the hook and plopped it on her head. Printed on both sides, it said "Beach Bum" with a big red flower. Definitely from the thrift store, like most of our stuff was. It was amazing what nice things people give away. Mom said maybe they still liked these clothes but had outgrown them. Or maybe they had died, but I didn't like to think about that.

That day, I had hoped maybe Grandma would forget I was home and just go outside without me. Right.

"You." She didn't turn to look at me but still pointed her finger at me. "Come to garden."

Hmf. This was not a question. I set down the tea to follow her into the heat.

Flip flops for my feet; I didn't like going barefoot because I've stepped on so many dead or sharp things. I put on my equally dorky floppy hat; mine with a cartoon starfish printed on it.

The real me, perched in the attic, wished right now I had that dumb hat to put on in the relentless, hard wind.

However, imaginary me got the other basket out of the closet, put on gloves, and picked up the clippers. If we had gotten all the way down there without the clippers, she would have said, "You lazy girl, get them." I was not going to break the second rule of living with a Tiger Grandma, which was: Be Prepared for Things She Is Thinking but She Doesn't Say. I didn't want to go up and down the stairs an extra time for no reason. If that's lazy, okay. Maybe it's smart. But I was not going to tell her that.

Before I got down the steps from the third floor, Grandma had already crossed the corner of the parking lot and headed around to the northwest corner of the apartment building. I crossed the parking lot, crossing right over the storm water grate. When I looked down, I could see the shining water just a foot below the metal grating. The water table was always really high. Or maybe it was that the ground was really low, so close to the bayou.

Real me perched in the attic knew that the metal grate and the parking lot now had maybe thirty feet of water on top. Thirty feet! Where was all the water still coming from?

In my mind, I followed Grandma on the path she had worn through the mowed grass and into the tall grass west of the apartments, into the tangle of swamp vegetation that hid her vegetable garden from the world. The long grass tickled my feet in the flip-flops. I'm not sure whose land it was, but it was swampy, buggy lowland just about twenty yards from the Johnson Portage. That bayou, known as Bayou Potash, connected with Bay St. Louis west of town, over by the Bay Bridge.

The salty-brackish water in the bayou came up and flooded the land regularly. I wondered why the ground wasn't too salty to grow anything. Obviously, all the crazy jungle was doing fine, whatever shape the soil was in. Grandma grew all kinds of vegetables in that soil. Tomatoes, peppers, eggplants, pole beans. Cabbage, turnips, broccoli. The melons took up a lot of space, but that didn't matter in her hidden-away garden. The plants were just as big as the ones in my other grandparents' vegetable garden in Nebraska. Maybe all the chicken fertilizer she put on the garden helped. Well, really, it was me, not her, carrying all the chicken poop. What a great memory.

I never had harvested the rest of the vegetables after I ran away on Saturday, and now, darn it, she was right again. The plants were pureed and swamped by now in the horrible deluge.

One day we'll get back to regular life. Next time I'm supposed to haul a bag full of chicken fertilizer down there, I'll try to enjoy it more. I mean it. Compared to this, that would be delightful any day of the week.

I opened my eyes to see how Mom and Grandma were doing, balanced up here above the chaos. They had their eyes closed too, and I wondered what they were thinking about. It was blowing so hard, if we really had to talk, we'd have to yell even though we were close together. We just kept hunkered down, because all we could *do* right now was to stay where we were.

7

Monday, August 29 - 9:55 a.m.

When I was little and we first moved here, I used to complain about all the steps up to our place. Sometimes Dad would carry me up a few flights of steps. My legs were short and wimpy, since I was only in kindergarten then. We did more fun stuff together when it was just Dad, Mom, and me, though.

It's been a while since they had to carry me, but I decided that if we did survive this natural disaster today, I was never going to complain about those steps again. If we were in a lower building and didn't have all those steps to deal with, the storm surge would have reached us a long time ago and washed us out into the Sound or slammed us into a floating car. Maybe we would have disappeared like those people on their roof next door, fighting the wind and the waves that moved up and down like a machine without stopping. Ever.

Mom, Grandma, and I balanced our butts on the wooden beams. It already felt like the circulation in my legs was messed up, sitting like this. How long could we wait here?

But what choice did we have?

We had most of the roof still over us, so Grandma's black chicken, Penelope, now sat on the wood beam next to her. Penelope liked roosting on a wooden stick, since that's what she did all night. Grandma kept one arm around her side to keep her close.

How could it get worse? But it did. Something a million times stronger than the roof grabbed onto the edge and pulled with all its might, hoisting another huge section of it into the air high above our heads with a shearing sound as the wood splintered and the screws ripped out of the wood. Diagonal wood pieces along the top—were those the rafters? —separated from the horizontal beams we sat on. A bigger section of the attic was open to the rain and wind now, but most of that damage was over Miss Akana's apartment next to ours.

You don't know what 'puny humans' means? One time on a sleepover, Mary and I peeked from my room, where we were supposed to be asleep already, into the living room. My dad was watching an action movie about the Incredible Hulk, where the big green monster was trying to win against the 'puny humans' who kept trying to defeat him in more and more horrible ways. We got scared totally out of our minds by that movie and couldn't sleep at all that night, but as my dad said, it was 'very well done,' even though it was too violent and we should never have watched it. My eyes can never un-see some of the things in that movie. I'd rather watch 'Kim Possible', or even 'Dancing with the Stars', any day.

Puny humans tried to create strong buildings with sturdy structures to protect us, but nothing could be stronger than this wind and waves combination weakening everything. Palm trees try to survive by bending in the wind instead of being rigid, but I even saw some of them broken right off, if that tells you anything.

When all that happened, we had nothing more to grab onto than the skinny wooden beam (Mom called it a "joist") that we sat on, and the one in front of us, and with all the upheaval, I slid off, crashing into the other beam and then between them, down through the waterlogged ceiling and slipping into the churning water in the kitchen.

The water that filled the apartment felt hot.

Not warm, but actually hot!

It was less windy down there, and I grabbed onto the kitchen cabinet to keep from being pulled away by the water, so I could try to climb back up through the ceiling. The chair was gone, so I used the shelves as a ladder again—the cabinet door was ripped away now—and Mom pulled me back up between the beams.

Meanwhile, the vicious wind pulled Grandma's last chicken off the beam and flung it into the air, smashed it, hard, into the underside of the attic, and then spun it out into the sky in a cloud of black feathers. She screamed and screamed, trying to stand up on the skinny wooden beam to catch it, but it was impossibly too difficult and too late.

She slipped down off the beam and crashed through the ceiling into the water just as I had, sobbing and sobbing about the last lost chicken. Mom and I helped pull Grandma back up, but after another long while, Grandma purposefully slid back down off the beam and into the hot water filling the kitchen. She grabbed onto part of the cabinet and then tried to close her eyes and float on her back, but the surges of waves and the junk floating around kept jostling her. She must have given up on "not touch water."

Down in the sloshing water in the kitchen, Tiger Grandma cried, "She my only friend. She gone. Penelope leave me."

Monday, August 29 - 10:30 a.m.

Eventually, we got Grandma to climb back up. We held on, and on, and on.

Then Mom said, "Listen, Jessie."

"Huh?" I didn't hear anything. We didn't have to yell to be heard. "Mom, is it over?" I asked, but I knew it wasn't. We couldn't do this for three or four more hours. We just couldn't. I felt so wrung out. Wet. Shaky. But what else was there to do but hold on?

Mom shook her head. "No. It's not over."

"I know," I said. "I think that was the eyewall." I remembered that from the hurricane test. The wall around the eye was the most intense part of the hurricane. The eye would pass us, and the rain and wind would come back in the rain bands on the other side. "That's what took Penelope away."

We looked around. We were in the calm center of the hurricane, and sunlight shone down. No rain or wind. The sky was blue. The eye of that humongous hurricane I'd seen on the news yesterday was directly over our heads.

"The eye," I said. It gave us a break and a chance to talk without yelling.

She sighed. "Let's eat something while it's quiet, Jessie." She motioned for me to turn so she could reach my pack, still on my shoulders, and get a can of soup out, and I got one out for her from hers. I slurped the soup without a spoon or anything. I had some water too. How could I be so thirsty with so much water around us and on top of us?

Mom grabbed one of the lids from the plastic chicken tubs as it floated by, to give Grandma more to sit on. Soon after that, I was able to grab a small rug, which was soaked and super heavy, but Mom and I hoisted it up for another way for her and me to relieve the pain from sitting on the narrow beam. That edge cut into my hinder the longer I sat on it.

Grandma was not herself. Just the fact that it was Mom, not Grandma, who was getting me to eat soup, was weird. I mean yes, we were sitting in the attic above our apartment, with a big part of the roof broken off. At least we had a short break from the wind trying to rip our hair out and pull us out into the crazy, undulating waves.

"Mom, I have to pee."

She chuckled. "Okay, honey, go ahead," she said, with a funny look on her face.

I waited for her to tell me how to do that, exactly. Her eyes looked down at the water and then back at me. "Go right ahead."

"Oh, that is gross!"

I had no choice, though, so I got it over with.

The rules do change in natural disasters.

Grandma didn't say anything more and couldn't eat. For the first time in my whole life, Grandma was the one who was not okay. Tears ran down her face and she stared at the pretty blue sky with hatred. She had not said any more since her cry when Penelope blew away.

"Mom, you know how Grandma always says she hates the water?"

Mom smiled a sad smile.

"Is this why?" I gestured with my head at the chaos around us.

"Yes, sweet girl, this is why."

"Oh." I thought some more. For a kid who can think of the word "undulating" in the middle of being trapped, I am definitely a dumb-head. "Is that why you said to her, 'you've done this before'?"

Mom nodded.

In the eye of storm, the wind had died down. But the tears of my grandma filled the world with her sorrow and her fear, because she knew what was coming. She had done this before. We were only halfway through the storm. And soon the wind would pick up again, coming from the west instead of the east, with the shearing eyewall hitting us first. Oh my gosh.

Mom looked so tired and bedraggled, but she still smiled at me. Maybe she saw I was figuring something out. I saw she waited for me to ask follow-up questions. And I did.

"What happened to her in China, Mom?"

She looked at her mama and back at me. She pursed her lips sideways while she gathered her thoughts. "Oh, my." She took a big breath. "It's a lot."

Guangdong Province, 1955-1973

Mom began, "Jiexen was born in the province of Guangdong, in southern China." Just hearing Mom use Grandma's real name that way reminded me she had not always just been a grandma. It hit me, she had been a baby, a little girl, a teenager... once upon a time. "During her childhood, her family lived in the city of Guangzhou, which used to be called Canton City more than a hundred years ago. It's the capital of Guangdong province, and it's on the Pearl River Delta."

A lot of new geography. Oh! I thought of something. "We have the Pearl River here, too!"

Mom nodded. "Yes. We do. It's about the same distance from us as that one was from them." Mom laughed. "You'll like this, Jessie. Guangzhou was where the more complex Cantonese language comes from, as opposed to Mandarin."

I made a joke. "You mean, Mandarin is easier to learn than Cantonese?" We both laughed. Neither one of us could write in traditional Chinese characters, but Mom could speak Cantonese, and I could understand it enough to follow what Grandma said. Mostly.

Grandma's eyes followed Mom and showed she was listening. "She hasn't told me everything about her childhood, but I did research later so I could understand her better. That was when we lived in Nebraska. David's mother helped me look up background information at the library in town." It felt weird when she said "David" instead of "your dad," but it made me try to imagine him as a teenager named David who had just become a father to a little baby who was me. It was hard.

I nodded for her to keep going. This really was unbelievable to not know any of this, really nothing about Grandma. I was already amazed that Mom's usual depressed lack of energy hadn't stolen her away from me today of all days. I was so grateful to have her here.

In the quietness, Mom said, "Well, when she was about seven, there was one horrible storm with a terrible amount of rain, and it hit at the same time as a high tide. It was called Typhoon Wanda. They had the winds like we're having today." She shook her head, looking around at our precarious situation in the ruined attic of an inundated apartment building.

She said, "I read a newspaper article in the South China Herald. So many people were killed, and maybe 100,000 people lost their homes, over the whole area." I kept listening. "There were tidal waves, and the storm surge on top of the high tide, and rickety wooden buildings collapsing everywhere. The article called it 'Hong Kong's Day of Terror.'"

"Hong Kong? Wait, I thought she lived in Guangzhou?"

Mom nodded. "Yes, it was all in the same neighborhood, as far as that typhoon was concerned. Guangzhou, Macau, Hong Kong. From Guangzhou, one way to get to Hong Kong, which was a British colony, was to go down the Pearl River and the wide estuary leading to the South China Sea about 80 miles. The north side of Hong Kong shared a border with mainland China, and then there are islands that are part of Hong Kong. It's surrounded by water on three sides."

This was complicated already. I asked, "When she went from Guangzhou to Hong Kong, they were two different countries?"

Mom nodded. "Yes, the border was shut tight. That's an amazing story. She was one of the 'Freedom Swimmers' who escaped. But that was later, when she was sixteen or seventeen years old."

"Oh. First, she was in China, and there were lots of typhoons?"

"Right. That only added to the misery they already felt. The storms came along in addition to all the bizarre social and political experiments the government was doing on its own people, and the famines and death they were causing. And every time a typhoon came along, it caused even more horrendous suffering."

"Oh, gee," was all I could say. "But it was already bad?" She used the word misery. That was so different from here. Everything was pretty good here two days ago, even though my friends and I had been whining about our lives. I listened some more.

"Mama said it was a lot of suffering there in the south when she was growing up, but they heard it was even worse in the northern parts of China, because it got so much colder there and it was harder to grow food. The beginning of her life was during the Cultural Revolution. That was a human-caused disaster on such a gigantic scale, I can't begin to tell you about that. So many people starved for reasons that could have been avoided."

Grandma surprised me by murmuring something that

sounded like, "They kill all swallow. Four Pest Campaign." Then she clammed up again.

Mom nodded and said, "The Great Leap Forward," as if that meant something to me. How did I not know this already? Social experiments? Famine? Why did we have to have a gigantic hurricane like this for me to just get to sit and hear about this from my mom? I sighed.

She read my thoughts. "Jessie, I'm sorry you haven't heard about all this before."

It might have helped me understand Grandma better. Well, maybe. I'm very mature for a seventh grader, but on the other hand, this was a lot.

She kept talking. "In every one of the typhoons, all the fishing boats got smashed up onto each other or onto the buildings onshore. Even big ocean-going ships ended up tossed on the beach with their hulls ripped open. Or thrown on top of other ships, or up on buildings on shore, or onto the wharves."

"Oh my gosh." I stayed quiet for a minute. "Mom," I asked. "Do you think that's going to happen here this time?" That casino barge bobbing up and down yesterday must have been destroyed by now. It couldn't have survived all this.

Mom nodded. "Probably, yes." She thought and looked around at the damaged roof and the apartment full of water below us and pushed some tangled hair back out of her face. The braid I'd made in her hair was long gone. "This is bad."

"And we're not done yet, are we?"

"No, Jess."

We were only halfway done. I could not imagine another long siege like we'd already survived. "Were there more typhoons? In China and Hong Kong?"

"Oh, yes. They had all the smaller ones in between, like we do here." We exchanged grim smiles. I felt like such a grown up, for a change, talking like this. "The next really horrible one was in 1971, so Jiexen would have been about sixteen."

Again, I tried to picture Grandma being a sixteen-year-old girl named Jiexen. Just a few years older than me, I realized. Hm!

Mom continued. "That was the time when neighbors denounced whole families to protect themselves from the Red Guard, so they were already stressed out from those lies flying around. No one knew whom they could trust. Urban high school kids were 'sent down' to the countryside to be 'reeducated' by the peasant farmers who really didn't want them there in the first place, because they were ignorant city kids, but that's another story, too." She looked up to think.

"That next big one was Typhoon Rose, I think. A bunch of boats and ships got washed far inland, many miles away from the sea, with the storm surge, and people drowned and were even electrocuted as wires broke." She stopped talking and looked at me. I nodded and she kept going. "Well, I don't know if you can imagine, but there was no one to come help, not really, after the storm. That was the worst part, Mama said."

We looked at Grandma, and this time she nodded but didn't look at us. Her eyes looked flat and dull.

"Mama told me all the high school students like her and Baa were rounded up to do horrible tasks like searching for … you know, searching through the rubble of the collapsed buildings to find any people who had died."

"What?" That was horrible. "Did they know how to do that?"

Mom shook her head. "No, but there was no one else to do it, she said. The Red Guard was in control, but they were just kids too, and they operated through fear and intimidation," Mom explained, "The buildings were just homemade wooden shacks built on stilts, not solid at all. Everything was broken into splinters." Oh geez. "Landslides blocked the roads. The electricity was out for a long time. Thousands of fruit trees blown down. Pigs and chickens killed. Grain storage flooded. That meant even more hunger."

"I didn't know."

Mom shook her head, mirroring mine. "No, you're right. We never figured when would be the time to tell you stories like this." She adjusted her position on the carpet on the uncomfortable wooden beam. "No time like the present, though, I guess." I wondered if she would say more. I didn't know what follow-up questions to ask.

She said, "It was hard for her, I know, trying to raise me by herself after my father disappeared." She looked reflective. "She met him in high school in Guangzhou. Baa was a gentle, intellectual man. I knew that even as a little girl. China ate him up and spit him out. Jealous, lazy people had labeled him as one of the Five Black Categories, who were declared enemies of Mao Zedong Thought."

I shivered, even though I didn't understand this.

"Then they planned for a long time and swam to Hong Kong for freedom, and eventually earned money to get to San Francisco and start the noodle shop, but then some bullies in America found Baa and finished him off." Her eyes were unfocused. Was she going to say more?

Mom took a sharp breath and said, "Mama used to tell me, 'Don't bully the sea,' when I was about to stir up trouble, like arguing with a teacher about a grade I'd gotten, or even standing up to what she said to me." She grinned sadly and stared at the horrible brown waves around us. "Yes, a great deal of her life was influenced by the sea."

There was more to my Tiger Grandma than I ever realized. I shook my head. How could I take all this in? No wonder Grandma said I didn't work hard enough. Oh my gosh.

And then Grandma spoke in a normal voice for the first time since the storm had wrenched her last chicken away from her. "No drink water from sea. Water bad. Make people sick."

"That's right," said Mom, coming back to the present. "A lot of sickness spread after the storms, because the clean water sources all got contaminated with disease and chemicals and salt water."

I didn't think we'd hear another word from Grandma about the typhoons, but she told us a story, quietly, about her escape. "All my life, Red Guard soldier come and take food away. Make us stop school learning. Make us dance like sunflower to worship 'the sun in sky,' worship Chairman Mao." She shuddered and took a deep breath to keep explaining. "Make all stop worship God. Take people away to punish, they from Black Families, landlord, professor, Christian. All good thinker, accused, sent work in countryside. Make stop creative, make more stupid. Why?"

Her eyes were unfocused, remembering all this horrible unfairness and fearful times. "Good people tell lies so they be safe. Mao take all food, books, teachers. The typhoon come. All typhoon. More people die. Lots people. More lies." Her voice was ragged. I'd never heard her tell about any of this.

"Then we have pay lots money, make false document, ride bus with guard watching us, pretend to visit village, run in night, hide in dark." Mom and I were quiet, listening. "Soldier find us during escape, take us to detention center, women sleep on cold floor in building. Men sleep far away in other building on floor, all crowded like pig. Food in bucket like for pigs!" Her eyes were wide. "We lock up many month. So cold. People die. Then they take us back to sent-down village for more education by peasant." She spit in the water.

"One day, I find Baa again!" She smiled slightly in her memory. "We pay, get more document. Go again on bus to south. Wait in the dirt for clear, calm night. We swim in huge, cold river, all night, whole night long, swim with jellyfish and shark and river current. Friend die in water. We swim all night, to escape China."

She closed up her face and lowered her head, tears falling silently. "We freedom swimmer."

8

Monday, August 29 - 10:45 a.m.

*A*nother daydream in the attic. My brain took me back to a conversation with Mom from earlier this summer, when she and I were at the park in Waveland.

"So, Mom," I had started. "Um…why does Grandma think it will make things turn out better when all she does is yell at people?" There. I had said it.

Mom had bitten her lower lip when I asked that. She had the prettiest eyes, narrow and dainty. Same Chinese eyes as Grandma and Baa, she said, but it seemed to me that she saw things differently through them than her mama did. "Yes, the yelling…" She blinked and looked down at her lap and a few tears spilled onto her cheeks. "She's… she's just been through a lot in life, Jessie," Mom said. "She didn't have much support."

"Oh."

Mom hadn't said it like this before. "Emotionally, I mean." She paused. "I remember Baa being so talkative with the customers, but it wore him out. He was not a big talker with

Mama. We lived in the one room above the kitchen and the noodle shop, and I could hear everything. The most words were from Mama giving orders."

"You said Baa was a professor before, in Canton?"

"Yes." She nodded. "A math professor."

"You said he had really long fingers."

She smiled, and I could tell she was picturing her dad. "Yes. Graceful. He was an intellectual, and a thinker. A teacher." She stopped. "It must have been unimaginably degrading for him when his coworkers lied about him, when he was just trying to make constructive suggestions—as they had actually been asked to do—and to be banished to the countryside. He was forced to be an unwanted, unskilled laborer on a farm, though he had helped so many students learn and ask questions and become problem solvers." She huffed out air. "To be a laborer is hard work for anyone. But he had never planned to work in the fields. He knew he had a future in the university where they respected him. Consulted with him. Looked up to…"

Something dawned on me. "What about Grandma?" I asked Mom. "She's so good with the chickens and the garden."

"She grew up on a farm, but she did well in school and got on the university track. For being a thinker, that's why she got punished and had opportunities stolen from her. She might have managed the physical work better than Baa did, but she still hated doing what Chairman Mao ordered. It was all so stupid. She is a smart lady, but she didn't get a chance to show it. The Red Guard executed people for making any suggestions since they were seen as criticism of Chairman Mao."

"That doesn't make sense."

She sighed. "No, but the people who survived found ways to make their quota of required suggestions into praises of the way things were." Mom closed her eyes and shuddered. "Messed up."

I thought about Grandma Jiexen as a smart young student. "But she learned three languages. Cantonese, Mandarin, and English. And she ran the business in San Francisco."

Mom nodded. "Yes. And evaded the patrols, and got documents forged, and escaped by swimming across six miles of nasty, violent, salty sea currents full of sharks and stinging fish.... Right," Mom said quietly.

That was a lot to understand. "So why does Grandma even do gardening now? Doesn't she hate it?"

"No, she does it now because she is free. You couldn't make her do it, but she chose it."

I smiled. "Like me!"

"My Baa must have hated being a cook in a restaurant," said Mom. "But at least by then he owned his own place and could make his own decisions."

At least we didn't have to grow algae to eat, like all the desperate people did when there was starvation in China.

I thought I heard a puppy barking somewhere nearby, but I couldn't think about that. And it stopped as soon as it had begun.

Monday, August 29 - 11 a.m.

"Mom, that makes me wonder, what was Grandma like, before she lived with us? When she ran the noodle shop?"

Mom smiled into the distance, then turned to me. "You mean, was she already ferocious and harsh then?"

I grinned. "Um. Yes."

She looked away. "I should tell you more about that, huh?"

"Yes, please. While it's still quiet?" I looked into her black eyes, waiting. Her eyes were more alive today than some-times. She felt better, I could tell. Once she had told me clinical depression was like that. Kind of up and down.

"Okay," she inhaled. "You know, when I was little, Mama and Baa ran the restaurant. The year I started kindergarten is when he disappeared. I realized it much later, that I think I saw him getting abducted, thrown into a car by one of the Chinatown gangs. But we don't know."

"That is so scary," I said. I was learning to get Mom to talk more by making little comments like that, even if I had no idea what follow-up question to ask. And by doing that, I was learning all sorts of things about my family.

"Right, not only for me, since I was so little, but also for Mama. She and Baa had clawed their way to freedom in America..."

I interrupted. "That's the name of Mary's dad's boat!"

Mom smiled. "Yes, *Free in America*. He probably has a story to tell, too."

Oh. I hadn't thought of that. I wanted to ask him about that when this was all over. I wondered if Mary knew that story.

She went on. "But after they got here, it was money trouble for a long time."

I shrugged. "Like now?" I ventured.

Mom laughed softly. "Not exactly." She sighed. "We do have all the debt on David's truck. But we're keeping up with the payments and the rent..." She looked at Grandma. "Mama hates debt. And for good reason. She's afraid of it because it literally stole 'the husband' from us. Her husband! A smart man who had made it out of such a dangerous, oppressive regime in China, only to lose him to a street gang."

I nodded and watched her eyes.

"So, when Mama and I were on our own in San Francisco, she did it all herself. Bought food, did the prep and cooking, served the people at the counter and the four little tables, rang up the cash register. We were only closed on Sundays so she could drag me to church." She took my hand. "I helped more and more as I got older. But she always pushed me to do well in school so I could go to college."

Gulp. That's where I came into the story. I said, "But you didn't go."

"Nope. David and I got married after high school graduation, and you came along, right before Christmas." She let go of my hand and wrapped her arm around my shoulders. "You were the best Christmas present since Jesus," she said. "In the middle of a Nebraska blizzard."

She always said that. But I didn't know why, because she struggled with church as much as I did. It was more like, "this ought to work" than "God from whom all blessings flow," like the song said in church. What were we doing wrong? Was it Grandma's fault or our fault?

Despite not understanding God, I did like church, because it was a change of pace for me and it felt reassuring somehow. When Mom and Dad went to church, they would talk with the other adults. When that happened, it felt like we were a whole family with a normal social life. Singing hymns was fun, and I had figured out how to read music. I could tell how the different symbols were like fractions that show how long to hold each note, and they also showed what notes to sing, which was harder for me, but I was getting better at going up or down the right amount to make it sound like a real song.

Our pastor and youth pastor knew everyone and greeted us by name, one at a time, during communion. I liked the forgiveness messages and all that, like the one from Ephesians that said, "Be kind to one another, tender-hearted, forgiving each other, just as God in Christ has forgiven you." It felt peaceful and hopeful at church.

But as soon as the pastor taught us one thing, Grandma pulled out her Cantonese Bible and read along with the verse during the sermon and came up with a different perspective on everything he said. She was always mad or impatient. Why didn't any of the fruits of the spirit — love, joy, peace, patience, etc. — seem to be part of her when she had been a Christian since she was in high school in an underground church? Even if she had had a terrible childhood?

A new word I learned in language arts is hypocrite. I wondered if Grandma was a hypocrite or maybe her Cantonese Bible had a different message in it than the English one did. Because I didn't see her forgiving anyone. Not Chairman Mao, which made sense. Not her husband, who disappeared. Not my mom. And especially not me, the incurable problem child.

Our pastor said grace was a gift from God, a free gift for us. But it wasn't free for Jesus, who paid the highest price imaginable to save us. I did not understand this, but one thing was certain, even though Grandma—a woman named Jiexen with her whole tragic life story behind her—had been through all that bad stuff and I should be more understanding of her history, there must not be a good translation of the word grace in Grandma's Cantonese-English dictionary.

Monday, August 29 - 11:29 a.m.

The other side of the eyewall hit us even harder, maybe because now we knew what was coming. The wind—the vicious, wet, stinging wind—started up again, reducing us to yelling if we wanted to talk. Now it blew toward the east, so it loosened things that might have survived the first hours by coming at them from the opposite direction.

The water touched the ceiling inside the apartment below us. More of the plasterboard fell off and pink insulation fell down as the waves sloshed. That plastic lid and piece of carpet to sit on helped a little to give us a secure place to sit. Down in the living room and kitchen, the stools, chairs, sofa, and even the dining room table all tossed up and down, upside down, right side up. The boxes and stuff we'd left packed by the door swirled around, some of them washed out the broken window or the front door, others smashed on top of other things. Everything was soaked and broken and ripped apart and twisted with other things. I wondered if anything wasn't broken down there.

I did not want to be out there in those wind-blown, scary currents full of flotsam. The waves made a checkerboard, alternating sections going up and going down, nowhere for the water to actually go. It stayed where it was and got deeper and deeper. The rain didn't stop. The wind didn't stop. We couldn't stop holding on, but we kept our eyes closed and prayed hard for it to be done.

It was mesmerizing. Numbing. We couldn't sleep or rest because we hung onto the wood beams, tried to sit on them in different positions. Nothing was comfortable. Or safe.

We couldn't talk again, it was so loud, and there wasn't anything to say, anyway.

The wind whipped and whipped and whipped at us through the broken side of the roof, daring us to let go and be washed away or blown away. I had no doubt that if the wind got into the attic and got hold of me, I would fly away like that cow in the *Wizard of Oz*, gone forever. They might never find all the pieces of me. I shuddered again.

The more I thought about why we were stuck here, the madder I got. First at myself, but I'd been doing that for almost two days already. I was still mad, but now I was mad at Mom, for delaying leaving, and at Grandma, because she was so unpredictable and made me upset enough that I ran away. But in my heart, I knew I had a lot of blame for why we were now hanging on for dear life in our broken attic in a hurricane, instead of cuddled up with Dad at the farm in Nebraska, waiting for the storm far away in Mississippi to pass so we could go home.

What home? It was all getting wrecked.

Oh, my gosh.

Through the hole in the roof, I saw a metal school desk chair blow by. Part of a small boat. More pieces of wood. If something did hit one of us, that would be the end, because it would happen so fast there would be no way to duck out of the way. It was all luck that a part of the roof was still there and protected us from getting knocked down or knocked out, even though the wind came from the other direction now.

How long had we been here? We'd been here for years already, hadn't we?

Grandma fell through the beams into the water again, and we helped pull her up. "Mama," Mom asked her in Cantonese if she was hurt.

Grandma sat on the plastic tub lid propped on the joists and showed her scratches on her arms and face from fighting against all the junk in the water. "Anna," she said to Mom. "That was refrigerator floating." Then she slumped to rest, pushing down on the wooden beam to stay upright. She had her feet stretched out to the beam in front of us for some balance.

Minutes ticked by like hours.

I had to give my brain something to do, so I tried to remember the names of the plants we'd learned about. Live oaks. Magnolias. Date palms. I saw the tops of all the trees sticking out of the water, sunk up to their tippy tops in disgusting, brown, salty, Gulf water full of black silty mud and broken bits and maybe even our car and our refrigerator now.

I tried to keep my eyes open so I wouldn't fall into the water in the apartment. I was so wet and tired and cold from the wind. It blew so hard, even in the shelter of the roof, it was like sticking my head out of a car window. Once I had done that when Dad was going sixty-five in Mom's little car, and I did not like it. Now the wind was twice as strong, at least. I might be bald by the time the wind stopped. If I were alive then, I would care.

My throat got all hot and pinched again. I hadn't cried this much in so long, but this weekend, I cried every time something happened, which was about every ten minutes. I let the sobs just come up into my throat, and the wind carried them away.

The roof made a screeching, tearing sound again, and another huge piece and even some of the diagonal rafters got ripped off on the west side, exposing us to the wind coming from that way. The roof was mostly gone. Now I could see more of what was being washed by the waves past the building from the west. I wished I couldn't, once I saw it.

A big dirt clump floated by on the upheaving water.

A floating dirt clump? What! "Mom! Grandma! Look there!" I yelled above the wind.

They looked where I pointed on the surface of the storm surge waves. They didn't seem to know, but I did. It wasn't a dirt clump. It seethed and moved, and I could tell even with the rain messing up my view. Mrs. Porter had showed us a video about this last year.

Fire ants.

If they floated into our attic space, they'd sting and sting and we'd be covered with itchy welts. It would be horrible!

The water was pushing everything toward the apartment building. Sometimes floating things crashed into it and then flowed around us, moving on to the east. I prayed hard for the fire ants to just float on by. And you know what? They did. But next I wondered about all the snakes and other creatures that might be displaced by all this water and floating around, looking for a place to hide, or something to eat.

I might have been a dumb-head, but I was no dummy. I didn't want to get eaten, or stung, or electrocuted, or impaled on some broken bit sticking up where it was not supposed to be. Grandma was usually the boss of us, because she sucked all the energy right out of Mom, who faded into the background. And my vote didn't count because I was a problem child, as Grandma reminded me all the time.

But you know what? I was proud of Mom today. She had been so strong. Grandma's face looked all defeated and small since the water came up and we lost the chickens. It was a good thing we were all together, Grandma, me, and Mom, so we could help each other. But I couldn't remember Grandma ever being this quiet for this long. It was the total opposite of her normal personality.

9

Last Monday, August 22 - 11:30 a.m. - remembering

How could it just be one week ago? After school last Monday, I went to Kendal's Seafood. Not her location near the harbor, but the retail store and little restaurant, east of my school, on Second Street. I parked my bike against the cement wall near the back door.

"Hi, Miss Doreen!" I called from next to the gigantic freezer, walking toward her workbench in the back room.

"Hi, Jessie!" Fish guts covered her hands, as usual, and her blond hair was pulled back in a practical ponytail. She could fillet a red snapper faster than anyone I'd ever seen, even faster than Grandma. "How's seventh grade starting out for you, kid? Do you have a boyfriend yet?"

I smiled. "No way." A picture of Tyrell flashed in my head, but I put it aside. If I had a boyfriend, Grandma and Mom would both probably kill me. Dad would just laugh and joke about making sure he was rich, so he could retire sooner. "Boys are stupid, anyway," I told her. I looked around the work room. "It's Monday. I'll take the trash out."

Miss Doreen shrugged and kept working. "Suit yourself. Sure helps me out now that my dad's not here." I'd never met Mr. Kendal in the year I'd been showing up here, but her dad's old-timey black felt hat and coat hung on the hook by the door in his office as if he were going to come back and put them on, even though it was her office now. I never would get to meet him, but she told me stories about him a lot. She wiped her eyes with her arm. "Thanks, kid."

After doing the trash, I swept the whole place out and washed the few dishes in the sink. Miss Doreen worked to get a ton of food ready to make fried shrimp po' boys and other amazing choices like seafood gumbo for the dinner crowd. I wanted to stay there all night instead of going home. Miss Doreen never yelled at me or questioned my floor-sweeping skills.

But it was time to just get it over with and go home. I said goodbye and was about to slip out the back door when she said, "Hey, Jessie."

"Ma'am?"

"Are you going straight home now?"

"Yeah, I guess so." I pictured the apartment with just Grandma in it, waiting to pounce on me.

She gestured with her shoulder to a white plastic grocery bag on the corner of her worktable. "Would you like to take that snapper? I bet your dad would like it." Her eyes crinkled when she laughed. "I didn't fillet that one yet. Thought your grandma might do that."

I nodded in thanks. Sometimes Miss Doreen sent shrimp home with me to thank me for appearing out of nowhere to do chores, but this was the first time for a whole huge fish like this. It must have been almost two feet long. I told her, "He's on the road this week. He left this morning. But Mom and Grandma will be really surprised," I said. "Thanks!"

"Nah, thank you, kid." She watched me take the heavy bag

and turned back to de-veining shrimp with her sharp paring knife, tossing them onto a pile of ice. A huge silver pot of shrimp shells sat ready to simmer for stock.

I took the fish home, and Grandma accused me of stealing it. Oh brother.

Monday, August 29 - noon, maybe, but who knows?

I watched Mom and Grandma near me, huddled on the beam, legs stretched across to the next one. They both had their eyes closed. The wind hurt less that way, but it was too unreal, and I had to keep opening my eyes to look around and see this was all really happening to us.

Yep, it was. For hours and hours. My teacher Mr. Cohen had given us another example about how hard the wind blew, and he'd been right. He said, "You all know how big a truck with a semi-trailer is, right?" He smiled at me, knowing my dad drove one for work. "Just the trailer is more than fifty feet long and about eight feet wide." We nodded. "So can you imagine a truck like that is parked at the side of the road, and you are able to climb up there and walk around. No problem, right?"

"As long as you don't fall off," said Tyrell.

"Right, if the truck is not moving, you could sit up on top and have a drink or play a board game." Where was he going with this? "But if the truck driver came back and drove the truck onto the interstate, all of a sudden you'd drop what you were holding, because you'd be going seventy-five miles per hour, and you would probably fly off!"

A quiet kid in the back said, "And if the storm got worse, I mean, if you were still on top of the trailer, you couldn't even hang on if it was going a hundred twenty-nine miles per hour down the highway."

Mr. Cohen said, "Yes, you figured out where I was going

with this. Now picture if you were stuck on the roof of that truck, going way too fast, and it kept driving, at that dangerous speed, all the way from Pass Christian to Memphis, Tennessee?" I liked how he said TEN-ah-see. But I didn't like what he was saying. That trip would take hours and hours. You could never hold on that long if the winds were that strong. It would be miserable.

Except that was exactly what we had been doing for so many hours now.

Our first goal had been that we were going to evacuate. But that didn't work.

Our next goal, I guess, was to just wait in our living room for the storm to blow over us. But that didn't work.

Then, our goal was to climb up above the storm surge and avoid the turbulence from the water. We were kind of doing that, but if the water went any higher, we would be out of options. We would be like those bees trying to stand on the rocks in the bee bath but getting washed away and drowned.

Did I have a goal in my life? Wasn't this just how it was with me and Tiger Grandma? Ever since she moved in with us, I'd tried to anticipate what she was going to be mad about next so I could do better and keep her from getting mad at me, but it never worked. I tried to do it her way before she yelled at me, but she was already mad at me when she got up in the morning. Ever since I was born, I was a mistake. So, I just tried to stay out of her way, stay away from home longer, but eventually I had to go home to sleep. Then she ambushed me like a tiger.

Granddaughters were not supposed to be treated like prey. They were supposed to be special. When we were done with this storm, if we all survived this storm, was our family going to be just the same as we were before? Or would something change? It had to change. I didn't want to live my whole life as a mistake.

And here we were in Hurricane Katrina, hanging onto our last goal of crawling up into the attic space, but maybe we needed to change that too. Grandma had no energy. Mom must have been wearing out. I didn't have strength either, but I was younger than they were. When in doubt, I had to think more, like Mrs. Porter said, and maybe even pray more, like our pastor said. I had to find a way to get some more energy. Or an idea.

What was the new goal going to be today? We couldn't just sit up here forever. Would the storm surge rise even higher than it is now? When would the water go down? Could we hold on long enough here to get back down to the ground? Was there any real earth left under all this water?

What was going to be left after the whole world washed away?

I went ahead and cried for a while. It seemed like the right thing to do, and maybe if I cried enough, I'd run out of tears and then they would just stop. I looked over at Mom and Grandma, who leaned shoulder to shoulder next to each other, eyes closed, just waiting. Maybe less than waiting. Just clinging on to a shred of energy.

I wondered what it was like for them when Mom was a little girl, growing up with her mama above the noodle shop, or before that when it was just Jiexen and the mysterious Baa, "the husband." How did those two ever get from Hong Kong to America after they swam across to Hong Kong? Would she ever have enough confidence in me for her to tell me that story?

Probably not.

Well, what did I have to lose then?

I opened my eyes and really looked at the stuff blowing by, hoping for an idea. Trying to think and pray. I remembered a joke the pastor told in church once. "Once upon a time, there was a huge flood, and the waters rose so high, the man had to climb up on the roof of his house. As the waters rose even higher, a rescuer in a rowboat appeared and asked him to get in. The man said, 'No, God will save me.' And he kept praying. Then a motorboat came by, and the people offered to pick him up and take him to safety, but he said, 'No, God will save me.' And he kept praying. The same thing happened with a rescue helicopter. He said he had faith the Lord would save him. And then the floodwaters washed the man off the roof, and he drowned. When he got to heaven, he asked God why He didn't save him. God gave him a puzzled look and replied, 'I sent you two boats and a helicopter. What more did you expect?'" I always liked that one.

I saw something coming toward us in the water that made me think. At first, I was afraid it was a body, but then I saw it was really an old tarp, maybe from a fishing boat. It was all crumpled and gray and had rips in it, but what if I could snag it as it went by? We could use it for a big wind break, maybe?

What was the worst that could happen? Either I'd get washed away, or else I'd survive and have to keep living with Grandma. I had to try snagging it, if it came close enough.

I'll spare you the gory details. I never even got my hands on it, and it floated away. I didn't fall in the water, but it was really scary there for a second.

"Jessie, that was … really stupid," Mom laughed at me. The wind almost stole her words.

"You're welcome," I laughed back into the wind. Like the man with one eye in the kingdom of the blind, I guess. No one else was doing anything.

If I had gotten washed away, though, maybe Grandma would start talking again. I bet she missed her chickens more than she would miss me, the problem child, if I blew away in the hurricane.

Monday, August 29 - 12:45 p.m.

"Do you hear that?!" I said through the wind. I guessed after so many hours of sitting in a storm that sounds like a freight train, we just got used to it.

A puppy was definitely barking in the apartment next door.

"Mom," I yelled. "When did Miss Akana get a puppy?!" A topic like this was worth spending the energy trying to talk and be heard. Yell and be heard, I mean.

She yelled, "Maybe late last week? Grandma mentioned it Friday while you were at school!"

We heard more faint barking through the gale force wind.

"How can it still be alive, Mom?!"

She shook her head. "It must be floating on something! I don't know!"

It was just too loud to talk, but that quick exchange had revived both me and Mom a little. I wondered what it looked like and how it was still alive. No idea.

I closed my eyes and searched out a place for my brain to take me next, away from the noise and rain and wind. How about science projects? The idea of setting up a control and then testing the one variable was so organized and methodical, it made me happy. And I liked collecting information and presenting it in an organized way. And yes, if my teachers praised me for it, I'm all about that too. So, sue me.

Last year I had an idea for a science project about the chickens. I wanted to test if the chickens laid more eggs if I fed them more insects and not just grain and food scraps. I asked Grandma, "Could I be 100% in charge of the chickens for two whole weeks?"

"Okay. This for school project?"

I nodded. "Yes, the science fair. I have to follow the scientific method and so the experiment has to be done a certain way."

She stuck out her chin at me. "You get good grade, make chickens proud of you."

I couldn't believe she was going along with this. "So, you understand, starting tomorrow, you cannot feed the chickens at all, because it will mess up the controlled part of the experiment." Three of them were supposed to just get their usual kitchen scraps diet, while the other three got supplemental nutrition and play time with live insects, too.

Every day, I went outside and caught beetles and grasshoppers in plastic bottles, then brought them upstairs and sprinkled them on the left side of the balcony for the chickens who got to eat them. I put some more chicken wire in between them. The right-side chickens got some more kitchen scraps at the same time, so they would be eating the same amount, just different food. I counted the eggs every day from both sides and marked it in a notebook which I kept on the counter by the kitchen. I couldn't wait to take all the numbers and make them into charts showing the results.

Near the end of the two weeks, the results were still not what I was expecting. The amount of eggs was the same for both groups. Maybe my hypothesis was wrong. I got home after school and saw Grandma on the balcony, talking to the chickens. At least she wasn't yelling at them. But wait...

"Grandma, what are you doing?" I asked, moving toward the balcony screen door. Just then, she dumped a bunch of grubs and beetles from a bucket onto the floor on the right side. "Hey, Grandma, you said you would let me feed the chickens! You said you would stay away so I could do my experiment!"

"This not fair to those chicken. Why you not feed those chicken same as these?"

All the energy went out of my legs, and my shoulders

slumped. I wanted to yell and say, "You went to school! You know how this is supposed to work. How can you mess up my science project like this!?" But I didn't say a word. It would not help. I just picked up the notebook from the counter and threw it in my backpack. I quit feeding the chickens for a few days.

So, my controlled experiment got out of control, all because of Grandma.

And I had to explain this in the presentation, even though I didn't name her by name. I made all the nicest charts and added photos of the chickens, but it wasn't enough. They had to grade me down for not finishing the experiment and not having a control group.

"Why you not win prize for science project? Use my chickens and not win prize? They beautiful chickens. Why not win prize?" Her voice reminded me of a clucking, biting hen.

Her words stung my soul. My eyes filled with tears, just like every time she did something like this. And just like always, I tried to defend myself, despite one of the main Rules of Living with Tiger Grandma: Quit Trying, Because You Just Won't Win.

"You messed it up, Grandma!" I said. "You said you'd let me do it, and you messed up the results!"

But it was like she was hitting me with a gun when all I had was a slingshot, and my bullet-proof vest was just a paper bag.

"You not work hard enough. You need try harder."

I didn't get it. Grandma dragged me to church, and they talked about loving each other and taking care of each other. That was what we were all supposed to do, to show how Jesus's love had filled us up to overflowing and was now spilling over onto other people — our friends, family, and even our enemies. The fruits of the spirit were joy, peace, patience, kindness, gentleness … and all that. The pastor said we would show these qualities when the Holy Spirit was working in us. Well, I didn't think the Holy Spirit realized how crazy Grandma made me.

Grandma had been a Christian since she was a teenager, but she spoke English as her third language, so maybe she just misunderstood what the pastor said.

No, she didn't.

What was spilling out of her was not love. She was just mean, that's all. She hated me.

Well, what could I do about that? Nothing. I wish I had the peace in my heart that Pastor talked about.

I couldn't change Grandma, but I didn't have to give up on myself.

Stuck in the hurricane, I decided to daydream about if there were a good science project I could do with the puppy, if we ever found it. Maybe we would need to get a second puppy, so we could have a control group. Which puppy would be happiest, the one that got dog food or the one that got home cooked chicken? It made me smile to think of having two puppies. Even though we didn't have any puppies yet, the old comic strip was right: "Happiness is a warm puppy."

I yelled to Mom through the gale. "Where's Miss Akana, Mom?!" It was such a miracle, today of all days, that she was sticking with us; not disappearing into the background.

"I saw her at the Quik Mart on Saturday morning!" She shook her head. "Since then, I haven't seen her!" She thought some more. "On Saturday night, I knocked on her door, but she didn't answer. I figured she'd left like everyone else by then. No lights on…" she was lost in thought. "I hope she's okay!"

I tried to picture old Miss Akana and the new puppy huddled up in their apartment together, safely, but that couldn't be right, because there was just as much water next door as there was here, and we were up in the attic because of it. Why hadn't she answered the door when Mom was looking for help? Maybe she just didn't make it back to the apartment. Her car was working on Saturday morning, before she went to the Quik Mart. Maybe we could all have evacuated together. Confusing questions with no answers.

And now, where was she, and where was the little puppy?

Monday, August 29 - 1 p.m.

So, I was even more lost in my thoughts than usual, picturing that helpless puppy bobbing around next door, clinging onto a floating table or something, wishing it could eat some dog food, or some home cooked chicken, while the floodwaters bounced it around near the ceiling and it got muddy, salty water in its mouth.

I kept having a bad feeling about old Miss Akana, wondering if something had happened to her, even maybe before the storm. I couldn't think about that, so I put all my energy into imagining the puppy. That made me feel warm inside.

"What kind of puppy is it, Mom?! What color …?!"

That's when a particularly wrenching wind gust, maybe it was even a tornado, took hold of the entire west side of the roof, rafters and all. The full blast of the wind hit, and all three of us screamed at the same time and tried to grab onto each other. We all fell backwards onto the beams. That hurt!

Mom got herself free first since she was on the other side of Grandma. The plastic tub lid was cracked after all it had been through, but she tried to use half of it under her butt to get situated. Then she helped Grandma onto the square rug with me. I've seen and heard how mean Grandma can be to both of us, and even so, Mom was so gentle and patient right then.

The wind laughed at our attempts to get seated again. If we had been hanging onto the top of a moving tractor-trailer since this storm started, like Mr. Cohen had pictured, I think we should have reached Dallas, Texas by now. How long could this keep blowing so hard?

Since the roof was now mostly gone, it was easy to see next door where old Miss Akana ought to be sitting up on her own beams now, with the puppy in a box or wrapped up in a blanket. She was the sweetest, nicest old lady. I wished sometimes she could be my grandma, instead of Tiger Grandma. Nobody was over there, though.

But the puppy was whimpering, so quietly we would miss it over the wind if we hadn't heard it before. Was the water level getting any higher or had it stopped rising? I wondered if I was right about him floating in a tub or a box, banging into the ceiling when the waves sloshed. Poor little guy.

At least down there, he would be protected from the hurricane. Up here, it was like standing in the wind tunnel simulator on our field trip, except the wind was twice as strong and it definitely did not shut off after sixty seconds. Or sixty minutes. Or sixty years.

"Mom, should we get down from here?! Since the roof is gone?" Why was I the one asking this question? Who was in charge around here anyway? Not me. Not Mom. Was it God?

She shook her head, looking down through the floor into the kitchen. "We can't go down, we can't stay up," she said. "I'm so sorry, Jessie!"

"Mom, this is not your fault!"

She shook her head and readjusted how she sat on the broken lid, a little bit away from us.

We heard the puppy again, so faintly. We felt like that too, wrung out and abandoned. Cold and wet. Hungry. Thirsty. "Hey, little puppy. We're here! We hear you! Don't give up!"

He must have heard me, because he barked again. His tiny puppy bark.

"Oh Mom, I wish we could help him!"

Mom nodded. "I think Mama said he's a black Lab, Jessie."

I imagined his little black head, all soggy with storm water. His eyes closed, little pink tongue probably hanging out because he was thirsty. I was thirsty, too. My tongue felt dry.

Mom looked over toward the other apartment attic, probably thinking about how to get the puppy to safety. She was so softhearted.

Oh my gosh, look at that. "Mom! Is the water level going down?!"

"What?" she didn't look at me. She was analyzing something about the attic above the next apartment.

I pointed east of us, out across the inland sea that used to be our parking lot. "See?" I had to yell. "Aren't there some more roofs poking up there?!"

She turned her head back to look east where I pointed. "I think so, Jess. And look," she said, turning a little bit north, "the waves aren't reaching as far up the live oak by the pier like they were before, either. I can see more of the branches now." She turned back to the south again, toward the next apartment.

We just needed to hold on a while longer and we'd be able to get back down into the apartment. And go find out about that puppy and old Miss Akana. Then we'd all be safe.

Monday, August 29 - 1:45 p.m.

Through the blowing wind, I heard a lady's voice screaming — it wasn't mine or Mom's or Grandma's—and I turned to look west of us. Coming right toward us was an entire live oak tree, half submerged in the broiling waves streaming toward our apartment building. The other half of the tree had far-reaching branches stretching up like a giant octopus flailing on its side.

One time, Mary and I had tried to measure a live oak at War Memorial Park, and it was about forty feet wide. So how could this huge tree even be moving like that without getting snagged on something, considering all the long branches that must be below the surface?

But who was screaming? All I could see was the tree.

In a flash, I could see someone hollering for help. It was a lady within the branches of the live oak, hanging on for dear life. Honest to Pete, she was wearing a bright red coat, a red life jacket, a blue helmet, and she had on the brightest red lipstick I had ever seen, even in a magazine, except she was soaked and clinging to this tree. She was so bright and so red, this was all clear to me even though she was surrounded by the thick branches and leaves of the live oak and the swirling blue and brown water and the heavy rain.

Mom had turned from looking toward the puppy to see what the yelling was about. She saw the whole far-reaching tree, headed straight for us in the unprotected attic space, and she started waving her hand to get the lady's attention. "Hey! Hang on!" Mom yelled over the wind and rain. "Let go and you can stay here!"

The lady must have heard Mom, because she shook her head. I don't think I would have wanted to let go of that tree either, if it were me. It all happened so fast. Mom was holding on to the rafter just above us and balancing on the beam, trying to walk toward the edge where the tree was headed.

"Mom!" I kept yelling. Was she trying to save the lady? I had no idea. I held onto the beam I sat on and watched with horror as the floating tree plowed toward us. One of the long branches swung right into Mom, knocking her off the beam she stood on. She lost her balance in so many ways at once, and she grabbed onto that tree branch by reflex. If she hadn't, the branch might have knocked her in the head or something.

"Mom!"

The lady in red screamed at the same time, "Hold on!"

Mom desperately held onto the branch while the whole tree kept barreling on by us, sweeping her out of the attic. She and the lady in the bright red water suit blew right past us, around the north end of the building, and kept going east, swirling in circles.

Mom was gone.

Grandma screamed, no words, just a terrible scream that sounded like someone stabbed her.

I thought I was screaming, but my throat was so dry I couldn't even swallow. Mom was gone!

The wind blew harder.

My stomach felt like someone had punched me so hard, I could not breathe.

I could not cry.

I could not think.

My throat ached with pain with all the screaming. Finally, I did cry, and my eyes could not see because of all the tears.

Mom was gone. Mom was gone.

I made myself look at the waves where Mom and the lady in red and the tree had gone, past the building, floating on the inland sea, out of sight.

I made myself look at Grandma, and she looked at me with the most terrible eyes.

But she still didn't say one word. I longed for her to yell at me. I was used to that, but this new total silence scared me. She didn't seem to be able to think enough to boss me around, and that's what scared me the most. Her eyes focused back at the place where Mom had been sitting with us, then back at me, and back out at the waves. Then she closed her eyes and screamed that horrible scream again.

What were we going to do without Mom here? And without Grandma giving orders?

But I couldn't just give up, or Mom and Dad would kill me. "Grandma! It's me, Jessie! I'm right here in front of you!"

She did look at me, but with these flat eyes. She still didn't say anything.

It was only me and Tiger Grandma against the hurricane now. Where was Mom? Could we ever find her again?

The wind gusts paused for a brief second, long enough for me to hear the puppy whining next door, but it was getting quieter and quieter.

Mom might already be dead. We were all going to die.

10

Remembering July 4, 1999

I need to tell you about when Grandma first arrived in the Pass. Now that I'm getting better at noticing things, it's important that I do, and you're welcome to listen in as I think. It was the summer of 1999, when I was six going on seven. Since my birthday was in December, I was always one of the oldest of my classmates. How can I be digressing already?

Dad was home from a truck run, and Mom had the day off, and they packed the blue cooler one morning and told me we were going on a fun family adventure. We had lived in Mississippi for long enough now, I knew exactly what that meant. We were going to the beach! We drove there in Mom's little green car, which was already a clunker back then. She said Long Beach had an Independence Day parade we could have gone to, but we just skipped that, and instead, we set up a sun tent, played in the warm, shallow water, and built sandcastles. A lot of other kids ran around and did the same things. I watched big kids playing beach volleyball.

Dad built a campfire, and we roasted hot dogs and marshmallows, and we also ate yummy food Mom had made: Mu shu pork rolled into pancakes, and sesame chicken and broccoli. We drank Barq's root beer as a special treat, saved just for holidays, because Mom found out it was invented in Biloxi, and also because it was so sweet and yummy. They let me have two whole cans to myself! I burped all afternoon, and my teeth felt sticky.

Mom and Dad laughed and told stories about when we first moved from Nebraska to Mississippi in the middle of the summer. They both thought they knew what humidity was until we got here, and the air always felt like a warm, wet towel. I got to tell my story about the first time they took me to the Mississippi Sound when I was five, and the sea was so flat, I thought I could walk on top of it, but instead my little foot went right through the surface, and I fell in. Dad scooped me up, and they let me splash around in the water in my clothes that day.

All three of us took naps on our towels on the hot sand, with Mom and Dad snuggled together on one towel, which looked too hot for me considering how hot the air was, but they did a lot of snuggling and laughing. We spread out dominoes on the towels. We played charades, and some of the other kids even joined us for a while. When it got dark, they took down the sun tent, Dad bundled blankets around me, with another big blanket for him and Mom, and we watched the fireworks lighting up the sky over the harbor in Long Beach.

Mom and Dad told me how school was going to change a little for me this year since I was a big girl going to first grade, and they got me all excited about what I would learn there. I was already a nerd then. Mom was going to work more hours at the convenience store while I was at school, but she would always get me there and pick me up, like she had this year.

Life was perfect.

The next morning, Dad was already gone on a new truck run, taking some girders somewhere in America, and the phone in the apartment rang.

Mom answered, "Hello?"

The other voice was piercing, so I heard it from where I sat on the sofa. It said, "Come to bus station. Biloxi. Come now."

Mom spluttered as she said, "What? Where?" More talking on the other end. "Today? Really?" She set down the phone in its cradle and looked at me. "Jessie…" She sat down next to me and put her head in her hands, then took a breath and looked at me. Big sigh, eyes closed, eyes open. "Jessie, we need to go to Biloxi. Could you get your shoes on, please?"

On the way there, she said, "I don't know what this means, sweet girl, but my mama is in Biloxi, at the bus station. We're going to pick her up. She is your Grandma Jiexen."

Huh? "I thought my grandma was Grandma DeGroot."

Another sigh. "Yes, she is also your grandma. You have two grandmas."

Oh. "I do?"

"Yes, but you have never met my mama. She lives in San Francisco, and she runs a noodle shop in Chinatown."

Oh.

Grandma Jiexen was waiting outside the bus station door with one suitcase and a light blue plastic flight bag slung across her back. She tapped her foot in its gray rubber sandal and Mom parked at the curb, turned off the car and got out, motioning for me to unbuckle and get out too.

"Why you take so long, Anna!"

Mom shrank a little but then replied, "Mama, you came to Mississippi! I didn't know you were coming!"

"I ride bus 34 hours. It two thousand three hundred miles across America to get here."

Mom tried to be polite, but I sensed something was uncomfortable already. "Mama, this is Jessie. She's your granddaughter: Jessie." She held me gently around the shoulder and drew me closer to her. Her arm shook. I wondered why that would be.

This was Mom's mama? Why hadn't I ever met her before? She didn't look like Grandma DeGroot who had gray hair and was squishy all over and easy to cuddle in her lap and smelled like butter and gingerbread. This Grandma was shorter than Mom, had mostly black hair, wrapped in a bun on the back of her head, and was built like a coiled metal spring, ready to react to anything that happened around her. She didn't hug me or look at me.

On the way back to the Pass, Mom said, "I know it's your first time on the Gulf Coast, so why don't we show you the Mississippi Sound as we drive home?"

"Too close to water, Anna."

Mom obeyed her without a question and took the interstate instead of the highway along the beach.

The apartment got smaller right away when Grandma was in it. Mom gave her my bed and showed me a fun way to pile up blankets on the sofa so I could sleep there while Grandma was with us.

In a few days, Dad got back from his trip. "Hello, Jiexen," he said, and Grandma winced at how he pronounced it, even though it sounded right to me. She tipped her chin up at him, looked at him, and said, "Oh, the father come home."

She announced she had found a spot for a vegetable garden behind the apartment building, near the bayou. "I need ride to flea market. Get seeds, shovel, bucket." Mom took her and left me home with Dad for hours and hours, and we played dominoes. Mysteriously, he gave me an extra Barq's root beer, and it wasn't even a special occasion, but I drank it up.

Mom and Dad talked with raised voices in their bedroom.

Then Dad said he was going to the thrift store and came back with another whole bed and mattress. He and Mom lugged it up the five half-flights of steps and set it up in the other corner of my small bedroom. "You can sleep in your bed again, Jessie. Grandma's going to sleep on this one."

What does a little girl know? That's what this new Grandma always said to me. "What does a little girl know?"

She scrounged up a bicycle somewhere and used it to get around town. I never saw her drive the car. She found discarded items on the curb and used them to build walls for her raised garden beds, a bench on the balcony, and stuff like that.

Soon, she took over the balcony with a project I didn't understand. She looked at Dad when he was in town. "The father. Go get." She handed him a list and had me come outside to work with her in her new vegetable garden. The next day, Dad was out on the balcony hammering chicken wire from floor to ceiling. Grandma slogged home with some old plastic tubs that she set on their sides in there, too. Why? Soon enough, we found out when she got a box in the mail. This was remarkable, because she never got any mail that I knew of, and this box actually chirped. It was full of baby chicks! And they sent them in the mail!

They grew bigger, and she made little harnesses for them out of materials she scavenged, and she took them down the stairs and out into the swamp and yard for a walk so they could have a dust bath and search for their own bugs to eat.

Obviously, Grandma never went back to San Francisco.

Mom slept a lot when she and I and Grandma were home

together, and she was at work more hours than before. Mom shrank.

School started. Mom took me on the first day and met my teacher, but she said after this, Grandma would be the one to drop me off and bring me home. That was it.

My seven-year-old self said, "No way. Me, I'm not shrinking. I'm not letting her treat me like that. No way."

And Tiger Grandma and I were off to the races.

Monday, August 29 - 2:30 p.m.

Grandma looked down at the water and furniture and stuff roiling around in the apartment underneath me and her for a long time. Then she glanced at me, closed her eyes, and went back into herself. Maybe she was just ready to die, now that Mom was gone and all her chickens blew away in a hurricane. She was not that old, but maybe she was just done. Maybe this was too much.

I sat there with my eyes wide open. The wind was blasting them dry, and even so, more tears tried to spill out. I blinked a lot to make them stop. My lips pressed together into a frown that quivered a lot. If I let go right now, I would completely lose it.

Where was Mom? And the lady with the red life jacket?

What was Dad going to do if he found out we all got lost at sea—while sitting in our own apartment?

No one was coming to save us.

This was not fair. This was ridiculous. I wanted to scream. Run. Disappear. But No!

Our youth pastor told us this verse once. At the time it seemed inappropriate, in my righteous sixth grade mind, to share with a bunch of kids who were just trying to have fun at youth group. But today, I thought maybe it had been appropriate after all. Maybe he knew this day would come.

Oh, my gosh. What I could remember was: Give all your worries and cares to God, because he cares for you. Stay alert. Watch out for your great enemy, the devil, who prowls around like a roaring lion, looking for someone to devour. Be strong in your faith. And after you have suffered a little while, God will strengthen you. And place you on a firm foundation.

Or something along those lines.

It got my attention, because I was so mad at our youth pastor that day. What the heck was he doing, talking about the devil and trying to scare us like that? I had enough problems in my life without worrying about a lion prowling around, trying to devour me.

And then, he even played a song for us with the same verses in it. Besides my fury at him that day, it was the music. That's why I could remember the words now. Yes, I remembered the song, in a mournful, slow, rolling melody. "Cast all your cares on him, and sing again. For God's love makes me smile through heavy pain. And oh, when his dear face the dark clouds dim, I am not all alone. I am with him."

Hm. Seriously?

Wait a minute.

Maybe that was exactly what he meant. My life, all the weird behavior of Grandma's, and Mom sleeping so much, and Dad always gone... maybe that was the roaring lion. Maybe I was supposed to remember I was not the only person in the world with a stupid life. People like Mary's parents who escaped from Vietnam had it a lot worse.

Oh, and so did Grandma and all those people in China too. But she still was a Christian. Or so she said. It was easier to see it in Mrs. Ngo, and even Mom, than in bitter, unpredictable Grandma Jiexen.

"He will strengthen you." I was starting to realize I was not the first person to be overwhelmed by despair. There were people all around the Pass right now, this very same moment, having this same argument with themselves and God, I bet.

We were sure trapped. Well, I didn't know what Grandma's problem was this time, but I was not old. And I was not done! I had to keep trying. I had this new, odd feeling inside. She was the one who should be helping the most, since she'd been through all those typhoons, but she just couldn't do it now. Maybe she wasn't just giving me the silent treatment because she was mad at me. Maybe something was really wrong. She seemed frozen. Maybe she really didn't know what to do. Or maybe she knew too much and had given up. Maybe she was worried about her daughter who wa washed away. Yes?

"Grandma, will you talk to me?"

Nothing.

"Come on, you talked to the chickens before. Odessa and Penelope, remember? Can you talk to me too?"

She shook her head slowly, but at least it was a response. She absentmindedly rubbed at the scratch on her arm, but now it was all nasty looking. It was bright red and inflamed all down her forearm.

She had said not to touch the water, but we had no choice. And now I looked at her infected skin.

Monday, August 29 - 3 p.m.

My brain raced. The fog cleared away, and I quit feeling sorry for myself. Like Mom said, Grandma had survived storms like this already. They had been as bad as this, or maybe worse. A lot of dead people. No food. No help coming then or the next day or the next week, it sounded like. I knew it would come, here, though. The helpers of Pass Christian wouldn't just never show up, the way no one helped her when she was a kid. But maybe she didn't know that. Maybe the vast amounts of water, and this storm, paralyzed her so much. It touched inside her where I had no idea she was so—what's the word—traumatized.

More lights flashed on in my head.

The youth pastor's words about the fruits of the Spirit. Peace, patience, kindness, goodness, faithfulness, gentleness, and self-control. That second one, Patience. I always just skip right over that one in my hurry to get through the list and finish singing the song. How can I be patient when there's so much going on in my head? And so much to figure out?

Dad had a sticker on the cabinet inside the cab of his truck. It said, "Be patient. God isn't finished with me yet." I never understood that. I thought he was trying to apologize to Mom for being such a doofus sometimes.

Hm.

Maybe Grandma does not blame me. Maybe she was just trying to keep me from failing and actually might have wanted me to succeed, but her way of motivating me was the complete opposite of what I could understand.

When she said, "No be lazy girl," did she really mean, "Go, fight, win!" like Edna Mole, the scientific superhero costumer designer in *The Incredibles*? When she said, "You need work hard," was she just worried I was going to depend on other people, which was risky, because they would let you down? Did she want me to remember what the pastors at church said, which was: God will be with you all the time?

I was being my own worst enemy. It wasn't really Grandma. It was me.

And you know what, maybe that's just what happened to my mom, too. Maybe her mama just had exactly the wrong reaction to just about everything she did, even though they were both trying so hard to win, but they might have been using the same words, like 'trust,' 'strength,' or even 'family.'

It's like they were speaking different languages. Mom was really a great person, unless she was with Grandma, and then she melted away into herself. Maybe that was why.

Having had these ideas, I wanted to understand more about the way Grandma talked to and treated my dad, whom she called 'the father,' the same way she'd called Baa 'the husband' before he vanished. Was Grandma worried something would happen to my dad as had happened to 'the husband' in San Francisco? The light was dawning in my head!

And do you know what? After hanging onto the top of a semi-trailer long enough to drive from here to Oklahoma, the hurricane winds slowed. It was calming down!

And the water really was going down. The roofs of buildings and tops of trees and telephone poles showed above the surface again, the ones that weren't broken or collapsed, anyway.

And after six years of being battered by the unpredictable, unforgiving rising tide known as Grandma, maybe the water level was going down there now, too. Maybe I wouldn't have to keep crouching on the counter or on a beam in the attic to escape from her. I desperately prayed that Mom was safe, but I still couldn't lean on her.

I could make decisions for us, at least right now. I had to. Mrs. Porter said once, "If you choose not to decide, you still have made a choice." She made a joke about it being a quote from a progressive rock song, but no one laughed. There was no way she had ever listened to progressive rock, whatever that even was. A band called Rush? She was way too old. Wasn't she?

I had ideas. They might even be good ideas. First, we had to survive.

And get the puppy.

And find Mom.

Then find Dad.

Monday, August 29 - 4 p.m.

You know, on Saturday I was only twelve years old. But by the end of Monday, two days later, I felt more like I was almost thirteen. If I was the only one in charge now, I really had to pray, like our pastor said, and think, like Mrs. Porter said. So, I started talking to Grandma out loud, instead of just thinking thoughts in my head, just in case she was listening. Even if she wasn't, it helped me think.

The wind was slowing down. Now it was only enough to blow me over on my bike, instead of blowing me off the edge of a cliff. I wish Mom could come back. But meanwhile…

"Grandma, the waters are going down, and in a few hours, it will be dark," I said. "We need to get down from the attic now." She didn't argue with me.

"See, look through the ceiling. The water is below the counter top down there. I can almost see the top of the coffee table." I got her to scoot toward the big gap in the ceiling over the kitchen cabinets, braced my feet on the beams, and grabbed the strap of her plastic airplane bag to try to guide her as she fumbled with her feet and then found the cabinet shelves we had used to get up.

She climbed down, putting her foot on the top cabinet shelf. "That's good, Grandma." Her right foot found the next shelf, but as her left foot found the bottom shelf and put most of her weight on the cabinet, it ripped out of the soggy sheetrock wall and hit the countertop. She tried to brace her right foot on the counter, but it was slippery, and her ankle twisted under her, bending her ankle in, as the cabinet fell on top of her, and then crashed down and fell into the water, and she was so off balance, she almost fell off too. She screamed so loud. Oh no.

I got down after her, trying not to step on her leg or foot.

"Grandma, sit still for a minute," I said, even though she was already sitting still. Her face grimaced as I lifted her pant leg to check out her ankle. Above her wet sneakers and ankle socks, her right ankle was already swollen and bright purple on the inside.

Oh, no. Oh my gosh, what did this mean? It probably meant I better pray harder than I had been. Out loud I said, "Dear God, this is really bad. Grandma is hurt. Please help me figure out what to do right now! Amen."

Words from the babysitter's first aid class popped into my head, and I said it out loud. "Ice, we need ice." I might as well look in the freezer. "You never know," I said. I stood up and walked along the slippery countertop, over the sink, to the refrigerator. I knew the power had been off forever, and the fridge had been floating in the hot water, but had the doors opened, or was it still cold in there at all?

I took a gel pack out of the freezer. It was cool, at least. "Look Grandma." She held it on her ankle.

Next order of business. "I'm thirsty. Do you have any water left in your blue bag?" She unslung it from her back, and I looked in there, but both the bottles she had were empty. I took off my backpack for the first time in over a day. Mine were empty too.

"It was a good idea to fill up the bathtub with water, Grandma. I see what you were thinking yesterday," I said, shaking my head. "Now I understand, anyway. But the water got too high. It must be all disgusting in the bathtub now."

I looked around. "But what about the water you made me put on top of the cabinets?" I stood up and looked, but all those pitchers and bowls were gone, except for one big glass bowl that now held muddy salt water.

"Grandma, I can't give up. What am I missing?" Not that she was going to answer me. "What about those plastic jugs with the lids that I filled up? Where are those? Maybe they're still okay?" I spotted one kind of bobbing in the water between the sofa and the coffee table. When Grandma had made me fill up the pitchers and jugs, I was doing a pretty bad job of it, and I didn't fill them all up all the way. There was a plastic jug that I'd only filled about three-fourths full before I screwed the lid back on. Probably saying some mean things under my breath at the same time. Yeah, probably.

But I remembered that one of my science teachers said if someone is drowning in a pool and you don't have a life ring or a stick, to throw them an empty milk jug. This would give them something to hold on to and calm them down enough to keep their nose above the water while you go call for help. You can't push a beach ball under water because it's full of air, so it's buoyant. If I had filled the jug up all the way and pushed out all the air, it would have sunk because it wasn't buoyant. But since I'd left some air in there, it was just hanging there in between sinking and floating, and I got down into the water and brought it to the countertop.

Better than that, I had screwed the lid on tight, and so it was clean water! We could drink it! We both refilled all our smaller water bottles, and there was still water left in the jug. How about that?

"Grandma, can you get down from the counter?" She shook her head. When I want to learn something new, I look it up in an encyclopedia or a book. I wished I could look up what to do about Grandma's ankle. It was swollen and purple, and I didn't think she could put weight on it.

Miss James at the town library knew what a nerd I was, and when the library had to update their encyclopedias for new ones, she let me take the old ones home. They were heavy books, so I could only do one or two at a time in my backpack. By the time Katrina hit, I was up to the letter S. They were all on a shelf in the back of my closet, which was now all filled with disgusting sandy seawater filled with chemicals and crap, literally.

Such a waste.

"Grandma, I don't think we can leave the apartment, even when the water goes back down."

She nodded, but her eyes focused somewhere out the window.

"Because we have to wait for Mom. If we leave, she won't be able to find us. Or Dad, when he comes to get us."

Grandma nodded again but closed her eyes. Her fingers touched the swollen purple ankle.

And because of your ankle. Okay, fine, I said to myself, but then out loud. "If we are staying here, and it's almost night, we need a place to sleep." I hugged my arms around myself. "And I want to light a fire."

No objection from her. I was sure she might have had some kind of opinion about how dangerous it would be to stay in this building that might fall down on our heads, but she didn't. Maybe she hadn't noticed that the balcony where her chickens lived was completely ripped off, or that a bunch of the neighboring apartment buildings were not standing anymore.

We ate the last can of soup from my backpack. I hoped Mom was somewhere eating soup now, too. And I hoped Dad would come find us soon. I prayed really hard.

Monday, August 29 - 4:30 p.m.

What else did Mom throw in my backpack? An assortment of things. A beautiful assortment of emergency things, and you know what? Now I remembered bringing this little hurricane emergency zip bag home from school when I was in fifth grade, Mr. Cohen's Mississippi Studies class. He had told us so many stories about monitoring the weather when you lived near the Gulf of Mexico. He told us how he went out in his motorboat—he called it a runabout—to go fishing, and so we made these dinky little kits. "You never know," he told us little kids.

I saw some antiseptic wipes, band-aids, and antibiotic ointment. While Grandma and I sat on the counter, I made her show me her arm so I could wash it with the wipes and try to cover up the bleeding parts, but it was not good.

There was also a little bag of chocolate candies, which must be stale by now but they looked so good, I shared the chocolates with Grandma right away. The sealed zip had kept everything dry. There was some gum, and some nail scissors.

And a tiny box of matches!

I wondered how many of my classmates from fifth grade were pulling out their dinky emergency kits right now and finding that precious box of matches. There was nothing dry for a hundred miles, but one thing I knew was that we had matches and I wanted to light a fire. I was so wet, I couldn't remember what it felt like to not be wet. I wanted to be dry and warm.

The wind blew less and less. I could almost hear myself think.

But we waited and waited on the counter top. At last, there were only a few inches of water. I lowered myself onto the floor again, glad for my soggy sneakers, because there were sharp and broken things that must have washed into the apartment from out in the swirling, broken world. My feet were tired of being wet, but I could not take off my shoes until it was safer.

Grandma had more room on the countertop without me there, and she stretched her legs out straight and leaned against the wall where the cabinet used to be. She wasn't going anywhere, but at least she wasn't all scrunched up now.

I hadn't built a campfire by myself before, but I'd watched Dad when we did fun beach days. He always brought some newspaper with him to use as the first kindling, which he crumpled up and then put skinny dry sticks over it in a tipi shape, or sometimes a log cabin shape. Then he had a match, and when the flame caught, he would put bigger sticks on there, one at a time. He never got the match out until he had all the kindling and the sticks ready to be lit. I'm glad I bothered noticing him do that.

So that's what I did, on the cement landing outside the missing front door. For kindling, that needed to be dry, something that would flare up as soon as the match touched it. I got some pages from my wet encyclopedias in the closet. I laid them on the steps outside so they could dry while I looked for more things I could burn. I found more cans of food tossed around on the floor, all dented up, and I opened two more of those to eat, handing one to Grandma with a spoon from my pack. A few still had their labels, so after we opened them, I saved the labels for more kindling. What else would catch fire easily? It had to be light and fluffy and dry. Oh, how about cotton balls? Sure enough, in the bathroom cupboard there were cotton balls and cotton swabs, both in sealed plastic zip bags. I had enough kindling now.

For the small sticks and bigger sticks, I found some wooden pencils in a drawer in my desk. Broken pieces of the front door and pieces of wooden furniture were scattered on the floor in the apartment and the balcony. I found a broom wedged by the refrigerator and used it to scoop the splinters and pieces up and added them to my pile on the stair landing. Oh, there was one of Mom's shirts in a soaking mess on the floor. I hung it up on the railing on the stair landing with more wet clothes and random stuff that could get dry and burn. Or maybe we could wear the clothes later. I didn't know.

I thought about the sofa cushions. They were foam and would burn. But they would be toxic and horrible. That's what one of the firemen said when they came to our class to explain about Stop, Drop, and Roll. He said if your house catches on fire to make sure never to stand up and breathe the air, because the toxic smoke from the sofa and beds would be worse than regular smoke. Hm. I didn't want to burn them.

The sofa frame was smashed into the corner, and the three sofa cushions were wedged around the apartment. I gathered them and brought them out onto the landing, but not for the fire. I got some plastic trash bags from the kitchen—the cardboard box had disintegrated, and all the bags were tangled inside the cupboard—and laid them over the soggy, smelly, ripped up cushions to make a soft, dry place for Grandma to sit against the wall, or even sleep on, if she ever came out here. Who was in charge around this horrible disgusting mess, anyway? Me, that's who. Who was going to argue with me? No one. That was more than unusual. This silence from Grandma. Just not right. She wasn't giving me the silent treatment. She was just completely silent.

So, I was praying about self-control and trying not to cry. I got the ingredients for the little fire set up on the landing, the wood splinters and kindling and all, and then I looked around to make sure it was safe to try to light something on fire. I'd been noticing all the spilled gas and other chemicals that I'd noticed on the surface of the puddles and that must have soaked into everything. What if I got a spark and a fire, but then something exploded? What if the wood pieces I had gathered were now full of more than just wood? Noxious horrible chemicals that might have seeped in there.

But here we were, miserable and scared and alone. I had this fire ready to light in the middle of the cement landing, with metal railings around us, and no roof above us now since it was ripped away and gone. And I was so wet and cold. So was Grandma. We had to get dry. We needed something to focus on. I decided to risk it.

I took out one of the precious wooden matches like I had seen Dad do, struck the end against the sandpapery strip on the side of the match box, and the match came to life! I tried not to move for a few seconds to make sure it stayed lit. Then I held the flame under the thin wood splinters and cotton balls. After the first ones caught, I sat with it for a while, trying to keep the flame going and giving it more fuel when it was ready. I added thin slivers of wet, broken wood I found in the living room, and curls of smoke came out of them but then each one caught fire. It worked!

As soon as I got the fire going, I told Grandma, and I helped her get down to the floor and helped her hobble outside. She sat right on those cushions, on the landing, leaning her back against the wall under the broken living room window. She watched me adding sticks and stuff for a little while, then laid down, and I bet she fell asleep instantly.

I sure wanted to sleep too. And I want to collapse in a pile of tears and worry.

But instead, I looked around in the apartment for any other clothes, shoes, or items that could help us, and I hung them on the railing outside, or along the landing, to dry. Unbelievably, I also noticed Mom's pink and white glass dish from Grandma DeGroot. It was coated with brown silt, but it was still in the muddy wooden cabinet in the corner, and it was not broken. Nothing made sense.

I made sure Grandma had that one clean jug of water and another can of mystery food. And even though I was so hungry and tired, I had one more thing I had to do.

Save the puppy.

11

Monday, August 29 - 4:35 p.m.

iss Akana's front door was next to ours, and it was totally gone, probably pushed off the hinges by the surge of water from the Gulf, just like ours had been when the water smashed its way in. Until now, I hadn't let myself look inside her place. When I went in, I saw the surges of brackish water had destroyed, added to, and subtracted from everything in her apartment, the same as in ours. And it was covered with black silt.

"Miss Akana? Are you here?" I didn't think she was going to answer me, because I really didn't think she'd made it back to the apartment before the water came up or something, so I focused on the puppy. Where could he be?

"Hello, puppy? Are you here?" I walked carefully, sneakers squishing with each step, trying not to get hurt by a sharp metal thing or wooden splinter. Some walls had pieces of wood jammed right through them, and a big chunk of the west wall was missing. Most of someone's washing machine was in the middle of the living room, and living room furniture was gone. So were the windows, just like at our place.

The bathroom door was closed, and behind it, I heard a tiny sound. That made sense. She might have been using the bathroom as a kennel for it, in case it had a potty accident inside the apartment. She must have left it in the bathroom when she went to the Quik Mart. Maybe that's how the puppy survived? But how did it swim or float for that long when the water rose up so high?

I peeked in, slowly, trying not to scare the little guy. It was pretty dark in there, with only sprinklings of light coming through the missing roof and the holes in the bathroom ceiling. "Hello, little puppy. It's me, Jessie."

It whimpered but it didn't get up. It was in the bathtub, which was filthy but had drained out now, and inside that was a rubber tub where the puppy was curled up. Maybe when the water rose up to the ceiling, the puppy floated in the rubber tub like in a boat and didn't fall out, because there weren't any waves in here because the door stayed closed? The poor little thing was limp and wet and shivering at the bottom of the tub, with a terribly poopy, smelly, soggy blanket crumpled at the bottom.

"Puppy, can I pet you?" He had coal black short fur, and the biggest paws and floppy ears. "Can you hear me?" He opened his big eyes to look at me. They were the brightest black I'd ever seen.

I wanted to just take the little thing in my arms and cuddle it, but he was so filthy, peeing and pooping in that tub for a long time, and I had no way to clean up, so I brought the whole rubber tub out to the landing by the fire, and he didn't move a muscle, but he seemed to accept me being in charge now. I pulled the disgustingly dirty blanket out of the tub and threw it over the railing into the mud and debris scattered across what used to be the grass and the parking lot.

I searched two rooms at Miss Akana's place. Dad would probably laugh and ask, "What do we have among our assets?" and smile this silly smile at Mom. I never understood why that was so funny, but he said it all the time, and she smiled every time, too. Sweet, but I really didn't understand married people.

Anyway, in the bathroom cabinet at Miss Akana's, I found a case of bottled drinking water, which was awesome, and a bag of soggy dog food to feed the little creature, but it was probably just as contaminated as everything else, so I kept my eyes open for canned foods we could all share. I found some towels and blankets that were soaked and muddy but probably not poopy. I used some of them to wipe off the puppy and hung up the rest to dry outside so at least by tomorrow he would have a warm, dry bed even if everything was stinky with that sludge from the bottom of the ocean.

In the kitchen, I found more canned food with no labels and brought them all back out to the collection of them near Grandma. I poured water in a little dish and put it in with the puppy. I also found a package of baby wipes, which I used on my hands after I messed with all this gross stuff, and I hoped I would find some soap and water, or more wipes, for me and Grandma. Not that I could get the black stuff off of me. It was gross!

Dear God, I know we are supposed to appreciate everything in our lives, because it all comes from You, and right now what I miss most is being able to take a shower with soap and hot water and get clean. I'll never, ever take that for granted again, as long as I live. Amen, and no kidding.

The fire on the landing was bigger now since I'd kept adding sticks to it every time I went by, pieces of broken furniture and whatever I found between our two apartments.

It helped me breathe to have that warm fire glowing, making me remember the beach parties with Mom and Dad. Where were they now? Did they think I was dead? Are they… Oh, I couldn't even ask that question.

The puppy was perking up, so I picked him up and set him on the cushions with my sleeping grandma, and he scooted close to her instantly. She held the puppy to her chest and said something incoherent in Cantonese. I wanted to be the one snuggling with the black Lab puppy, but I didn't even know where I was going to sleep. I put more cans of mystery food near Grandma so she and the puppy could eat while I futzed around.

My wet shoes drove me nuts, but I couldn't take them off and go barefoot with all the dangers spread everywhere in the apartment. So, I took the broom again and made a clearer path from the landing to the kitchen and then to my bedroom, so I could walk with bare feet without getting an infection, even if there was no way I could get all the salt and sand out, and then I took off my socks and shoes, hung up my socks on the railing and put my squelchy sneakers near the fire. Then I unlaced Grandma's soaked sneakers, pulled off her soggy socks, and put them by mine. Her swollen ankle was deep purple and yellow.

Grandma gave me this grim look, from me to our shoes and back to me, right in the eyes. I said, "We're not going anywhere right now. We'll just get them to dry out some, Grandma. Okay?" She didn't want to step on something horrible and hurt herself, and I didn't either.

I covered my bed mattress with trash bags, so I wouldn't get wet from the disgusting soggy mattress full of mud and dead sea creatures and whatever else the water had scooped up as it swirled through every car, house, and trash can in the Pass. I thought I'd be able to sleep since it was at least softer than the floor, and I stretched out to try. Hm.

That wind. It had been like having my head pushed out an airplane window or a fast-moving train, for so many hours in a row. Non-stop. Pulling my hair. Blowing my eyes open when they wanted to close. My ears still felt like the roar was in them, even though the wind was gone. My hair distracted me from settling down now, it was so tangled. I wondered if maybe I should cut it all off and start over instead of trying to wash it and get all the snarls and junk out. That was worth consideration.

I kept tossing on the bed.

What had happened to Miss Akana? A voice in my head tried to tell me I'd seen something in the bedroom in her apartment, but I had not gone in there, and my brain didn't let me think about it. I had convinced myself she hadn't made it back to the apartment before the storm. But if I'd really seen what I thought I might have seen, it was too terrible to contemplate.

I was so tired. I wanted so much to sleep. But the echoes of the wind blew through my ears and my brain and my eyes and wouldn't let me rest.

Dad was supposed to get home from his trip today. It's Monday, right???

How could it be just Monday? Isn't today the day the storm surge started? Was that just this morning?

Tuesday, August 30 - morning

I must have fallen asleep, finally. I dreamed about Grandma and Grandpa DeGroot. They both spoke with a neat accent because they came from the Netherlands. They let Anna and David live in their basement after they got married, and then I was born, so then Anna and David became Mom and Dad. Their Nebraska cow barns smelled putrid in the summertime, and flies flew everywhere no matter how many fly bucket traps he set up. I didn't miss that. But I did miss them. Grandma DeGroot always baked scrumptious sweet desserts, with lots of cinnamon and sugar and chocolate. She was starting to teach me about baking when we moved away to Mississippi so Dad could start with trucking.

As I woke up, I tried to remember what was going on. Oh geez. I was on my soggy mattress in our dark apartment. The world smelled horrible, worse than any manure-filled cow barn, and it wasn't just my body or the clothes I'd slept in. It wasn't just the carpet or everything else in our apartment that was wet and now must be growing all kinds of mold or mushrooms.

The rottenness was the air itself. Our whole town. The whole world. Plants and animals and furniture and houses starting to decay, mixed in with all the stuff in the water that should never be mixed in. I was smart enough not to turn on the water tap; even if it worked, the water would be awful.

But there was nothing I could do about needing to breathe this air.

I heard the puppy whining out on the landing and walked out there. My leg and shoulder ached a little, but not as badly as before, and I walked carefully in my bare feet along the path I'd cleared.

I took my long pants and some less-dirty underwear off the railing. The air was already hot and sticky, I had to really concentrate to pull on those pants, but my grandma's warnings echoed in my head about not touching anything. Yesterday I'd found my rubber garden boots in my closet; they were full of mucky water, but I'd dumped them out and now they were dry, and I put on some different socks. All damp. Ugh. I was glad to have shoes at all, though. If I didn't have shoes or these boots, I'd really be stuck. Thanks again to my grandma.

The sun shone in a beautiful blue sky as if nothing had happened yesterday, as if to ask the residents of the Pass why we weren't all trotting off to school, or the beach, or to go fishing or something. I saw that Grandma had opened one of the food cans during the night for herself and the little guy.

All dressed, I sat down on the landing. "Hi puppy, what's your name?" I scratched behind his soft black ears, and he nuzzled his way into my lap. Today, his intense black eyes looked deep into mine. Those eyes and the black fur captivated me, and all I wanted to do was cuddle with him and scratch his ears and rub his tiny, furry belly lightly covered in fine black hair.

Oh, then I noticed she was a girl puppy, not a boy! I kept rubbing her belly.

Grandma moaned and rolled over on the sofa cushions but didn't wake up.

I picked up a can of something without a label—green beans, as it turned out—and the puppy and I shared them. I gave her some water in the dish I'd found and fetched the whole package of water bottles, and more cans of food, and left them by the cushions for Grandma.

I knew Grandma had used the bathroom in our apartment and had not flushed the toilet. I wouldn't have flushed it either if I were her. Knowing how destroyed everything was, who knew if it would just explode? But I avoided going in there altogether so she could have it for herself.

Instead, the puppy and I stuck together like glue and went down the steps to the ground. Puppy did her important hygiene jobs and looked at me, asking where we were going next, but first I really needed to do those same jobs. Um. Usually, there was a bush or something to hide behind when you have to go potty outside, so I squatted on the ground for all to see, only there was no one to see. I did my business right there next to where the puppy had, with my hinder sticking out in the air. Hinder was Grandma DeGroot's funny word for your butt. It made me smile to think about her. What would she do if she were here with us right now?

I decided to explore a tiny bit, without walking too far and risk getting hurt by a hidden danger. As far as my eyes could see was nothing but chaos and broken things.

The stench surrounded us. The muddy brown stench. It was gut-wrenching, awful, muddy, green, rotting stench that even hurt my eyes, not just my nose and the inside of my head.

Then it was the quietness. No sounds at all. No wind trying to rip out my hair or spear a piece of wood through a wall or a person. There were no sounds at all.

No bugs buzzing.

No birds chirping.

No car tire noises on the pavement. No honking.

You know, I couldn't even hear the hum of the power lines now. They were dead.

The air seemed dead and heavy. I spoke out loud to make sure my ears still worked at all. "Jessie, this is Jessie. Come in please." I smiled a little. Okay, I could hear.

My feet tried not to trip on all the piles of everything imaginable in the mud that used to be our yard. And it wasn't just like some trash blown by the wind. There was a refrigerator in the middle of the parking lot. The huge trash dumpsters were missing, just missing, replaced by piles of branches, and bottles, and insulation, and twisted metal, which I went around. Plastic sheeting and ropes and a Barbie Dream House. A heavy metal toolbox, upside down and empty. Over in the trees by Bayou Potash, I saw a runabout like the one Mr. Cohen showed us, but it was hanging up high in the tree branches, upside down. More gaps in the line of trees that used to stand along the bayou.

I looked for Mom's car on the other side where we left it,

but it was not anywhere I could see. Even if I had found it, would I recognize it? Would it still be green, or would it be dull graying brown like everything else on the ground?

I heard a helicopter far away. An actual sound!

I heard a big dog barking, from the direction of the animal rescue place. Did all those hundreds of dogs and cats get saved? Oh, I sure hoped so.

The air turned into a regular hot August day on the Gulf Coast. Except it smelled musty. Moldy. Spoiled. Putrid. I wanted so much to escape from here.

We just had to stay here until Mom got back. Then we would wait for Dad to find us.

Tuesday, August 30 - a little later in the morning

Puppy bounced up the five half-flights of steps and started to go into Miss Akana's apartment, where she used to live. I didn't stop her. She stuck her little head in there but then whined, backed out, and galloped back to me and Grandma on the landing. Smart little girl.

"Grandma, why is everything brown? Why aren't there any colors?"

She looked out at the gray-brown world and shook her head.

No green leaf. No yellow or purple flower. No lady with red lipstick.

We sat there on the landing, not looking at each other. No talking. Just staring into space. We sat and watched for any sign of life out in the world, but it was just silent, with no hint that we were in a town of almost seven thousand people.

Eventually, we found stuff to do. She sat on the cushions and blew life back into the fire. I looked around the apartment for anything that survived. A credit card. A jar of loose change with a lid on it.

I brought her more little piles of rubbish from the apartment that she could add to the flames, gradually, and keep it going. It felt good to get a tiny bit of the junk cleared out. And to sit by a warm fire, even though I wasn't so cold anymore. It was comforting.

She still didn't talk.

I found a comb in a drawer in the bathroom and handed it to her. She combed her own long hair, taking her time, got the snarls out, and put it into a bun again. Then she gestured that she wanted to do my hair. The braid Mom did for me on Sunday had not held up in the hurricane winds, and I was sure it was too tangled to ever be combed, especially by someone like Grandma who usually jerked the comb through. But today, she was careful, and eventually she made it into one braid in the back, not two like she used to do for me, and she didn't pull so tight that my eyebrows moved back to my ears.

It was nice to have the sticky hair off my neck and all the loose strands not blowing in my eyes. And it was nice to just sit with her like this, even though life was upside down and she wasn't talking. Maybe I wouldn't need to cut all my hair off and start over, after all.

"Grandma, do you remember when I brought you some frogs to cook?" I had caught them in the bayou right there next to our apartment one evening last year, and I put them in a plastic bag. She had told me before, "in China we call that Heavenly Chicken." I thought she would cook the legs right up. But the frogs were still alive, and I hadn't thought about that part. She put them in the refrigerator that night, then moved them to the freezer in the morning so they would die peacefully. The next evening, after marinating them in milk, she sautéed them with butter and garlic.

I was testing her that day, to see if the story about Heavenly Chicken was true. I didn't know anything then about her surviving any famines. And she had tested me right back, to see if I would eat them. I did, even though at first it was a new flavor, kind of like bayou-flavored, tender chicken.

When she appeared in my life, it took me a while to get used to her cooking, and at first it was weird, even though Mom was a good cook and she had learned everything from Grandma, cooking at the noodle restaurant. Mom stuck to more basic food that suited Dad and used ingredients from the local grocery, but Grandma would cook absolutely anything.

Bonus points for me: when we did the frog dissection in life science, so many of the kids screamed when Mr. Hartman took the frogs out of the glass jar to give one to each team. I stayed calm and collected. But the smell of formaldehyde is not good, trust me.

"I hope the kids in my class are okay. We were supposed to go floundering on the beach over Labor Day weekend."

Grandma was listening, for sure, because her head snapped up and her eyes flashed at me.

"Yeah, Grandma, we were going to go near the water." She harrumphed and petted the puppy some more. I said, "And we were going to go shrimping from the pier too." So there, I had confessed. Shrimping was fun, to take the small circular weighted net and fling it into the water, then drag it back up to empty the shrimp into the cooler. Someday, I hoped I could learn how to catch soft-shell crabs, too.

I needed to go look around, farther than I had before, but all the warnings about "No touch water" and toxic sandbags worried me.

"Grandma, I just thought of an expression you would say now, about me going out to see what happened," I said, nudging the puppy over to her so they could keep each other company while I was gone looking for…for what? For information? People? Food? She looked at me and waited. "I'm riding a cow, looking for a horse." She smiled and put her chin out, indicating I should get on with it. Victory for me! What would I find in the mangled up, flooded, dangerous world that used to be my town?

Tuesday, August 30 - twenty minutes later

My bike was not in its place at the bottom of the stairs, and neither was Grandma's, but in their place was a gas can on its side, some sunglasses, a car bumper, piles of branches and leaves, and some patio lights wrapped around part of the railing. Anywhere there used to be bare ground, there were huge piles of wood, insulation, and twisted metal.

North of the building, the bayou was all torn up. The marshy plants that should have been there were gone, but lots of other trees and pieces of boats and cars and roofs filled it up instead, hanging from branches.

I began to follow the trail north and west of the building in the grass to Grandma's hidden vegetable garden, but the ground was super squishy, still full of water, and so much junk lay across the path that I skipped that part and went back to the parking lot.

Maybe half the buildings in the apartment complex were either collapsed or gone. Nothing, and nobody, moved.

I moved south through the parking lot, hoping to see Mom's car. And I finally did find it, down by the entrance on North Street. Her little car was upside down and wrapped around a live oak branch, hanging way up above my head. I stayed away and stepped carefully around splintered wood beams, metal twisted into scary shapes, dead animals, and trash bags with the ends blown out so they just lay there, empty.

I didn't see how Dad would ever get down here to find us, because the streets were full of appliances and cars. A desk. A baby's crib and several torn up mattresses. Piles of pink insulation and sheetrock. Another little fishing boat. A huge fishing boat.

Smoke drifted toward me from some fire east of us. I realized it wasn't just smoke blowing this way. There were sparks as big as tiny coals floating through the air and landing on things. Mostly it didn't matter, because everything was so wet.

"Oh, look!" I said to no one. A six-pack of sports drink, still held together by the plastic rings, and it looked like the orange drink was still inside. Worth saving. Now my eyes knew what to search for: things we could actually use. I also found a can of something with no label, but it had a pop top, so maybe it would be edible.

I saw a plastic shopping basket, the kind that has fold up handles and wouldn't hold very much, but I knew I needed it to hold all my treasures. It was pushed up against a fence and tangled against it in a huge green shrimping or fishing net, the kind Mary's dad had on his boat. I thought again about him and where he was, but this net was no use to anyone anymore, not even him. I took off the backpack and rummaged in the bottom for the folding knife Mom made me carry. It took me a minute to figure out how to get it open and lock the blade in place, and then I cut through the net, retrieved the basket, and put the drinks in it so I could look for more useful things. It took me even longer to figure out how to close the knife, but then I put it in the pocket of my pants instead of in the backpack.

On my way treasure hunting again, on the other side of North Street, something big and bulky lay in the black silt dredged from the bottom of the Sound. It was wearing clothes. I stayed away. I knew it wasn't Mom, because of the clothes, and that's all I could do right then—stay away from it. I didn't know if it was a him or a her. I didn't want to know.

My attention moved to something hanging out of a second-floor window—was it a canoe or a kayak?—and then as my eyes were looking upward, something sharp grabbed at my knee, grabbed it hard, above the top of the boot.

"Noooo!"

I pulled my leg back, hoping I hadn't gotten a snake bite. We'd learned all about those in Mississippi Studies too. We'd learned there were fourteen kinds of aquatic snakes, and they weren't all venomous, but they would all bite no matter what. I had all those thoughts in a microsecond, but when I looked down, it was a piece of barbed wire fence that had reached up to grab me. Those hot boots and those hot, sticky, long pants, had saved me already. Grandma had saved me, again, yes she had.

Oh, then I saw my bike, or what was left of it. It would never carry me along with my hair blowing behind me anymore. But soon, I found someone else's bike hung up in a tree, the wheel skewered by a branch, so one of the spokes was missing. I took it down, very carefully so I wouldn't get hit by it, and I squeezed the tires. They seemed like they held air, so I sat on it. It was just about my size, but because of the mess on roads, it was impossible to really ride, and I walked my new bike with the grocery basket on the back fender to collect a few more things. A can of what might be tuna fish. An unbroken bottle of beer, which I took for Grandma.

Sometimes I saw a person far away, but they all were walking like zombies. Was that how I was walking?

I noticed the metal part of a car wheel standing by itself in the road. And a little girl with blonde hair, maybe three years old, stood behind it. She wore a little yellow sun dress with pink flowers. Some more kids wandered around behind her. She just watched me go by.

Grandma wasn't kidding about not touching the water, even when it looked clean, but now every puddle just looked muddy, oily, or scary. Were there more snakes? Where did the fire ants go? Everything smelled like it was rotting, or coated in rotten stuff. The sewer water mixed with the flood water from the Sound. The dead animals. All the wet clothes and papers and gas and everything that was in our houses and now all mixed together and getting moldy and stinky. Even dead fish. You would think fish would survive a hurricane because they lived in the water, but it was hard for a fish to survive if it got slammed against a house or a pier or run through with a metal wire. Even if you were a fish, a hurricane could kill you.

It was repulsive. When Mrs. Drummond taught us that word, I didn't think I would need to remember it. But today was the day. I wondered where she was. I hoped she evacuated to her daughter's house in Hattiesburg.

I got back after an hour or so. Grandma was asleep with the puppy on the landing, but there was another empty can of something next to her, and she'd added wood to the fire. That made me glad.

Mom wasn't back. Yet. I gave the puppy some more water and we shared a can of tuna fish. Then we sat together and watched the fire. I watched Grandma sleep and thought about the stories Mom told me about the typhoons they'd had in China. And how people ratted out their own friends and family to survive, because if they didn't make up lies about their neighbors, they would be suspected of being what people called a "monster or demon," whether there were floods, or famine, or not. And no one came to help. Not ever. People painted Big Character Posters full of twisted truths and unfair accusations about strangers, family, and friends to escape being targeted themselves. No wonder no one had wanted to tell me about the Cultural Revolution.

Grandma drank the bottle of beer when I wasn't looking.

We managed through the day. Me talking, Grandma not talking, and the puppy keeping us both covered in puppy nuzzles. I searched the apartment again for anything else that looked important that we might keep—all the papers were mush, but I found a few items–if we could wash it or salvage them, to give to Mom or Dad when…we found them. My library book, *Magyk*, had all the pages ripped out of the cover. Miss James would understand. Basically, everything was ruined. I had a feeling my library book was not the only one turned to mush, and it made my stomach ache to think about it. I wondered what the library building looked like right now. Was it still even there?

By nighttime, even more was missing than Mom, Dad, and all the colors in the universe except brown and black. There was no light. The moon had been waning, and it was just a sliver. Not one electric light shone anywhere in the Pass. No glow from Biloxi or Gulfport or Long Beach hit the clouds east of us. Nothing from Bay St. Louis. But the darkness was actually more full of stars than I'd ever seen in the sky at night. We sat by the fire on the landing and saw the most beautiful sky full of stars. It was like Mr. Cohen said, if you were out on a boat out in the middle of the Gulf of Mexico. Just me and the heavens completely jam-packed with millions of stars I didn't even realize were there until all the other lights completely disappeared.

But they'd been there all the time.

12

Wednesday, August 31 – sun is up and shining

In the morning, I had another good idea. "Grandma, I'm going to make a Thinking Map to help us decide what to do next." No argument from her. I kept voicing my thoughts. "We use them in school all the time to organize our thinking, so I don't see how it could hurt." I loved making Thinking Maps with Mary for homework, and with how fuzzy my brain felt, maybe it would help me to think about my own thinking. Mom would call this a 'God sighting,' to have the perfect idea right when you needed it most.

I fetched a yellow pencil and the damp Kim Possible spiral notebook and drew a large circle with a smaller circle in the middle and labeled it Storm Problems. Around it in the big circle, I needed to brainstorm all the problems that seemed so impossible right then.

Hm. A list of problems might have been obvious on a regular day, when I took everything for granted, but now, when it was stressful, nothing was obvious, not even the problems. There were too many. "When in doubt, think and pray," I told myself. Okay, just do one problem at a time. I added these around the big circle: "1. Mom lost. 2. Dad lost. 3. Grandma injured/infection. 4. Limited food and water. 5. We need to find help. No one is around. 6. What about puppy? 7. Grandma not talking." That was a lot of problems. Well, the last one was not a problem. She was nicer when she didn't talk.

Outside of each problem, I noted a possible option, one at a time. "1. Stay here and wait. 2. Go find help. 3. Search for more food. Etc." Next to each one, I narrowed it down even more on both categories, such as for "go find help," I wrote ideas about how we would travel, what we could take with us, and what street might be the best.

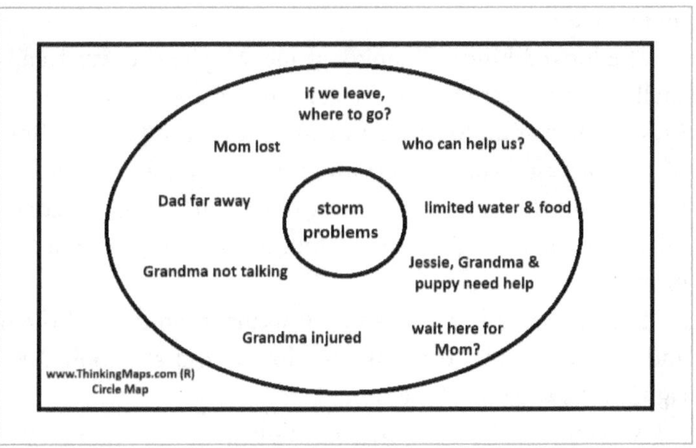

We were staying here for now, but how long should we wait for Mom to come back?

If we left, where would we go? I spoke out loud to myself.

"I think we would have to go either north, toward the interstate, or else east. The ground is higher that way. We can't go west, because we would end up by Bay St. Louis, and

Henderson Point is probably under water." I thought a bit more and then said, "And to the east is Gulfport. That's where the hospital is. We should go find Mom before anything, right?"

No answer, but I wanted to explain this to myself, at least. "If Mom couldn't come back here, why would that be? And where would she go?" Grandma looked at me and petted the puppy. "Well," I answered myself, "If she got hurt, someone might find her and take her to the hospital." I swallowed and added, "And you too, Grandma." I pointed at her ankle, which still was purple and yellow and twice its normal size. "You need a hospital too." Even if we weren't looking for Mom, we needed to get help for Grandma. But we couldn't walk, or at least she couldn't.

"Grandma, if we could get you downstairs, could you sit on my bike?"

She looked kind of blankly at me. Maybe she was totally shell-shocked and really wasn't understanding me at all. Maybe she was all foggy like I was. "I forgot to tell you. Both of our bicycles got washed away. But I found another one that's about the right size." Was it stealing if I took someone's bike without asking? Even if I found it hanging from a tree branch?

She squeezed her eyes shut, thinking, then opened them, and nodded at me, three times, slowly, and she looked me right in the eye the whole time.

Awesome. "Thank you, Grandma." Maybe that was another God sighting. Thank you, God. "Should we just get ready to go, then?" She didn't argue.

We both ate a can of soup and shared one bottle of sports drink. I already had on a long-sleeved shirt of Mom's, the sticky long pants, and socks inside my rubber boots. I wished I could find my stupid gardening hat against the hot sun. Grandma was already wearing long pants, the same ones she'd put on Sunday. Really smelly and muddy, but for now it was better than trying to get her to change clothes, even if I could find more for her, because of her ankle. But she did accept a different shirt that I had dried on the railing.

It took a long time for her to put her sneaker on that right foot since her ankle and foot were so big. I helped her get it on and we left the laces wide open.

"Oh!" I said, "We should tell them where we're going, in case they come to find us!"

Grandma nodded slowly.

I ripped a page from that spiral notebook and wrote in pencil, "Mom and Dad. We are OK. We have Miss Akana's puppy. We are going to Gulfport to the hospital. Love, Jessie and Grandma Jiexen." I drew a doggie footprint at the bottom and stuck the note onto the refrigerator with a magnet that hadn't budged in the waves. Just in case, I added "David and Anna DeGroot" at the top, in case anyone needed to know our whole names.

Then I hauled up two buckets of water and drowned the fire on the landing, just like we did when we lit camp fires at the beach.

I held my breath and snuck into Miss Akana's to find a leash for the puppy. I collected the last of the water bottles, some cans of food, the old towel that the puppy snuggled in on the landing. I found a plastic container just the right size for the pink and white dish and packed more soggy notepaper around it to try to protect it. The can of coins and the credit card. And I got the plastic zip bags – her mysterious one full of papers, and mine that said, "Jessie's Hurricane Kit." Thank you, Mr. Cohen. I put on my backpack and picked up the dog's leash and the grocery basket and realized I needed to make a trip down on my own with the first load, tying the puppy to the railing at the bottom.

Meanwhile, Grandma slung the plastic travel duffel over her shoulder.

Now freed of my first load, I couldn't really help her walk, but I put my hand under her elbow as she hopped on one foot down one step at a time, holding the railing. We took forever getting down the five half-flights of steps, but those steps had saved our lives, and I was grateful for every single one.

We both drank some water after all that exertion. The air felt hot, humid, and extra stinky. This was going to be a long slog to get… somewhere else.

I flicked the lever under the bike seat to lower it as low as it would go. Next, I attached the grocery basket on the back fender of this bike which had a rack on it just for carrying things, and I got the puppy to settle in, wrapping her in her towel. She was small enough to nestle in with the other items I had salvaged around her. Grandma climbed on the seat and leaned toward the left so she could push herself along with her left foot. Slow. Slow. Slow. Even if she were not injured, we still had to go slow, just to avoid pitfalls, but also because the damage was so much to comprehend.

We saw how high the water line had been by looking at the marks way up on the buildings that still stood. It was so high, I had to really bend my neck backward to tilt my head up to see how high the water had reached and stayed so long. We walked around tree branches. So much wood from buildings. Piles of mystery fluff. More dead cats and dogs. Oh, my gosh. A half of another shiny black piano, with all the white keys splayed out from it. We walked around the whole roof of someone's house.

Bit by bit, we saw people coming out and walking around in a fog, just like we were. At first, they were just sitting on their front steps, staring into space. Sometimes the house that was supposed to be behind the front steps was missing.

Other times, it was picked up and set on the ground next to the foundation. Or smashed flat nearby. Or leaning at a forty-five-degree angle.

We didn't talk to them, but if they waved, I would wave back.

At one house not too far down North Street, we saw a lady crying and holding her baby. I remembered seeing her walking around this summer, with her new baby in a stroller. She was such a nice lady, always smiling and helping people. I wondered where her husband was now and hoped the baby was all right.

But in my heart, I didn't think he was all right. Oh gosh.

We had to keep going.

The houses that weren't on stilts were either all gutted or completely missing. But even houses that were built up on stilts to avoid storm surge all looked wrecked, too. I saw a piece of wooden slatted fence hanging out the window up near the attic on one of those elevated houses. This storm was worse than Camille, I bet, even though I hadn't been here for Camille.

I noticed something and wondered. How could we be having a "hundred-year storm" less than forty years after Camille?

At the intersection of Menge Avenue and North Street, people were gathering and trying to share news. Someone had put up a canopy near what used to be the little restaurant that sold pop and hamburgers. The windows were all broken, and the roof was missing. People sat on the ground and rested in the mud, leaning against the walls, but maybe that was better than staying at their homes. Or where their homes used to be.

We stopped there for a rest, though we'd only gone a few blocks. I set the puppy and the basket on the ground, and after Grandma got off, we laid the bike down right next to her as she rested near the cluster of gathered people. I recognized some of them from the Quik Mart. They nodded as we settled down and got our water bottles out.

One lady I knew from visiting the Quik Mart asked me, "Honey, are you all doin' okay?" We both laughed a little at the ridiculous question. "You know what I mean," she said gently.

"Yes, ma'am, we're doing okay." I rubbed the puppy's ears and she gestured to ask if she could hold the puppy for a while. In the next minutes, what a comfort that puppy was to each person we met. I wondered again about all the animals at the shelter, but I didn't ask, because I didn't think I could handle the answer. We just sat and listened, and soon I heard Grandma snoring next to me.

One of these refugees, a big man with a red beard, said, "I saw St. Rose today."

This was the Catholic church near my middle school.

"I was just at Mass on Saturday night," he said. "Fr. Myladiyil was going to have Mass again Sunday morning, he told me."

The man's face got all red and he wiped his eyes with the back of his muddy hand.

"When I walked around this morning, the seminary buildings were still there, and when I went in the church, the mural of Jesus with his arms outstretched was still there, just as normal, hanging from the wires like they were getting ready to say mass. The glass doors facing the Gulf were fine too, and the prayer book the Father uses for mass is still on the altar." We all waited while he finished his story, because we knew there had to be more. "But the roof and windows were broken. All the prayer books and hymn books..." He turned away and cried for a long time.

No one tried to say anything. That seemed like the best thing to do.

Wednesday, August 31 – late morning

We went south on Menge Avenue and had to cross the stupid railroad tracks that made me fall off my bike; the ones that everyone said would stop the storm surge from washing that far back into town. Not true.

Up on top of the railroad tracks sat a shrimp boat that looked just like Mary's dad's boat. But the name didn't say *Free in America*. Someone else's dream of running a shrimp business was smashed. How was he doing? Did his boat survive? Did he tie up to a tree or a bridge in the Pearl River, or did he just float up and down and sideways? Did his boat get smashed, too? Was he alive? Where was Mary?

"I won't go close to the water yet, Grandma. Let's keep going on Second Street for a while. Maybe there's less junk in the road here." Well, that was overly optimistic of me. But soon I realized my choice had been right for another reason. We rolled along the north edge of War Memorial Park, parallel to the highway and the beach. The park, where Mary and I had spent so much relaxing time in the shade of the live oaks, was torn up, filled with flotsam, and so many of those ancient trees hadn't made it through this storm. We kept going east.

Second Street was a little higher above sea level, and as we went east, more of the houses here looked like they survived. Fewer of them were pushed off their pilings. We had to push up the gentle hill, which was hard for Grandma on the bike, but we didn't hurry. We went around whole trees and cars and piles of unknown debris and mud and sand. I wasn't sure about power lines, but I tried not to step on anything that looked like a wire. It was such slow going.

"Do you smell that barbecue grill, Grandma?" She nodded, and right then, the puppy also noticed that good smell in the air that almost competed with the rotten, spoiled, devastated smell. "What's going on up there?"

We poked our way east on Second, and I saw a group of people around the front porch of a two-story brick house. A lady saw us coming and walked out to meet us with a huge smile. She hugged me and patted Grandma on the shoulder so she wouldn't knock her off the bike.

"Oh, Sweet Jesus, look at you two dear ones." She looked us up and down. "We're so glad to see you," she said, as if we had a hotel reservation or something. "You come on in here and we'll get you cleaned up a bit and get you some food."

I shook my head, but then I changed my mind. "Wow, yes please, ma'am. That would sure help, ma'am."

"I'm Kate. You can just call me Kate."

I shrugged and helped Grandma off the bike, putting the basket and the puppy down and laying the bike next to it. "All right, Miss Kate, ma'am."

The first miracle was that she had two buckets of water to wash off, first with soap, then with cleaner water. Grandma washed her infected cut, but Miss Kate didn't have much she could do about her swollen ankle.

Her smile looked familiar and made me wonder something. I asked her if she was related to one of the ladies Mom always talked to at church, Miss Caryl. I described her, Miss Kate laughed. "Well, how did you figure that out? Yes, sweet girl, she's my cousin on my daddy's side. My daddy and her daddy were brothers."

Like I said, we have a lot of cousins around here.

She took some wipes and helped us wash up a little more, which felt so good, but I felt like it would be long time before I could really get clean. We'd already used up the wipes I found at the apartment. Then she filled our plates with red snapper and shrimp.

"Miss Kate, why are you cooking up all this food and giving it away?"

She smiled and hugged me. "Dear girl, if we don't cook it, all of it is gonna spoil, and that's no good, so eat up and get your strength!" She smiled and served up some more helpings of the delicious food for all of us, including the puppy. She brought out an apple, and I washed the folding knife and cut it up so Grandma and I could share it. Puppy ate the scraps, but not the seeds, because Miss Kate said those were not good for dogs.

While we sat and rested, she told us about the fire I had smelled yesterday. "Do you know, something caught on fire near the apartments east of here, and the coals from that fire have been blowing over here and landing on our houses!" I looked at the amazingly intact house next door, and wouldn't you know it, that was our friend Mr. McDermott waving from the roof, holding a shovel? He looked exhausted and disheveled, just like everyone else.

People came and went, bringing a propane tank or a cooler with food in it, or more drinks. Everyone stopped to scratch the soft, black puppy's ears or her tiny tummy, barely covered in black hair, but with some pale pink skin showing through too. Two great big men who were dressed as police officers even stopped and schmurzeled with the puppy, and so did Mr. McDermott, when he took a break from shoveling coals off his roof. The puppy was all into it.

Grandma fell asleep with the puppy as soon as she had eaten. I slept for a little while on the muddy slope in front of Miss Kate's house, surrounded by all these people I didn't know. No one bothered me. I felt safe. Another God sighting.

Wednesday, August 31 - evening

I couldn't get myself to move at all from Miss Kate's

comfortable haven and good company, and we rested and talked all afternoon. I helped the new refugees find the bucket of soapy wash water and helped serve them food that Miss Kate and her friends just kept cooking. Sometimes people hugged me. Sometimes they didn't. A few were completely silent, like Grandma.

"Dear Jessie girl, do you know where you're heading next? When you're ready?"

I nodded. "Yes ma'am. I want to get to the hospital to..." All of a sudden, the tears I hadn't cried for a whole day all spilled out at once. Miss Kate hugged me and got another clean wet wipe for my face. Finally, I could finish my sentence. "... try to find Mom." I sniffed.

She said, "That's a good idea. You're doing a lot of good thinking, Jessie my girl. Now listen, let me write down all your names so I can share them with the Red Cross. They're keeping track of everyone we find and what, well, you know, what condition you're in."

I wrote down what she needed and who we were looking for too.

"Tell me about your puppy, Jessie."

That made me nervous. "Well, she's not mine, ma'am. She was my..." I found myself fighting back a bunch more tears and wiped the back of my hand across my nose. "Mom and Grandma said she was our next-door neighbor's puppy, but I don't think... I don't think..." I burst into tears again, wondering if what I had seen in Miss Akana's apartment bedroom was really what I thought it might be. And I worried about where Mom was, and if she was okay or if someone would find her the same way I had seen... whatever I had seen at Miss Akana's. I shuddered.

And what if we didn't get to keep the puppy, after all? We'd have to give her back if we found Miss Akana. That would be amazing good news if she were alive, but at the same time, I would have my heart wrenched out. Maybe she'd let me take care of the puppy sometimes, when we were all back here and life was normal.

Miss Kate found me some tissues, gave me a side hug around my shoulders, and when I could talk again, she got me to write down Miss Akana's name on a different list than the one where she'd written down Grandma's and my name. On that other list, I also wrote down the location for the lady with the baby on North Street. Miss Kate had a third list where we listed Anna DeGroot, when we last saw her, and what she had been wearing, blue jeans shorts and a gray t-shirt that said Fisherman's Wharf on it. Oh my gosh, that was hard.

"Jessie and Jiexen, I know you're planning to go in the morning, and I would offer to drive you to the hospital in my car …"

My mouth dropped open. "You still have a car?"

"Yes, well I did. It didn't get flooded here. The water came up, don't you worry about that. It sure did come up and leak in the car doors, but it didn't swallow it up." I found myself nodding at her, waiting for her to tell us to get in. "So," she said, "my car still works, but the fire department has taken possession of it now to do rescuing."

My face fell, but who were we kidding? "That makes sense, ma'am," I said. "Thank you for thinking of it, Miss Kate. I hope you'll get your car back from them after… you know, later." I was about to cry again, picturing how long 'later' might take to get here. I'd seen the absolute destruction east of our apartment, and from what Miss Kate and other people had said, it was even worse farther west on the penin-sula. That's where my school was, and the high school, and so many houses and churches like St. Rose. They must have had whole football fields of water surround them and cover them two or three stories deep. It would have crushed anything under it, even if it weren't flowing and blowing and undulating, but that extra force must have left absolutely nothing. I wondered about Bay St. Louis and the big bridge, Waveland, and Clermont Harbor on the other side of the bay bridge. Did they get clobbered too? "Thanks for all of this, ma'am," I managed to say.

That night, the flying embers from the fire burning out of control blew through the air in fiery waves. I saw her next-door neighbor Mr. McDermott, who stayed awake shoveling them off the flat roof to keep the coals from burning down his house.

Thursday, September 1 – first light

After that good long rest, I went to find Miss Kate and give her a big hug. She was already up, ministering to everyone, handing out more plates of amazing grilled seafood to people who straggled in after us. The only un-horrible thing about this was having shrimp for breakfast. The adults oohed and aahed over the instant coffee she'd heated up for them. Grandma listened to everything, I could tell by watching her eyes, and she ate a plate of food for breakfast, but she still didn't say one darn thing, even as she drank some of that coffee from her water bottle.

Miss Kate took me aside and said, "Jessie, sweetie, I think you should leave your grandma here with the puppy, alright?"

My stomach clenched. "What? We have to get to the hospital."

She hugged me again. "Yes, sweet girl." That made me almost cry too, because that's what Mom always calls me, but I swallowed and kept listening. "Jessie, they could just rest here and you take the bicycle, okay? Go on and find your Mom, and maybe you can get someone to send more vehicles in here to get the rest of the refugees out. Do you think you can do that?"

I swallowed again and wiped my eyes with the back of my hand, then I took a big breath. "Yes, Ma'am. I can do that."

I said, "Miss Kate, thank you for taking such good care of us." She hugged me again.

I went over with her to tell Grandma the new plan and make sure she and the puppy were set, sitting together on the slope near the sidewalk. We all cried, even Grandma. That was all we could do.

Miss Kate started back up toward her house, but Grandma waved at her to stop. She reached in her light blue flight bag full of rescued items and plastic zip bags and fumbled around for something. She opened one of the plastic bags, keeping the opening covered up by bending low over it so only she could see. She brought out one, dry, one-hundred-dollar bill, and she handed it to Miss Kate without saying a word. She still couldn't talk, but Grandma's face was looking more human again and less like a robot as she zipped up the blue bag and scratched the puppy's ears.

Miss Kate blubbered like a baby and thanked Grandma and the puppy got more ear scratches.

Wow. Could that really be my Tiger Grandma?

Thursday, September 1 – morning

When you're heading straight east on the Gulf Coast, and the sun is just above the horizon, it's really hard on your eyes. I couldn't look forward anyway. I had to keep my eyes on my feet and the ground in front of me. No way I could ride the bike yet because of all the dangers scattered and piled across the road.

I had to cut south to the highway along the beach to go farther east. It was full of people like me, walking, or limping due to injuries or just because they didn't have shoes on. My boots were hot, but it was so worth it. Others were hobbling in bare feet, and I wished I'd brought my soggy sneakers to give to someone. Hardly any flat road was left at all, and what there was had a layer of muddy sand, mixed in with more boats and rocks and pieces of houses and upended sections of the road. Believe it or not, this road was more passable than where we'd been.

And of course, absolutely not one car was on the highway along the beach. Not driving, I should say, but there were *so* many cars flipped around and upside down, blocking the way. A backpack, two metal shopping carts stuck together, another bottle of beer that still had the beer in it which I put in my backpack to give to Grandma later. Sometimes I could identify what the piled-up things were, but a lot of time, it was just piles and piles of broken stuff in big rows, all tangled up, and it made my eyes tired. Where was my dumb floppy sunhat?

On my right, the Sound was calm, glittering with sunshine hitting the water. In no time, it grew sticky and hot. The brilliant sun in the cloudless sky above us heated up all the damp things. The wet ground and the humidity surrounded us like a thick coat.

I kept smelling the fire smoke getting stronger over by the Walmart. So, I guess there was some wind. But after a whole day of so much wind, and now it was so quiet, and hot and yes... quiet. I felt like we'd been abducted from the Pass by pirates in a ship, rattled around in it for a few days, bobbing around in the storm-tossed waves, and then gotten dumped out on a desert island, scattered with the broken pieces of our houses and televisions and books and projects and lives, in the middle of the sea where no one would ever find us or even look for us. We must have been blown right off the map.

I kept looking for Mary and her mom and brothers, even though I'd seen them leave days ago. There was no reason for them to be back already. I just wished I could see her.

On the bike, I could go a little faster. There was a cluster of people in front of me. A little toddler walked next to a lady, holding her hand and taking tiny, tiny steps. As I got up next to them, I saw Katrina, the girl from my class, next to the lady with the toddler. She looked just like Katrina but was older. She was probably her mom. Katrina had some water bottles in a plastic bag dangling from her hand, and her school backpack on her shoulders. "Katrina!" I said. "You're okay?" I didn't really know her; she was just famous because she was on Hook TV, but she hung out with different girls. We'd been in a few classes together.

She looked at me kind of blankly, then nodded. Then her eyes lit up when she realized she knew me from school. "You okay?"

"Sure." I got off the bike and walked it next to her. "Why not?" We both laughed. That felt so good. So very, very good.

She looked around and then back at me. "What's your name, again?"

"Jessie," I smiled. "Is this your family?"

She shook her head. "No, it's me and my mom." She gestured her chin sideways at the toddler, who was more filthy than the rest of us, and he looked like he had been crying a lot and was ready to cry again. He kept sniffling. It looked like he'd been pletching in the mud the rest of us were trying to avoid. "We found this little guy..." she took a funny breath and didn't say anymore.

"Oh. I think I know what you mean." My throat clenched up again, thinking about Miss Akana. "We found a lost puppy and... you know."

Katrina sniffed. "Yes, he needs us too. He doesn't have anyone else right now."

"Do you know his name?"

She shook her head. "Maybe my mom does." She pushed the hair out of her face and wiped tears off her face.

Both of us had greasy, stringy hair, and we both smelled like the worst B.O. ever. I was glad my greasy, stringy hair was at least braided to keep it behind my ears and out of my eyes. Otherwise, it would have been driving me crazy. Well, it still was, but I couldn't fix it.

So much I could not fix. No one could fix.

She looked serious. "Where are you going, Jessie?"

"Trying to find my mom first, and then my dad. He was out on a run. He went to Maine. Hope he's coming back here. Soon, I mean. To come and find us," I said. "And send help back to get my grandma and the puppy. What about you?"

Katrina looked at her mom next to her. "We're trying to get up to my uncle's house in Montgomery. Dad was doing a delivery to New Orleans, and we're not sure where he is now, but it makes sense about meeting at his brother's house. Mom says they might get the school back open in a month or so, but..." she pursed her lips into a frown and her eyes got watery.

"Did you see that fire?" I pointed to the smoke ahead of us. "A man in the crowd by the convenience store said it was an apartment building."

She started to say, "I wonder why the fire department..." and then looked down and sighed. Never mind. No fire department. No anybody. "Just us chickens."

We all kept walking, around huge missing sections of the highway, and piles and piles of broken, upside down, dangerous looking bits of the most confusing garage sale in history. "Hey, look at that!" Up ahead, I saw a child's red wagon mostly buried in sand, but the long black handle and the beginning of the red wagon box stuck out. Some ropes or long, twisted plastic lines tangled around the wheels and the handle. "Hey, Katrina, this might help you, if it's not broken," I told her.

I laid the bike down, and Katrina and I picked up bits of wood to use as shovels and scraped away the sand. Her mom dug in too, and we uncovered the little red wagon. It still had all its wheels! I took out my knife and cut away some twisted plastic bags tangled around it so we could get going.

Right then, the little boy really started crying, but Katrina's mom bent down to pick him up and set him in the wagon. "Look baby," she said sweetly. "Let's go for a fun ride, okay?" Her voice was bleak, but she added as much energy to it as she could. "You could even lie down and take a nap, okay?"

He fussed as if he wanted to be picked up again, but then he just sat there. He was worn out too. His eyes were flat, and he didn't have the energy to cry.

Some other people walking by saw what was going on, and they stopped to check in with our little group. One man, I think it was Mr. Spinney from church, held out a bottle of precious water and gave it to Katrina's mom, and a lady with him saw some kind of blanket hanging from a flooded car in between the two lanes of the highway, shook it out, and tucked it around the toddler with a tired smile. He drank a sip of water from the bottle held out to him and then curled up in the wagon on the blanket.

13

Thursday, September 1 - all afternoon

If we were in a car, it would have been a half-hour drive to Gulfport, and I would have gotten there yesterday morning. But walking and sometimes riding the bike, and all the breaks and rests, drew the journey way out. It made me remember a marathon my dad watched on television, where a father ran the marathon while pushing his adult son, who was disabled, in a special wheelchair, or pulled him behind him in a boat as he swam, so they could do marathons and triathlons together. The real winners of the marathons always got done in the quickest time, but this man and his son—who called themselves Team Hoyt—didn't cross the finish line until way after dark, taking a million times more energy to finish.

After so long, I finally got past the fire, which I could see was in the apartments near the Walmart, so now the smoke wasn't blowing toward us anymore. All these buildings were wrecked, too.

I still didn't see any cars. There couldn't be cars, the

highway was so full of holes and pieces of boats and buildings and cars. And all the cars that were still here had been drowned, anyway.

The rotten smell was everywhere. You might say I'm being repetitive, telling you all the stuff on the ground, but the truth is, what I'm telling you is just what I could see or smell. This was just part of it, a small fraction of all the stuff, from everyone's houses, pulled out and spread up and down the beach, the roads, the trees, the railroad tracks, and the whole town. It was more than I could absorb with my eyes.

After hours of rolling along, I heard a loud machine hum in the distance. I heard cars or trucks moving around. I got so close to the hospital that I could hardly bear it, but I wasn't there yet and had to keep going.

For the last mile closest to the hospital, a bulldozer had cleared debris off the streets, and I could really ride the bike now. The bulldozer was just starting to head west toward us. He waved from up high in driver's seat but didn't stop. He was trying to push stuff off the road. I saw him get to something too big to push with the machine, an entire house that looked like it wasn't damaged at all, but it was off its foundation and now sitting on top of the road. It was in perfect shape, except for being on the road. Then he smashed the bulldozer right into that house to push it out of the way.

I felt sick, hearing the wood scream as he smashed it and moved it off the road.

In the distance, on the shore east of us, I looked for the casino that looked like a riverboat. It was still there, almost, but it had been tossed up on the pier and was leaning over at a crazy angle.

Pretty soon, a man in a clean blue jeep drove up to me. I was still with Katrina and her mom and the toddler. "My name's Butler. Can I give you all a lift?" We just nodded. We didn't care where he was going as long as it was away from here, really. "There you go, ma'am," and, "You now, young ladies," in his deep, reassuring voice. He squeezed all four of us into the jeep and hung the bike and the wagon off the back. He wore a clean shirt, and had clean frizzy black hair and smelled good, even from where I was crammed in the back seat with Katrina and the little boy. The man was sweaty, like we all were, but I could smell it was just sweat from today, unlike the rest of us who just reeked. I wondered where he lived and why he'd come down to help, and I was so glad. Another God sighting. He said, "I'm gonna take you all up to the hospital so you kin get checked out, okay?"

We nodded again.

"That way you kin check in with them that you're safe an' sound, and look at the lists of names if you're tryin' to meet up with other people, okay?" He drove east.

Nobody said anything. We were too tired and thirsty and numb. Finally, I said, "Yes, please. Thank you, sir. Mr. Butler."

He picked up some kind of radio and checked in. "Car Two, heading east to the hospital," he said.

It made me think. "Sir, who can you call on your radio?"

"What do ya' mean, young lady?"

"It's just, can you send more people to help the people back there in the Pass? Miss Kate and my grandma and a bunch of others are back there. There's a lady on North Street, and she really needs someone to come help her... I think the baby is... you know," I looked out the window, but I had to tell him more. "And there's a whole group of people camped out on Menge... and..." I gave up and just cried.

"Sure 'nuf, we can. Yes, young lady. Let's get some more people back there to help." He promised to tell them so they could get a bulldozer in there and more cars, and find more of the refugees.

It wasn't too much farther now that we had a ride. Mr. Butler took us up to the emergency department entrance, helped us all get out and get our stuff, and made sure the people helping inside found us. Then he loaded up with fresh water bottles and drove off to find some more people on the highway of destruction.

The hospital had broken windows and missing pieces. I saw where the water must have surged up against the whole building and pushed its way inside, probably even up to the second and third floor, but it hadn't collapsed, and they were using it as a meeting place at least. Everything stunk here too, but at least the hospital was still standing. Big trucks kept rolling up full of boxes and people in clean medical clothes.

The people at the hospital had food and water right there outside the emergency room entrance. A lady gave me a bag of potato chips and a soda. They asked my name. "I want to find my mom, Anna DeGroot," I told them.

"You can wait here, young lady," a man told me. "I'll see if I can locate her for you, okay? Would you like to sit on these chairs in the front hallway?" I leaned the bike against the wall outside the door and sat on a metal chair in the hall. The floor inside was covered with sand and mud and junk, even though you could tell someone had tried to sweep it.

I spread out onto the next two chairs and rested my head on my backpack, listening to the very loud hum of the generators, which after the last few days of wind going twice as fast as dad's truck on the interstate seemed peaceful by comparison, and I zonked out.

Next thing I knew, someone was gently jostling my shoulder, and a nice voice was saying, "Jessie! Jessie, sweet girl, wake up!"

I opened my eyes, and there, looking into my face, was Mom!

Thursday, September 1 - 4:30 p.m.

I COULD HARDLY BELIEVE my eyes. "Mom!" I jumped up and gave her a huge hug, and we stood in the middle of the hallway. "Mom! You're here! I found you!" I could barely breathe. "What happened after you got washed away with the lady on the tree? How did you get here?" I didn't give her time to answer any of the questions, because I kept thinking of more.

"Oh Jessie, I'll tell you all about it." She hugged me, and I saw she still wore the same gray Fisherman's Wharf t-shirt, though it was torn and really, really dirty. "Let me look at you," she said. "I'm so glad to see you." And right away, she looked worried again. "Where's Mama?" she asked. "Is she okay?"

"Yes, Grandma is okay." As we walked outside, I told her all about how Grandma had hurt her ankle and arm, and she and the puppy were waiting for us at Miss Kate's. She laughed and reached around to lift the messy braid of my hair, then dropped it with a shrug.

Then I noticed the bandages on her left arm, because they were white and clean, and so was her arm, like they'd only had enough soap for just that one arm. "Your arm! Did I hurt when I hugged you?" I shaded my eyes against the setting sun, wishing again for the dumb floppy hat with the starfish on it. It was probably in Mexico by now.

She shook her head and smiled. "No, Jessie sweetie, it's okay. I'm okay." She got distracted when she noticed a lady leaving the hospital, holding a man's hand, and got all excited. "Lisa, over here!" She waved to them and the lady smiled. She wore bright red lipstick and a red wet suit. I had definitely seen her before.

"Anna!" she screamed, let go of the man's hand, and ran over. "Anna, we did it! Is this your family?"

"Yes, this my daughter Jessie."

The lady introduced her husband Jay. "You and I just hung on for dear life to that live oak. We had to stay safe to get back to our families. And here we all are!"

Mom's face clouded. "Almost all of us." She looked at me to see if I had any clue about Dad, but I didn't, and I just shook my head and shrugged. "Lisa, I'm sorry you got swept up in it too, but if that tree had to come and swipe me away, I'm so glad you were already there with me," she laughed. "In the brightest red wet suit I've ever seen."

Her husband laughed. "Mine was bright blue. We usually wore those when we went sailing," he said. "But Lisa's story is way better than mine. I stayed on our roof and waited for the water to recede. I didn't jump onto the first tree that washed by…" The lady started to be mad at him, but then we all saw he was teasing her. I noticed he had tears in his eyes. They all hugged again. The couple left, and Mom and I stood in the middle of the sidewalk to figure out our next steps.

Did you notice how I said "our" next steps? Yes, I did.

Mom said, "I heard there's a shelter open in the middle school. I was about to go there next and see what I could do to find you, but then a volunteer came and found me instead…" she burst into tears and pulled me close to her. "Jessie, I was so afraid you were washed away too. I didn't think I'd ever find you again."

"We're both okay, Mom," I said.

"I just can't believe it."

"But there's another thing, Mom," I said. "Grandma hasn't said anything to me since Monday when the last of the chickens blew away."

Mom didn't reply, but she nodded her head, thinking, as if that made sense to her.

I added, "You and Grandma packed so much useful stuff into the bags, Mom. I've used a lot of the supplies," I was glad to say. "We waited for you at the apartment for a long time, two days, I think. Is today Wednesday?" She nodded, then shook her head. "No, I think it's Thursday. Not sure." We laughed a little. "Okay. Yeah, but then I decided we should go look for help for her arm and her ankle, and find some more water. And I wondered if you were hurt and so we might find you at the hospital if you couldn't get back to us."

It was starting to hit me how much I'd had to really do to keep us safe. I started wondering what would have happened if I had just sat there like a scared, lazy girl. Would we still be sitting there in the apartment, waiting for someone to rescue us?

I thought about the lady we had seen sitting on the concrete steps, with no house behind her, holding a bundle wrapped in towels that must have been her baby. She cried and cried and cried. I wished we could have helped her, but I realized even if we could have given her a ride and food, that would not have helped her with what she really needed and could not have. I hoped Mr. Butler in the Jeep, or the lady at the hospital, had gotten someone there to take the baby. The poor little baby.

Thursday, September 1 - 4:45 p.m.

Oh geez, I blinked and realized Mom was trying to talk to me. "Earth to Jessie," she said, rubbing my shoulder. "I just realized you said, 'Grandma and the puppy.' Who's your puppy?"

I noticed she said "your puppy" from the get-go like that. My tummy relaxed some more.

I told her about how we had rescued her, and how soft her little black head and tummy were, and what I thought happened to Miss Akana, and I wished right then I could have been rubbing the puppy's ears. I forgot all about helping come up with our new plan, as I flashed back with memories of all the horrible things I'd seen floating in the water, and wrapped around other things on the ground and in the beautiful tree branches.

Mom was saying, "Jessie? Are you okay?" I sniffed and hugged her and nodded. "So, I was about to go over to the shelter to look for you. Maybe we should go there and find a place to rest and see if we can make contact with your dad and send them back for Grandma and everybody." She mumbled to herself, "Where are you, David?" I saw her eyes were tired and red. Of course they were.

"Yeah. That sounds good."

I asked a very clean lady in a bright yellow reflective vest. "The shelter is just over at the middle school a few blocks away, right?" I'd been there once to watch Mary play volleyball, and I indicated with my head where I thought we were going. Mom nodded the question at the lady too. "Can we stay there? And can they send help to go get my grandma and the puppy? And all the other people? They're stuck back in the Pass."

"The shelter? No, that's not where it is, sweetie." She shook her head. "That school close by got clobbered pretty bad. The shelter is much farther away. It's way over on…" I didn't hear her words. My head was spinning too fast. "…because of the puppy. Even if we got you over there, you can't stay in the shelter with a puppy, sweetie."

Oh, this was so unfair. My eyes filled up and spilled over. Mom started to say something, but I said, "No way. We can't go somewhere if the puppy won't be able to come in. I don't even want to go to the stupid shelter." Then I lost it, turned to the wall, and cried a lot. She and Mom might have talked a bit while I was falling apart, but I just needed to vent some more before I could pull it together to help Mom. She was doing better than I had seen her in years, but she was so fragile, and I wanted to help.

I sniffed and wiped my hand over my eyes, stepping back to Mom and the lady in the yellow vest. Mom had this tired look on her face. I knew what to say, now. "Ma'am, besides getting Grandma a ride here, what we really want to do is find my dad, David DeGroot. He doesn't even know if we're okay or where we are." She nodded and listened. "He's driving back to find us, but he's driving a truck, and I don't think he could drive down here even if he knew where we were."

"That's great news!" The lady smiled. "You know what, you're in a different situation than a lot of the folks who are going to the shelter, sweetie. They have nowhere to go, and no one is coming to pick them up." She looked from me to Mom. "I have an idea. Will you hold on just a minute?" She left us standing there and took off at a brisk pace without another word.

"Mom, let's sit down." We both sat down on the muddy grass, drank some water, and waited.

She came back with an old man named Mr. Adam. His clothes were clean and so was his hair, and he was freshly shaved too. He must have driven here from somewhere else, somewhere dry and safe. But here he was, ready to help us, even though he didn't know us, just like Mr. Butler had. He looked glad to see us, and he squatted down and stuck out his hand to shake Mom's hand and mine.

"You folks trying to get in touch with someone out in the world?" he beamed.

We nodded. How did he think this was a time to smile?

"Well, we have some amateur radio operators here near the hospital, and some more up by Interstate 10." He nodded excitedly, as if he'd explained everything we needed to know. He reached into his back pocket for a little notebook with a pen clipped to it and flipped to a clean page. His eyes noticed my confused face, and he said, "You know, ham radio operators?"

I looked at Mr. Adam from where I still sat cross-legged on the ground. I was so tired, and this wasn't making any sense. Why was he being so… obtuse? That's what Mrs. Drummond would say. Obtuse.… He looked at me and gave me his hand to help me stand up. "Dear ladies," he looked at us. "We can help get a message out with who you're looking for, and where you want to meet up."

"Huh?" Was all I could say. Mom looked blank too.

I finally began to understand when Mr. Adam asked, "He's in a semi-truck, you said?" I nodded. "Then it's best he doesn't try to get all the way down here, but the interstate exit up there would work."

I still didn't see how he could help, but I was getting hopeful at least. He said, "Give me your information, and I'll send it out on the network. We have hams all over the place helping folks like you who are stuck get in touch with their folks who have transportation. If your man does the same thing, we could tell him where you are and how to meet you."

"Oh, my gosh," I said, and my eyes brightened. "I just remembered something, sir. My dad has a CB radio. Is that the same as the ones you have?"

He smiled and said, "Well, no, but if you could give me his CB handle, I'll add that to the message going out about him. Some of the hams can help connect amateur radio bands with the CB bands, too."

This was great! "His handle is Dutch Boy."

Mr. Adam laughed out loud with delight and slapped his thigh. "That's outstanding. Dutch Boy! That will help a lot, young lady."

Mom finally said, with a slightly hopeful look, "I have a CB handle too. Mine is Art Mama. That might help. Good thinking, Jessie my girl!" She side-hugged me again.

Mr. Adam wrote that down, and then he found us a ride up to the interstate, saying to that driver, "Drop these ladies up at the club's tent next to the shelter tent at the home repair store."

I put on my backpack. Mom still had hers too, since she had been wearing it when she got washed away. We left the precious bicycle leaned against the wall for someone else to find.

In the five miles we went north, away from the Sound, I saw a lot more damaged buildings, and most of the signs for the stores were ripped off or broken, and I could see evidence the storm surge had brought waves and sand way up here. Epic flooding, way inland.

The sand and junk on the road was mostly pushed off to the side, and all sorts of people in cars and little trucks helped bring supplies and people back and forth from the interstate to the hospital. I noticed all those people who actually were there to help so soon after the storm. That was different than what Grandma experienced when she was my age.

She really had been the same age as me, once. Wow.

Thursday, September 1 - 6 p.m.

The land near the interstate was made entirely of parking lots, so it was never pretty in this part of Gulfport, and it was more desolate now that they were surrounded by damaged buildings. And anything that used to be pretty, like green grass, was now muddy gray or sandy brown or black. No colors showed anywhere. We got dropped off south of Interstate 10 in the parking lot near the home supply store, which was dark and looked broken. They had used a bulldozer to push debris off the parking lot into piles in the far corner. But the parking lot was buzzing with people and cars and little trucks. Our nice driver took us near where there were tents set up with people sitting at tables, but he drove on past them. Instead, he got us introduced to the volunteers in the radio club tent a little ways away from a huge RV with tall antennas poking up, and a loud generator running next to it.

Another clean, gray-haired man said, "Our club is helping people like you to get connected to someone who can come get you." This new radio operator, Bob, had heard on the Net that we'd already given some information to his fellow club member by the hospital, but he reviewed it with us since we were here in front of him. We made sure he had Dad's work number to leave a message, in case anyone there could even answer the phone or knew where he was. And we asked them to contact Uncle Joe in Nebraska with the same message. Mom knew both phone numbers by heart.

"That's great, ladies. Especially knowing he's got a CB radio, and what you've estimated about the route he might have been taking back down here, that'll help. We'll get the message to those places and as best we can out onto the Net. Meanwhile, there are a lot of other people in the same boat right here." He pointed over to all the people on the other side of the parking lot by the tents, spread out along the mud-coated edges of the blacktop. Sleeping, sitting, talking. A lot of them had pets, like we did. Plenty of dogs spread out or romping with each other or a piece of broken tree branch, some cats cradled in people's arms, and one lady had a bird cage on the ground next to her, with a noisy green parrot squawking in it. I found out later her name was Deena. "They're all working on getting a ride too, and finding their families."

Bob said, "I'll come over there and find you as soon as we hear something from the Net, alright? So don't wander off too far. There are porta-potties here, and I heard that the Southern Baptists will be here to set up a food tent tonight." I realized how late it was, how we'd been walking for two days, and we were going to be right here until Dad found us, however long that would take. For now, I realized how hungry I was getting.

Bob sent us to the other tent and we listened for what was next. I was so glad someone else was in charge now, I tell you. We swayed on our feet, but we just had to hold out a little longer. "Hello, ladies. My name is Susan. I'm a volunteer with Samaritan's Purse." She had gentle, friendly eyes, and she turned to one of the other volunteers. "Meridith, could you get us some more snacks?" Meridith brought us each a bottle of water, a granola bar, and a blanket.

Miss Susan said. "Won't you sit down?" She gestured to the folding chairs, and we both slid into them. I set my backpack down and so did Mom. "We heard we will have a food tent being set up tonight. There's a group of volunteers from Georgia, I think it's the Southern Baptists, bringing in their mobile kitchen team." She glanced at her watch and looked around. "Ladies, we also do have toilets available."

We had just heard that big headline that there was food and a toilet, and you know what, it was the absolute best news I had heard since I got an A on that stupid hurricane test. She was pointing nearby to the couple of porta-potties with a line of people. "I hope that helps. Now, if I can, I'd like to take your names down so we can add you to the list of good news."

I said, "Ma'am, we already gave our names to the lady at the hospital, and also to Miss Kate, over on Second Street in the Pass."

"That's good, that's good. But it might help if I document them again for the authorities." She then asked, "Now, who is Miss Kate?" I told her all about her and all the people she was helping, and the food she was giving away, and how they confiscated her car, and she could really use more help if they could send some people down there. And how Grandma was there and had a hurt ankle and needed help an that's where the puppy was. She wrote it all down and said she would get that done. "For now, that's all I have to do for you. Have a great..." she stopped herself. "I mean, I wish we could do more for you."

"Just help Miss Kate, and bring Grandma. Just send more people down to the Pass. Thank you, ma'am."

As Mom and I walked over to the grassy mud, I scanned the whole area, looking for people I knew from school or church or the convenience store or the library.

People stretched out everywhere, in little groups. A few stood up but most sat on the muddy, sticky ground, resting in the steamy heat of the evening, some of them sitting on the concrete curb stops at the edge of the parking lot. Some played with the animals. A few had a blanket to lie on or make a pillow from.

The Pass was a small town, and even though we weren't friends with a lot of people, I kept recognizing a familiar face and sharing a smile. Even if they were exhausted, hungry, and not sure where they would sleep tonight. Oh yes, they knew that; they'd be sleeping on the ground near the interstate exit ramp.

Nearby, another classmate of mine and her family straggled up. I wondered if they had walked all the way up or if they'd gotten a ride. Meridith handed them a blanket and some water, and I heard the other kind woman start again, "Hello, I'm Susan..."

We camped next to a family from our church. They had two boys in high school, totally cute and popular. Their dad had told Mom that their little house still stood, but everything inside had "gone-pecan—you know, got-gone by the storm." This evening, they were completely zonked out on the ground, snoring like two freight trains. Maybe tonight we could sleep hard enough to snore like that.

Mom was amazing, talking to the parents, considering how tired she was and all she'd been through with being washed away by the tree. "It's so good to see you. You made it … here!" She gestured with a smile at the interstate and the scene. The completely foreign scene. Mom seemed to have new energy, despite the sickeningly heavy humidity. I kept wondering how it could be even stickier and hotter than usual, but it was. She told people she knew, "We're waiting for someone to bring my mama here, and my husband David. I'm sure he's going to try to get down here and pick us up in his Peterbilt truck."

Though it was now dark, a few pickup trucks and a huge food truck trailer drove up and their volunteers began setting up the mobile kitchen, tents, chairs, garbage cans, and stuff like that. "Mom," I said, "I want to go help them set up, okay?" I was so hungry, maybe if I helped, we would be able to eat sooner.

She smiled, and I pulled my hot rubber boots back on.

I imagined Grandma right now, back at Miss Kate's house, cuddled up with the puppy and eating a plateful of grilled food. I squeezed tears out of my eyes as I walked over to the trucks.

14

Thursday, September 1 - 7 p.m.

Volunteers from Georgia mixed with refugees from Mississippi in the food tent. Most of us had been wearing the same clothes for three or four days, and slogging through the filthy water and mud, and it smelled pretty bad in there, but it didn't matter. They let us wash our hands at a portable plastic station that had water and paper towels. Then we walked up the folding steps to go through the food trailer for our tray of food, and I asked to load another one up for Mom too. We sat at white plastic tables, and all we could smell was how delicious those fresh cooked pancakes were, covered in butter from tiny plastic tubs and syrup from little white plastic packets. It was the most delicious food I'd eaten in my whole life. They had coffee in huge yellow plastic dispensers, and Mom must have had four cups, loaded with sugar and powdered creamer. I had lemonade, cup after foam cup.

I saw one of my teachers, Mrs. Ladner, sitting at the table near us and went to say Hi. I couldn't believe she was here in the food tent, a refugee just like us. She was muddy and bedraggled, in dress pants and a delicate light blue summer sweater, and she gave me a hug, saying, "Jessie. Look around us! The food tent. The great equalizer! Here I am wearing my fancy clothes for work." We both laughed at how muddy and destroyed her pretty outfit was. She said, "I really thought we would have school on Tuesday, and so all I packed was one extra outfit when we left for what I thought would just be one day." I told her about finding the puppy and making a fire and getting help. She got super quiet, but then she perked up again and asked more questions.

We looked around at the other people in the food tent. All types of clothing and situations, poor, rich, but all in the same boat. All sweaty, muddy, stinky, and hoping to not have to sleep on the ground another night. But grateful for the community, a place to wash up, and amazingly delicious food. Grateful not to be sleeping in a tree branch or alone in a ruined, dangerous house.

After a while, Mrs. Ladner said, "Jessie, I loved your story about finding your puppy."

My eyebrows went up. Where was she going with this?

"I was thinking, as I was looking around here and noticing all the people with their pets, they might appreciate a little bath too. They have soapy water in the waste tank for that hand-washing station. I wonder if they'd let us use that old soapy water to help wash off those dogs a bit more. Want to try it?" I must have looked hesitant, having my teacher sitting on the ground to help wash muddy cats and dogs with people's used soapy water, you know. She said, "Really, it would be nice to have something to do!"

I went and asked a few people who were close by who had dogs with them, while Mrs. Ladner talked to the volunteers. They got their dogs so much cleaner, and got themselves a little cleaner at the same time, and then my teacher held each one of them for the longest time, drying the pets off with some old towel we'd found, rubbing their ears, and their little puppy bellies if the owners agreed. Everyone was so thankful, and few more adults and kids stepped in to help out with the process. We looked around at all the pets and their owners who were now fast asleep, and Mrs. Ladner seemed to relax more, too. In her fancy, muddy school clothes, now also covered in black, brown, and white dog hair, she looked content.

People chatted around us. One girl said, "I heard there's a shark trapped in the pool of that house on North Street."

"There's a car in that swimming pool too."

"Yeah, there's cars everywhere they ain't supposed ta' be."

"I heard the Bay St. Louis Bridge collapsed."

"What? At Henderson Point?"

"Lawd. All that's left is the supports, but all the road pieces is clean gone, at the bottom of the Bay."

A lady asked a friend who showed up in the tent, "How'd you make out, Ellis?"

She replied, "I got slabbed." All that was left of her house was the cement slab.

The first lady shook her head and said, "I came out pretty well. I only got six feet of water."

"I saw a house on the railroad tracks." Nods all around. There were so many of those. And boats. And cars. A hot tub. And unknown pieces of things. Everywhere.

"I heard the police were trapped in the Pass Christian Public Library," said a man named Dan. He had a cool black mustache and a beard that only covered his chin—Mom told me that was called a goatee. He wore those glasses that automatically darkened in the bright light to look like sunglasses, but now they were just lightly shaded.

"Oh, no," someone said. "What else do you know, Dan?"

"Yeah, there were about twelve of them inside, and the

police cars were circling the building on a current of water, floating the squad cars."

Everyone listening oohed.

"Then one car crashed through the front door, made of glass tough enough to survive a Cat 3 hurricane, you know. The water poured in, well, you all just saw that yourselves, right?" A lot of the refugees around the table nodded. "Yeah, so the officers couldn't open the back doors because of the water pressure, so they pulled their guns and fired at least 50 rounds into the glass until it finally shattered. Then they made a human chain and climbed up onto the roof and spent the next three hours in the 130 mile-per-hour winds."

A man said, in a whisper, "Just like we did. How about that?"

Someone said, "So, the library is gone, too?" No one answered but just looked down.

A kid said, "Wow, Mr. Ellis, you should write a book about all these stories."

He nodded. "I just might do that. I already wrote nine other books, you know, but here we are again. We people from the Gulf Coast have so many stories to tell." He paused. "I just don't know if I can find the words for another book, but maybe if everybody sends me their stories, I'll get them printed." He closed his eyes. "They might never find all the police cars. They're probably in the Gulf, or washed inland somewhere."

"Along with a lot of other things," said a lady quietly.

I wondered what could be done if a shrimp boat was found sitting in the middle of a field. Could they lift it on a trailer and put it back in the ocean somehow? It would be so heavy. Or would it get smashed to smithereens like the house was when the bulldozer pushed it off the road? It was such a waste.

While we sat at the table, late in the night, a man got up

from the radio table in the tent across the parking lot and handed a piece of paper to one of the other radio volunteers. She wore an orange shirt that said Samaritan's Purse. She walked among the gathered families under the food tent. "Beauprez family? Francis and Salome?"

A man and woman raised their hands right away, before she had to go searching for them among the sleeping people camped on the ground. She said, "Your son Jacques just checked in up there at the exit ramp. He's driving down here now to get you." The man and woman hugged each other, and then they both hugged the lady, picked up their two white grocery bags each and walked toward edge of the parking lot so he could find them easily now. The bags were about to give way with all the rips in them. I hoped they made it to their son's car without tearing.

As they went past us, the lady stopped and handed her Red Cross blanket to Mom. "Here," she said. "Why don't you take this, if you have to wait for your mom and your husband."

"Oh, thank you so much," said Mom. "Thank you for sharing."

The lady smiled. "Now we're on our way, so we are blessed."

"When did you get here?"

"Yesterday. Or was it two days ago? The radios operators got here this morning, I think, and we have our Jacques here already tonight."

Mom's eyes spilled tears down her cheeks and she said, "Bless you." The two of them hugged. Then the lady turned to catch up with her husband, who had stopped a ways ahead.

Even later that night, Mom and I were stretched out on the mud, staring at the stars, which were still so unbelievably bright since there was no light polluting the sky. The same amateur radio lady from before found me and Mom and smiled. She handed us four more water bottles and a piece of paper from the radio table. "One of our radio operators contacted your husband David and reported your location to him." Mom and I hugged each other and thanked the lady again and again and cried a bunch, which felt so good. "He knows where you are. Now he's working his way down here. We'll get you more information whenever it comes through on the Net," she promised.

Mom said, "I hope he gets here soon. And Mama, I hope she gets here soon."

I imagined Grandma cuddled up with the puppy in the mud at Miss Kate's and felt a little jealous, but at the same time, I was glad she wasn't all alone. At least I had found Mom, and I wasn't alone either. I had a dream about Grandma holding Penelope, her favorite black hen, on her lap, but then the chicken changed into the puppy. I wanted to tell Grandma another quote from Kim Possible, the cheer-leader with superpowers, who had said one time, "You're weird, but I like you." I knew I could not quite bring myself to say this to Grandma, but I felt good inside for even considering it. I slept so hard that night, even better than I had on the ground at Miss Kate's. There still weren't any bugs. They must all have been blown to Mexico too, and that was another good thing.

Friday, September 2 - morning

When I woke up, I was so stiff. How did Mom and Grandma ever get to sleep on the ground when they were so old? Then I remembered what my mom told me about Grandma's months in the cold detention center in Guang-dong, sleeping on the cement floor and getting fed one time a day with slop from a big bucket. Hm.

I put on my socks and boots, walked back over to the food tent area, used the porta-potty, then joined the line for breakfast. It was so… civilized. Wonderful. I wondered if the same volunteers were cooking for us again, or if it was a new group. One lady smiled at me and said, "I hope you slept okay, sweetie," and I recognized her from last night. She had circles under her eyes but she looked happy.

"Yes ma'am, I sure did," I said. "I hope you did too. Thank you for being here."

I brought food to Mom, who met me under the tent.

We sat near a man who was telling a young kid, "I know this has been really scary, and everything is a total mess right now, but it is going to be okay, Chandler. You know that, right?"

The little boy smiled up at him and nodded with confidence and just said, "Yep. I know." The man looked startled, and the kid went back to eating his breakfast burrito as if it were no big deal.

But you know what? I knew that too. It was going to be all right. Thanks be to God. Even though this had all happened.

Meanwhile, we had waiting to do, so we sat a table at the edge of the food tent.

Refugee people straggled in at all hours. We told them our stories, and they shared theirs.

"I heard Robin Roberts came back to town. She brought Good Morning America with her, and all the cameras and everything." I didn't know who she was, but apparently everybody else did. "Her mom and her sisters are okay, I heard."

I decided to help some more with the kitchen truck, but they said they had enough helpers, so for a while I played tag with Chandler and his brother Preston who had some energy to burn. Then I wandered over to the amateur radio table again near the loud generator and the RV. Anything to distract my brain from all the buildings wrenched apart, the bleak, brown landscape, and the rotten, moldy smell. And the waiting!

The same man was there, Bob. He must have slept on the ground, too, or maybe in the RV. He looked a little less clean now, and more wrinkled, and he had headphones on his head, but only on one of his ears. The other headphone was pushed back. When he saw me walk up, he smiled. "Aren't you the one with the dad in an 18-wheeler?"

"Yes!" He remembered us! "Have you heard from him?"

He smiled but shook his head. "Not since last night, according to the documentation, but I'll tell you as soon as we do." He looked down at his notebook and flipped some pages back. "Your name is Jessie DeGroot, isn't it?"

I nodded. He took good notes in that notebook.

"How about you wait around with us for a while? I'll show you our emergency communications station."

That sounded great.

Friday, September 2 - slightly later in the morning

Dad had showed me his CB radio in his truck cab lots of times, but at this ham station, they had so many other kinds of radios, antennas, batteries, cords, microphones, notebooks, and pencils. They had a news station turned on, and Bob, the other hams, and I just listened for a while. I felt so grown up.

One of the men said, "You know, I've been listening to the national news since Monday, and I haven't heard them say hardly anything about here. Only hearing about New Orleans, and it's sounding pretty awful over there, no kidding. They're in dire straits. But…"

A lady who also wore her headphones on one ear said, "Not Pass Christian, or Waveland, or Bay St. Louis?"

"No, not really," he said. "New Orleans has people still trapped in their homes, still surrounded by the flood water, though it's been four, or is it five, days since the storm. The hams are helping call in rescues to people still trapped up on their roofs. No water to drink or anything."

"The storm surge couldn't drain away like it did here," said someone else.

"That's part of the problem," the man said. "Not only did they get the storm surge, but then the levees broke, and now the rancid water is trapped on the low side of those levees."

A lady said, "Well, some of the city is built below sea level, so the water can't drain out once it flowed in there. At least when we had 30 feet of water washing inland, it was inclined to slide back down below sea level again."

"They're going to have to use pumps to pump all the water back uphill into the Gulf or Lake Pontchartrain? Or who knows," someone said.

"Oh my," the lady said. "I can't imagine sitting and sleeping on a sloped roof for four days." She shook her head. "In the roasting sun!"

They all sighed.

She said, "But you say, they're not saying much about the damage here? Or Long Beach? Or even Gulfport or Biloxi? We got hit with the same hurricane."

I even spoke up then. "The eye of the hurricane was right over us." Everyone nodded at me in agreement.

"Don't you know it, young lady," he said. "I heard Chipper say we just went from the 21st Century to the 18th Century in nine hours."

The lady said, "That is a sobering thought."

"But he also commented that since it was a daytime storm, instead of in the nighttime, that did save a lot of lives.

People who were stuck at least had daylight to help find a way out, sometimes."

The lady said, "Yes, but it lasted nine hours with those ferocious winds. That's longer than anything I've seen before."

Bob, the gray-haired man nodded, put up one finger for us to wait a second, and put both headphones back over his ears to listen to something. He took a few notes in his documentation book.

"Hey, Miss Jessie? Could you come over here a minute?"

I listened closely.

"We got word he's close by. In fact, you might want to stick right by me for a bit." He asked a question into the microphone and wrote a note, then looked at me. "He's on his way to the interstate exit, Miss Jessie."

"What!?" I jumped up and down, trying to listen. "Right over there?!" I pointed.

He smiled. "When he gets there, we will give him directions to come in safely with a whole tractor-trailer." He listened to the headphones again. "Jessie, you could go tell your mom. He is working his way closer to you right now."

I was off like a flash, but when I got back over to Mom, I had an even bigger surprise. Grandma was there with the puppy! She must have come in with one of the car loads of refugees the helpers were delivering to the food tent. I couldn't believe it, but I found myself giving Grandma a big hug, and she hugged me back and didn't let go for a long time. She had her foot in a walking boot, and her injured arm was bandaged up, and she still had her blue plastic bag strapped across her back. The puppy tried to jump up, but she only reached my knees, and I rubbed her all over and picked her up, I was so happy. Grandma still wasn't talking, but she was back with us. Our family was getting back together.

"Oh, Mom! Grandma!" I finally got around to telling them. "The amateur radio people said Dad is almost here. He knows which interstate exit we're near, and he's going to come down here as soon as he can."

Mom and I got our stuff together, and Grandma held the strap of her bag and picked up the little grocery basket. We gave away our Red Cross blankets to some new people. Then I ran across the parking lot and thanked Bob and the mobile kitchen people on my way to the porta-potty. I found my teacher and gave her a hug. Then we waited by the edge of the asphalt in the mud, and I rubbed the puppy's head and she nibbled on my fingers a little bit.

And then nothing happened. Where was Dad's white tractor cab? How far away was he? Bob hadn't said, exactly.

A white semi-truck with a long white trailer pulled up on the other side to the food tent in the parking lot. The truck looked like Dad's Pete, but Dad didn't have a white box trailer like that, so I knew it wasn't him. I just watched and tried to be patient. The driver talked with some people who then started waving in volunteers to come help unload the stuff in the truck.

"Mom, I could go help them unload, okay? While we wait for Dad?" I was so tired of waiting and sitting and being hot for no reason. It would help to do something. I started across the parking lot, and as I got closer, the driver of the truck worked to get the back doors of the trailer open. It looked like the whole fifty-three-foot trailer was full of tents, sleeping bags, pallets full of canned food, bottles of water. I was close enough now and was about to join the people forming into a human chain to help unload it into a line of pickup trucks ready to take the supplies into the Pass for people. At least I hoped that's where they were going.

But then the truck driver turned around, lifted up his

baseball hat, and scratched his blond head, looking around at all the tents and people.

His eyes landed on me walking up to him, and he smiled this big goofy grin. At the same time, we held out our arms and ran into each other for a big, long hug. It was four days later than I wanted, and the restaurant on stilts above the harbor was surely washed up on shore or out to sea, but I really did knock him sideways, just like I'd been planning.

15

Friday, September 2 - slightly later that morning

Mom ran up to me and Dad hugging in the middle of the parking lot and we all held onto each other. Then I let go so Mom could have him all to herself. I jumped up and down like a silly little girl next to them, but I didn't care.

"David! You found us!"

"Anna!" His voice was almost a croak, full of tears. "It was so hard not knowing," he started to say when they finally stopped kissing each other. I don't understand why grownups like that, but, whatever! He said, "I was already headed back home Saturday. By Sunday night I was in Pennsylvania. By then we knew the hurricane had hit here so much harder than it did Florida, and it was worse than ever, and I kept heading back this way," he told us. "I got on the CB to find out about the road conditions."

Mom hugged him some more. "Oh honey, you're so amazing. Thank you for marrying me. Thank you for being you."

He lifted his baseball hat to scratch his messy blond hair. "Can't really help that," he smiled. "Take me as I am."

"Oh David, I love you so much," she said, taking his hand, then got practical again as we walked back toward Grandma and the puppy on the curb. "Let's go over to the food tent and talk with each other about everything that's happened."

"That sounds great. And food sounds great, too," he smiled.

We had just gotten to Grandma, and Mom said, "Oh, David, my mama's hurt her ankle so…"

Dad reached Grandma and crouched down in front of her, saying, "Jiexen, it's really good to see you. I'm glad you're safe." He smiled at her and touched her forearm. "Looks like you got all patched up already, too." Grandma nodded and looked right into his eyes with what was almost a smile. "May I help you to the food tent?" He reached out his strong, tan arms and practically scooped her up and carried her, and I got the puppy's leash and followed them.

I went to get food for Dad, and Mom related what happened to her after the tree swept her away, and I told part of our story. It really helped having the puppy on my lap to calm me down.

"What's with the white van, David?" Mom asked. "Full of sleeping bags? Did a church send it with you to bring the donations? Or was it a company?"

"Oh, that," he said, with an expression that looked just like mine when I got caught stealing a cookie. "Well, that van's ours now, Anna. I mean, the trailer is, not the sleeping bags. Those are all donations from people along the East Coast."

Her eyebrows went up. "It's ours?"

"I bought it on the way here. It made sense," he said. "I told people where I was going, on the radio I mean, and kept heading south. By the time I got to Tennessee on Monday, the CBers connected with churches and businesses, and next thing you know they told me I could take a pile of donations of food and water and clothes if I could just wait a bit longer to head out. I had to stay off the roads by then anyway, with all the tornadoes and rain." He looked sad. "I just wanted to get down here and find you, but..." he hugged Mom. "I told everyone I'd take the supplies they donated as long as I could get to the Pass first and get to you."

We listened intently.

"Anyway, I was just bobtailing it in the Pete then, and I didn't have a way to carry any donations, so between the CBers and the churches, they helped me find a guy who would sell me this dry van, and I loaded it up there and then at a couple more churches on my way south. Every church arranged for another pile of donations farther south, and I'd stop and there'd be another crowd of people wanting to load up and send stuff down to the Gulf Coast, it didn't matter where, just wanted to help all the people. By then it was Tuesday, and Wednesday, and yesterday, and we were hearing how bad it was. How really awful it was." He stopped, took off his cap, and wiped his eyes. "The whole interstate was full of trucks heading south."

Grandma was really paying attention to all he said, and she was nodding. Her eyes were wet, but she didn't wipe them away, so her cheeks glistened.

"I kept on the CB the whole time. Then along the way, one guy who was on the channel got me connected with a ham operator, who talked to the amateur radio club down here, and that's how I knew just exactly where to come find you." He hugged me again. "Good thinking, my dear ladies."

The volunteers had the whole trailer, I mean Dad's whole new trailer, unloaded already. "What are we going to do now, Dad?" I asked.

Mom shook her head as she held tight to his side and

looked up at him. "So, we own a dry van now? What about your job, David?"

He shook his head. "I've been in touch with them via voicemail messages, and it's gonna be some time before they need me to haul for them again, Anna." We waited to see what this meant. "Yep. And it sounds like, from what you've told me about the apartment, that this truck and trailer and whatever's in the cab is about all we own now in the whole world."

Oh. Yes. Wow. He was right. Anything we had was in our backpacks and what was in the Pete.

We all nodded. At least for now, there was no point going back there. Not today.

"What about this little dog?" he looked at me with a silly smile.

"Oh, she's ours now. We rescued her, Dad." I looked at Grandma. "She's been helping us too. She's so cuddly and warm and soft."

He obligingly ruffled her floppy black ears, and she shook from head to tail to paw, dust flying off her in the sunlight. "What's her name?"

I really hadn't thought about that since I'd kept thinking of her just as the puppy, and I hadn't believed we would even be able to keep her. Grandma looked at me and didn't look away this time, waiting to see what I said. Totally unaccustomed to that, have I mentioned?

I had an idea. "I kind of had a dream about that," I said, looking into my grandma's eyes. "She looks so much like Penelope," her favorite hen, who was pure black too. Or had been, anyway. "How about Penelope?" Grandma's eyes looked surprised. "But she's not a chicken. So maybe, Penny?"

Grandma nodded slowly, and Mom said, "Penny, that's our new puppy."

"As you wish." Dad brushed off his hands on his lap and stood up. "Let's go then. Let's get this show on the road."

We brought our backpacks and stuff to the cab, and I climbed up the ladder-like steps first so Mom could hand me her bag, and Grandma's, and the plastic shopping basket, and the little puppy. Dad helped hoist Grandma up the steps while I took the extra beer from my backpack and put it in the tiny fridge in the cab. Dad blew the air horn in the cab as he drove us up toward the interstate. Mom sat in the front passenger seat, and Grandma and I situated ourselves on the bed behind the driver's seat with Penny. We could look out the window back there.

He was so glad to see us, but he still had to tell a few corny jokes. Maybe he did it to avoid his real emotions. It didn't matter. "What do you call a row of trucks hauling nachos?" He waited only about two seconds. "A cheesy pickup line!" Then we laughed.

Another one. "Did you hear about the LEGO truck that crashed on the highway?" No, we hadn't. "Authorities are still trying to piece everything together."

He had the most handsome blue eyes and blond hair. Mom and I always laugh when he is trying to cheer us up. Today, even Grandma was laughing.

Friday, September 2 - mid-morning

"I've decided to head north, dear family, to get out of this terribly devastated, soggy country, but after we are clear of here, I am totally open to your suggestions," he said.

That caught me off guard. Where were we going now, anyway?

He added, "They said on the national radio that almost a million people had to leave their homes and find a place to stay, so a lot of the hotels are full, within a hundred miles of the coast. Of course, some people didn't evacuate at all because they didn't have gas in their car…"

"Or the car broke down…" added Mom.

"Right… or a friend to go too and didn't have any money, since payday was … today maybe?" He looked worried. "How are they going to get their paychecks when the banks are all washed away?"

I hadn't thought about that. So much I hadn't thought of yet.

"And how are we going to get our paychecks?" Mom asked. Then she said, "Oh David, the car…"

"Don't even think twice about it, Anna. We can go back for it later and…"

"Um, no dad." I shook my head. "No, we can't." When I told them I searched the apartment for anything salvageable and found not too much, I hadn't mentioned finding her drowned, smashed olive-green car a few blocks away.

She sighed. "It was a good little car. Except for letting us down on Saturday, I mean."

I said, "Mom, one thing didn't break. That white and pink dish was still in the cabinet in the corner. I brought it with us…" I trailed off. I hadn't looked at it since I put it in the little plastic tub, which was still in the shopping basket we had been using for the puppy. Then we had left the basket with Grandma at Miss Kate's. Hm. I took the little container from the basket, but I heard a clinking sound inside that shouldn't have been there. How could I have thought I could carry it? I didn't open the container, but I gave it to Mom.

"You brought this all the way from the apartment? Oh, Mama, and Jessie honey," she said looking back and forth at us. "It is amazing it even made it as long as it did. I can't imagine. Thank you for thinking of it and trying." We all shook our heads. I hadn't seen one other unbroken thing in the whole apartment. Mom had big tears in her eyes but there wasn't anything I could do about it then. Thinking about Grandma DeGroot filling the dish with colorful jellybeans made me happy and sad at the same time.

Dad said, "I guess I should know what you're talking about, but I have no idea."

Mom laughed a little, holding up the biggest of the broken glass pieces to show him as he drove. "It was from your mom, David. She gave it to us when we moved out of their house to come here." He shook his head. So oblivious.

It was quiet for a bit.

I said, "Dad and Mom, why don't we go up to Uncle Joe's in Nebraska first? While they clean up the mess at home?"

Dad snorted at himself. "Well, my brain is sure fried. I forgot we'd talked about that last week. It's been such an awful week…. Good idea, Jessie," he said. "That's smart. That'll give us a place to figure out our next plan."

I sure liked the sound of him saying that, "Good idea, Jessie," I mean.

He hadn't even been through the storm with us, but his brain was mush too. I was so glad we were sticking together. We were actually a team.

He rubbed his temples with his fingers. "For now, let's keep heading north and see if we can find a truck stop with showers and get you all cleaned up," he said, laughing, "because my sweet ladies are really smelling up the whole cab of the Pete." No one argued with that, and a few hours later, we were washed and wearing new clothes and shoes, and crossing the Mighty Mississippi River into Arkansas. They had bought me a Barq's root beer, and Mom and Grandma shared the beer I'd found. They also got me an Elvis Presley Graceland t-shirt which I kept for a long time after that, plus another extra thing I'll tell you about soon, to remember the good parts.

Dad said later today or early tomorrow, we'd cross the

Missouri River a few times, and then creep west into the nearest corner of Nebraska to the DeGroot dairy farm. I wondered if it would look like I remembered from when I was little. Even though they'd had a tornado, it might still look familiar. I didn't know.

I woke up from a long nap because Dad and Mom started laughing like crazy up there in the front of the cab. "What's so funny?" I asked from the back.

Mom could barely breathe, she laughed so hard. Whenever she tried to talk, either she or Dad would burst out with more laughing. Finally, she wiped the tears off her face and said, "David wanted to know if I thought we would get our security deposit back from the apartment complex!"

We all laughed through some more tears, and then for me the giggles changed into nothing but tears again. I had no idea what would happen to all the people who owned houses, apartment buildings, and businesses that had been destroyed. The bank. The library. The school. I kept thinking about Miss Doreen and her seafood business and restaurant, Mary's dad and his shrimp boat.

This far from the ruined shoreline, the landscape finally did look like it ought to in September in Missouri. I think we were in Missouri, anyway. The grass was green instead of muddy, and the trees stood tall instead of being bent and broken. The air smelled clean, and the bugs were making so much noise. How could I actually miss the sound of buzzing insects? Well, I did.

Dad drove a few more hours on the divided state highway, but his shoulders were sagging, and he pulled off at a tiny truck stop and sent the three of us over to a "pick-your-own farm" he knew about, "just over there." I even saw a Monarch butterfly on a milkweed plant.

Penny was already a great trucker puppy, though she needed to be lifted up and down the ladder of steps from the cab to ground level. She did her doggie jobs and then stayed with dad while we went to the farm. When we got back with sacks of apples, sweet corn, cantaloupes, and a cabbage that Grandma wanted, he and Penny were snoring something fierce on the bed in the back. We all squeezed in around them and slept.

When I woke up Saturday morning, he was already driving us down the road again. I watched the scenery go by as I tried to wake up and thought about all that had happened.

On the radio, we finally heard something that wasn't about New Orleans and the Superdome and the awful levee flooding.

Not that it was good news. It was news, however, where there had been none before. They said every single county in Mississippi had been declared a federal disaster area. The rest of Louisiana, Alabama, Georgia, and Florida experienced horrible ruin. People who had survived Hurricane Camille said this storm was worse.

All of a sudden, I knew what we should do. The idea hit me really hard. It almost knocked me over like a... storm surge.

Saturday, September 3 - morning

I slid off the bed and peeked around the bulkhead so I could see them in the seat. "Dad? Mom? I know what we should do. After we go to Nebraska, I mean," I said.

"Good morning to you too, sweet girl," said Mom from the front. She had her stocking feet up on the passenger seat and held a cup of tea. When had they stopped for tea this morning? How did I miss so much? I must have slept pretty hard. It felt so good to sleep in a safe, warm place. Anyway...

It surprised even me when I said, it, but I had to say it. "I don't think we should go back to the Pass."

Total silence. Mom and Dad exchanged looks up front.

I knew I was making sense. "You didn't see the worst of it by our place, Dad. It was like the man on the radio said before, how the whole Gulf Coast looks like what he imagined Hiroshima looked like after the atomic bomb. I have a feeling your jobs won't come back for a long time."

Mom said, "That was the governor of Mississippi, Haley Barbour, who said the thing about Hiroshima."

Dad just kept driving along, but his thumbs bounced up and down on the wheel.

I gained steam, though I wasn't even sure what my whole idea was. "I know our principal, Mrs. Favre, and Mrs. Ladner and everyone will get the school open again soon, because she was already talking about it when we saw her in the food tent, and it's a great school district," I said, "but it's hard to imagine everyone, all the families coming back right away with no buildings left to live in, you know?" I stopped. "I mean, there are really almost no houses or buildings left, from what we could see." I almost cried again, but I kept talking through it before they stopped me. "I would sure miss my friends and school and everything, and the Sound and the Gulf…" I could feel Mom and Dad trying to think of an answer, up there in the front of the cab, and I stepped back around to sit on the bed to let them think about what they'd say.

"We listen," said a croaky voice on the bed behind me. Unbelievably, my Tiger Grandma spoke for the first time since she lost all six of her chickens—and her daughter—on Monday.

She said, "Let us listen what Jessie say. She hard worker. She good thinker."

Gulp.

Then she said, "During storm, she step into boiling water and walk on fire." That was a Cantonese expression that meant I'd been brave. "Today is different from past."

I almost couldn't talk after all these compliments, but now Grandma, along with Mom and Dad, waited for me to explain my reasoning. Could you believe it? Good thing I loved using Thinking Maps and could do one on the fly, even just in my head; problem, ideas, solutions. I was praying to find out what was the rest of this crazy idea that I'd started, because this time I was working backwards in my thinking.

It came to me. God sighting?

"So how about we go to Colorado?" More silence, but Grandma was nodding at me. "For starters, it's really far away from the water. No hurricanes there," I said. Grandma smiled. "And Dad could maybe get a different trucking job, since he has this dry van now? Colorado has interstates, and the Rocky Mountains. And snow…. Right? Not hurricanes?"

The fact that it was Dad who said the next thing was even more surreal and cool. He said, "Wow, that's a great idea, Jessie. I've been through there a lot. It's got potential, I agree. Let's pray about it, okay?"

Everyone was super quiet for the next many hours, driving up to the farm in Nebraska. But it felt more like a happy, thoughtful quiet than an exhausted one. For once, Dad didn't turn on classic rock music on the radio. The only sound was tiny snores and whimpers from Penny as she slept.

By the time we'd spent the weekend at Uncle Joe's, we had talked about it some more and made plans. Mom told me she could get our mail forwarded once we got there, and soon I could meet my new classmates at a school in a little town called Garnet, north of Pioneersburg, on the Front Range full of pine trees and pronghorn antelopes. Didn't that sound perfect?

Back when we had stopped in Tennessee the day before, I didn't know why I wanted this blank book, but Dad bought it for me at the big truck stop when we got our showers and bought clean clothes. He was the one who said "Sure, Jessie," but then Grandma was the one who, in her walking boot, shouldered Dad out of the way, took cash out of the zip bag and paid for all our purchases without complaint. Dad was floored by that one, but he focused his tired, happy blue eyes at her and said, "Thank you, Jiexen," in a way that meant she didn't do that very often.

Anyway, on the cover of the blank book, it says, "Ready to Go?" and it's full of nothing but blank lines, ready for me to decide what to put in it. I'm going to write down everything that happened to Grandma, Mom, Dad, and me. It makes me proud to know how much I really did to help, and I want to document all my gratitude to God for our new chapter.

Hopefully Colorado won't be as full of natural disasters as Mississippi or Nebraska have been, but after I'm done with this story, I'll need another book for whatever happens to us in Garnet, Colorado.

The End

EPILOGUE

What I Found Out Later
by Jessie DeGroot

*I*f I'd known at that moment, when Mary and I said goodbye outside her house that I wouldn't see her again until we were both in college, I would have given her a big hug. But how was I going to know that?

UNDERSTANDING THE SURGE: "The world's fastest river rapids move at about 10 to 12 feet per second, and even the strong and brave people who enter those waters with life jackets, helmets and sturdy kayaks sometimes do not make it out. When Katrina's surge was just 10 feet deep, it could have been moving at speeds as fast as 16 feet per second, a speed that rises with the water's depth, said Joseph Suhayda, a Louisiana State University coastal oceanographer. 'Being in that kind of water is tantamount to being dead.'" From *Katrina: Survival and Revival,* by Dan Ellis.

The storm surge washed five miles inland from the Gulf

Coast, past the train tracks, and went as far as twelve miles inland following the rivers upstream.

ODDLY, Hurricane Camille was responsible for more loss of lives in 2005 than in 1969, when it had occurred, because some people who had survived Camille thought they could survive Katrina. They were wrong.

FLOTSAM AND JETSAM are terms for various types of property lost or abandoned at sea. Flotsam pertains to goods that are washed overboard and floating as a result of a wreck and may be claimed by the original owner. But jetsam is cargo that was intentionally discarded or "jettisoned" (to lighten the load of a ship in danger of sinking) and can be claimed by whoever discovers it.

I DID FIND out a month or two later, when Mom and Dad and I were in Colorado, all watching the news at our new place, that the school district had already gotten some of the schools re-opened in the Pass. The kids needed to ride the buses–and do Thinking Maps–again, which must have made it seem possible that one day life would get back to normal. To celebrate that huge milestone, Robin Roberts, a famous news anchor in New York City who had grown up in the Pass, and whose first job was as a school bus driver in our school district, came back yet another time to visit her family and the town and drive one of the school buses! How about that?

Like A Sunflower - Early 2006: "I tell the story of a little miracle that boosted our spirits and brought us smiles. In early 2006, big, fat sunflowers started blooming all over town. They bloomed in the middle of debris piles, under collapsed homes, in nasty ditches, and scattered throughout our own yards. They grew everywhere. We WERE those sunflowers: survivors, funny, cheerful people and just a little muddy. I believed it was God giving us something to smile about and giving us a symbol for our recovery!" --Wendy McDonald is a native of Bay St. Louis who moved back after Katrina to help recovery efforts and never left. Her full story can be found in *Blown Together: The Trials and Miracles of Katrina* by Fr. Sebastian Myladiyil, SVD.

SUNFLOWERS AND HOPE: "After the storm during the rebuilding, hundreds of sunflowers started popping up everywhere. Katrina had scattered the seeds from neighbor's bird feeders. We saw sunflowers as a sign of rebirth, resurrection, and resilience." – Lili Stahler-Murphy, co-founder of Waveland Ground Zero Hurricane Museum, past Waveland Alderman, and community activist.

FACEBOOK: This new technology showed up a year or two after we moved to Colorado. Mom and Grandma let me get an account when I was in high school, and that's how I finally got in touch with Mary again after so long. We didn't have a computer at home yet, but I went to the Garnet Public Library and used their public computer to communicate with my old friends and find out where they lived then.

THAT'S ALSO how I eventually found out that Kendal's Seafood and others like hers were back in business on the new wharf that Chipper McDonald worked so hard to get grant money to have built, so the fishing industry could come back. Doreen's business took a beating. But she's a winner, for sure. Eventually, she connected with shrimpers trying to go back to work, and she sold shrimp and fish out of a cooler near the wharf as she worked so hard to get a retail space to work out of again.

MARY'S DAD'S boat didn't survive the storm. At first he moved up to Hattiesburg and lived with the other shrimper families while they tried to figure out how to make a living. After a long while, he found a place to live with some of the other shrimpers and oystermen who were in the, you know, same boat. They tried to go back to their careers on the Gulf. But it took over a year for that to even happen, and then there was no place for them to buy fuel for the boat, or ice, or sell their catches. Some who still had boats sold the shrimp fresh, direct to customers, from coolers on the pier, just like Miss Doreen did.

HE FOUND work doing cleanup and construction back near Bay St. Louis, and then he opened his own small engine repair business which also helps install solar power on homes and RVs. I heard some of the other shrimpers became DJs or got jobs with the Department of Agriculture.

THE SHRIMP CAME BACK, but the price of shrimp kept dropping, and tons of imported farmed shrimp drove down the prices.

BY THE TIME Mary's whole family moved back to the Pass in 2006, Pirate Pride was really growing strong again. Many schools were rebuilt and creating a safe place for all ages of students. Mary's mom got super involved in a group called Boat People SOS that started a branch in Biloxi, and she's become a disaster case manager.

THEN THE 2010 Deepwater Horizon oil rig explosion sent millions of gallons of oil into the Gulf over the next 87 days. It was the largest marine oil spill in history, affecting the beaches, bayous, wetlands, and estuaries.

ELLIS ANDERSON PUBLISHED *UNDER SURGE, Under Siege: The Odyssey of Bay St. Louis and Katrina,* in 2010. That's where I heard about the term "Katrina patina," describing the sludgy, muddy, grimy, sweaty substance resembling black algae that covered people doing long days of "mucking out" after the storm and which could never quite be washed off. She said, "We, as well as our belongings, are vaguely recognizable, inalterably changed."

I DIDN'T DISCOVER until 2019 that the *U.S.S. Comfort,* a huge Navy hospital ship, arrived off the Gulf Coast a few days after Hurricane Katrina to help treat medical injuries. Do you remember the name Allie Jackson, who was the firefighter captain in *To Starve an Ember*? She had been a babysitter for my boyfriend Prentice and his brother when they were little. She was on that ship after Katrina, not far from where Jessie had lived. She understood what Jessie had gone through. But that's a story for another day, and another 'Ready to Go?' novel.

AUTHOR'S NOTE

Why did I write this novel?

The DeGroots will run into wildfires and blizzards ("bomb cyclone" hurricanes) in Colorado in 2019, and you can read about those disasters in *To Starve an Ember* and *To Melt a Snowdrift.*

But how did the Ready to Go? series get back in time to Mississippi, then?

I lived in Colorado when Hurricane Katrina hit the Gulf Coast in 2005, and the news coverage about New Orleans blew us all away, all the natural and human-caused trauma. But I didn't realize how much other damage occurred along the Gulf Coast until the next year when our church youth group went to Mississippi to help do hurricane cleanup. The high schoolers went to Bay St. Louis, which like all the other towns along the coast still had a huge amount of debris to deal with even before they could start rebuilding. I wondered why we had not heard about the Gulf Coast the year before, since so much destruction had happened there too.

Hurricane Katrina killed at least 1,392 people and

damaged at least $125 billion in property, mostly around New Orleans, Louisiana. In Mississippi, at least 238 people died, billions of dollars of bridges, barges, boats, piers, houses, and cars were washed inland, and all 82 counties in Mississippi were declared disaster areas for federal assistance after the storm traveled up the whole state. The storm dumped eight to ten inches of rain on Hancock, Harrison, and Jackson Counties. Hancock County: Waveland, Bay St. Louis, Kiln, Diamondhead, Pearlington; Harrison County: Pass Christian, Long Beach, Gulfport, and Biloxi were all hit with a twenty-seven to thirty-foot storm surge which failed to even pause at the railroad embankment and even crossed Interstate 10 in some areas.

My visit to Pass Christian in 2024 for book research was fantastic. What a lovely town full of helpful, positive people. I've fictionalized their stories here, but there's truth in all of it.

Like Chipper McDermott, the alderman who became mayor soon after Katrina, said, "We went from the 21st Century to the 18th Century in nine hours." He and I sat in War Memorial Park, and he told me how he'd helped earn grant money to build a new harbor expansion for the shrimp, oyster, and fishing industry to continue after the storm, but at that point the changes in the flow of silt from the Mississippi River, and damage from the Deep Horizon oil spill all but destroyed that whole industry. It was a beautiful new wharf, and that's where I met the real "Miss Kate" and "Miss Doreen," at Kimball's Seafood shop which I have fictionalized as "Kendal's," and I got to buy fresh seafood right there on the dock and gaze out at the Mississippi Sound. They told me every business on the shore is required to be housed in shipping containers. That way, at a certain alert level, they must pack up their shops and haul them to safety until the storm passes. Several times a year, this happens.

I met Meridith Bang through the miracle of the internet, and she guided me around the Pass on the phone and in person to show me what an amazing town it is in 2025. She had joined the Pass Christian School District in 1998 as a teacher and had just become the new principal of one of Pass Christian's two elementary schools when Katrina hit. I found out that within six weeks of the destruction, she and the school district managed to combine all the elementary students who were still there in one elementary school, uniting the students after the destruction and building a new district family, making sure those students didn't lose a year of education. She told me how she will always be "grateful for the donations, prayers, and many contributions of so many kind and giving people all over the United States and beyond. Being principal for so many incredible children in our district over the years brought me such joy, rivaled only by the ever-present joys of being a mother to two precious boys (now both amazing men)."

She and the school district are understandably proud of how they used Thinking Maps as an initiative to excellence, both before the storm (when 60% of the students were on free and reduced lunch) and after Hurricane Katrina, to "provide continuity in the midst of chaos," as Teacher Suzanne M. Ishee said. On top of searching for shelter and loved ones, the students continued earning academic awards. This was achieved despite 85% of the teachers losing their homes, too. Metacognition was not a distraction. It was a lifeline.

Once I had prayed enough, I crossed the Bay St. Louis bridge (I hate long bridges) and found Bernie Cullen, Board Chairperson, at Waveland's Lili Stahler-Murphy Ground Zero Hurricane Museum, west of Bay St. Louis. They say, "Our museum is not a memorial to a disaster, but a tribute to the strength and beauty of the human spirit." www.wavelandgroundzero.com. The tangible teaching style there, showing with a line on the wall how high the water was in that school, really hit me.

How can we pretend a disaster is never going to affect us?

Just as with wildfires, which you can't prevent, but just need to plan to live with, so it is with hurricanes, tornadoes, blizzards, earthquakes… depending on your location, certain types of disasters are more likely to happen. You'll find once you do begin to prepare for one type of disaster, it's easier to add just a few additional supplies to cover other contingencies. Even if there is not a large-scale disaster, you always need some first aid supplies on hand for a dumb accident with a table saw, and you never know when some odd reason might come up for, I don't know, maybe a two-week shutdown of the whole world? Make that six months? Buy a few extra boxes of pasta and jars of spaghetti sauce now, while you can, and rotate through them.

For a more straightforward set of lists to get you started, I love Kathi Lipp's term for preparedness, which is "pre-deciding." Her book *Ready for Anything: Preparing your Heart and Home for Any Crisis Big or Small* is another way to get yourself to do some "pre-deciding." I love her hashtag #PreparedNotScared. You could also check with your local office of emergency management, or see: www.ready.gov.

ACKNOWLEDGMENTS

Tony A., "The Laundry List." adultchildren.org/literature/laundry-list/

Ellis Anderson, *Under Surge, Under Siege: the Odyssey of Bay St. Louis and Katrina.* University Press of Mississippi, 2010.

Robin Adair, Pikes Peak Regional Office of Emergency Management and Community Emergency Response Team.

The Angels of de Montluzin, the tree that provided rescue for four survivors of the Bay Town Inn Bed and Breakfast, and when it died in 2005, was carved into a memorial by Dayle K. Lewis.

Marjann Kalehoff Ball, Ed.D., "Stories from Mississippi: Results from College to Kindergarten," Ch. 14 in Hyerle, David N. and Larry Alper (eds.), *Student Successes with Thinking Maps.* Corwin, 2011.

Meridith Bang, retired Pass Christian public school administrator who says, "Once a pirate, always a pirate."

Marge Gaylord Bardeen, one of my most influential teachers.

Natalie Barszcz, *Our Community News.*

Boat People SOS Gulf Coast, serving Mississippi and Alabama communities. https://bpsos.org/gulf-coast

Evelina Shmukler Burnett, award-winning journalist and co-founder of the *Gazebo Gazette,* soon after the hurricane, to help residents get information about their city's relief and rebuilding efforts.

Jeff and Arlene Cohen, Inquisitive World Explorers.

Bernie Cullen, Board Chairperson, Waveland's Lili Stahler-Murphy Ground Zero Hurricane Museum, www.wavelandgroundzero.com. "Our museum is not a memorial to a disaster, but a tribute to the strength and beauty of the human spirit."

Angie Curry, friend and proof-reader; M.A. in English Composition, Language & Rhetoric.

Darlene and Kay, from Kimball's Seafood, "fresh seafood daily since 1930."

Den Kwai Ying, multi-lingual citizen of the world and amazing cook who feeds me every time I visit her.

Dan Ellis, *Katrina Survival and Revival: A Pass Christian MS Story.* https://Katrina.passchristian.net/stories.htm. https://camille.passchristian.net/camille_the_storm.htm

Gulf Coast Pre-Stress Partners

Mark Hatfield, husband, gentleman, and geographer

Jenny Sue Horsey

Dr. Gayle Humm, M.D.

Suzanne M. Ishee, Pass Christian Middle School Teacher tells about Thinking Maps, "The Pass Story," Thinking Foundation, www.eggplant.org/tf/mom/pass_story.html.

Kathryn "Sally" Bishop James, who shepherded so many children and parents through the Pass Library, both before and after Hurricane Katrina.

Kathi Lipp, *Ready for Anything: Preparing your Heart and Home for Any Crisis Big or Small.* #PreparedNotScared.

Chipper McDermott, a past alderman and long-time mayor of the Pass, whose handprint was on every part of the city after Katrina, because of his vision.

Ross Meyer, LBF, ROG.

Mississippi Department of Transportation, *Hurricane Evacuation Guide.*

Mississippi Emergency Management Agency, *Hurricane Guide.*

Susan M. Moyer, ed. *Katrina: Stories of Rescue, Recovery and Rebuilding in the Eye of the Storm.* Spotlight Press LLC, 2005.

André Mouton, U.S. Department of Homeland Security, Fire Adapted Colorado, Pikes Peak Regional Community Emergency Response Team.

Fr. Sebastian Myladiyil, SVD. *Blown Together: The Trials and Miracles of Katrina.* Evergreen Press, 2010.

H. C. Porter and Marlo Carter Kirkpatrick (ed.), *Backyards & Beyond: Mississippians and Their Stories.* Backyards & Beyond, 2008.

Diana & L. Dow Nichol III and Elena Ruth Nichol

Steve Pate, *Our Community News.*

Randy Petrick, author of *The Soul Repair Manual* and creator of www.wordsofabundance.com.

Scott Rand, Medical Reserve Corps of El Paso County, Logistics Lead, Head Gopher

Rush, the band. www.rush.com.

Angie Sage, *Magyk,* Book One in the Septimus Heap series.

Gordon Saunders, mentor, editor, and cover designer. https://gordon-saunders-writer.com.

Ann Scelba, Ph.D., *Waltzing with Katrina: Courageous Stories from the People Who Stayed.* Pass Christian, 2006.

Byron and Susan Spinney, Hope Restored disaster ministry, https://hoperestored.org/.

Linda van Noordt and The Leddies

Michael Weinfeld, *Our Community News*

Joyce & Bob Witte, W0TLM Tri-Lakes Monument Radio Association

Kent Wong, *Swimming to Freedom: My Escape from China and the Cultural Revolution.* Abrams press, 2021.

Margie Wood, margiewoodwrites.com

Lisa Hatfield is an everyday citizen on a mission to get more people to take responsibility for their own readiness when it comes to natural disasters. Here, she's teaching kids to "pre-decide" how to deal with trouble instead of just pretending nothing bad will ever happen.

Photo by Kaylene Kohl, Pikes Peak Region CERT

As they say in the Community Emergency Response Team

(CERT): "We want you to be able to help yourself and others when 911 is not coming."

Subscribe to my newsletter at LisaHatfieldWriter.com and I'll send you a short story (PDF or MP3). The site also includes free book club resources and other extras. The intermittent newsletter will tell you about upcoming events for the **Ready to Go?** Series.

Books in the 'Ready to Go?' series
To Starve an Ember
To Melt a Snowdrift
To Ride a Storm Surge

I would be very appreciative if you would write a review of this book on the site where you bought it or at: https://goodreads.com.